Sugar and Spice

Sugar and Spice

Angela Britnell

W F HOWES LTD

This large print edition published in 2014 by
W F Howes Ltd
Unit 4, Rearsby Business Park, Gaddesby Lane,
Rearsby, Leicester LE7 4YH

1 3 5 7 9 10 8 6 4 2

First published in the United Kingdom in 2014
by Choc Lit Limited

A CIP catalogue record for this book is available
from the British Library

ISBN 978 1 47126 703 1

Typeset by Palimpsest Book Production Limited,
Falkirk, Stirlingshire

Printed and bound in Great Britain
by TJ International Ltd, Padstow, Cornwall

To my very own hero – my wonderful husband, Richard, whose love and constant encouragement are never ending.

CHAPTER 1

Lily admired the fact that her taxi driver didn't flinch at the enormous pile of luggage by her feet. Her two oversized suitcases, garment bag, carry-on, computer bag and handbag were all in matching bright pink leather complete with luggage tags encrusted with her name in fake diamonds.

'Can you fit it all in?' She cocked an eye at his old, and to her eyes, miniature blue car.

'No problem, love, although you might have to hold a couple of the small things on your lap.' He started to load and for a second Lily hesitated as a sliver of apprehension sneaked through her.

Last week this trip had struck her as a great idea – doing research for her new cookery programme combined with getting away from Patrick and all the hassles he'd put her through recently. She intended to prove that she didn't need him once and for all. Now, standing outside a rain soaked train station and shivering in the Cornish drizzle, Lily wasn't so sure. Sure it had been a hundred degrees and sweat-dripping humid when she left

1

Nashville, but didn't the weather here realise mid-July meant summer?

'Hop in. You picked the worst day to arrive. Saturdays are always a nightmare this time of year,' her driver said, with a shake of his head.

Were other people mad enough to consider this a desirable place to visit? Lily dredged up a smile. 'How long will it take us to get there?'

'About twenty minutes or so, love, give or take. Hop in,' he said again. She did as she was told and clambered into the back seat.

As least she wasn't stuck on the train anymore, trying to survive four plus hours of torment. It had been overcrowded, packed with screaming kids, irritated parents, and teenagers jabbering non-stop on their cellphones. She'd risked lunch from the buffet car and shuddered at the thin, tasteless sandwiches and lukewarm Coke. Another time she'd rather starve and for a serious foodie like her that was a sacrilegious statement.

'Ever been to Cornwall before?' the driver asked, glancing in his rear-view mirror.

'No, but I've heard a lot about the place from my secretary. She's originally from Mevagissey and recommended St Dinas as being quieter.'

He chuckled. 'It's that all right. Mevagissey's a zoo in the summer. Nothing much in St Dinas though, but maybe you want that?' the man probed, but Lily couldn't resent his natural curiosity.

'Yeah, it should suit my purpose. I guess there's public transport to get around?'

'The buses aren't bad, but they often get held up with all the traffic. They're all right if you're not in a hurry.' He shrugged in a resigned way.

Officially she wasn't, but Lily knew herself well. Workaholic was a kind term for her driven personality and rest one of her favourite curse words. Her mother made her promise to take a few days off before starting work, but Tricia Redman was four thousand miles away so would never know. Lily hoped the internet connection was as good as she'd been promised because without being able to use her Blackberry, iPad and iPod she'd be screwed.

The soft rain misting up the windows, combined with jet lag, lulled her into resting her head back against the seat. Lily allowed her heavy, tired eyes to shut and drifted off.

'Here we are, love. Cliff House. I'll get your gear out while you run up and get Betty to open the door.'

Lily jerked awake and gazed blankly around. 'Oh, right. Sorry. I fell asleep. I'm not quite with it yet.'

'That's all right. Better you than a car full of drunken yobs throwing up out of the windows.' He laughed and grimaced at the same time.

'I guess it is.' Lily opened the door and stepped out, surprised to realise that it had stopped raining somewhere along the way. She stared at the stunning view in front of her and her jaw dropped. 'Oh, wow.' An endless deep blue sea, miniature fishing boats bobbing around in a neat little harbour, and a soft blue sky dotted with fluffy

3

marshmallow clouds – Lily had never seen anything like it before. 'Oh, wow,' she said again.

A broad smile creased her driver's weathered face. 'We take it for granted 'til someone sees it for the first time and reminds us.'

Lily couldn't believe *anyone* would ever get used to seeing this everyday.

'Miss Redman?' A small, dumpy woman stood on the front step of the pretty, white-painted house. Lily smiled at the hanging baskets of exuberant red geraniums flanking the glossy black front door. They'd be nothing but shrivelled up twigs in Tennessee's searing summer heat.

'Yeah. Just coming.' Lily threw an apologetic grin at the man hauling all her bags out of the car. 'Can you manage?'

'No problem, love. I'll bring them up. You go on.' He shooed her away.

She opened the gate and picked her way carefully up the narrow path, the combination of uneven flagstones and her high heels were an accident waiting to happen. Lily admired the colourful flower garden on both sides still glistening from the recent rain. When she reached her new landlady she stuck out her hand, managing to remember at the last second not to initiate a traditional Southern hug. It had been top of her secretary's long list of *things not to do in England*.

'Betty Tremayne. Come on in, my dear. You must be fair worn out.'

Close up Lily guessed the woman was around

4

sixty, her brown wavy hair streaked with grey, the dark skirt and pale blue blouse giving the impression of a woman comfortable in her skin. Amusement sparkled in her soft blue eyes as she checked out her new visitor. No doubt Lily's wild red curly hair, tight white jeans, clingy pink T-shirt and pink stilettos were out of the ordinary for Cornwall.

Lily stepped into a hallway eerily reminiscent of her grandmother's home in rural Mississippi with its dark patterned carpet, plain cream walls, brown paint, framed family photos and lingering smell of cooking.

'I'll show you your room so you can freshen up while I make us some tea.'

Lily sucked in a deep breath and prepared to check out where she'd committed to spend the next two weeks. A small knot of excitement unfurled in her gut as she followed Betty Tremayne up the steep narrow staircase.

She stifled a groan as her new landlady opened the door to the tiniest bedroom she'd ever seen, wondering where on earth she could put all her luggage.

'I had the en suite put in last winter,' Betty said with great pride, pointing to a small cubicle taking up one corner. 'There's one of those newfangled electric showers, but if you want a proper bath you can go along the landing and use mine.'

'Thanks.' Lily looked around the sunny room, amazed to see it managed to contain a single bed, a chest of drawers, something Betty declared to be a wardrobe but she'd call a free-standing closet, and a straight-back chair. The overwhelming effect was of blue flowers – lots of them in various shades on the wallpaper, the bedcover and curtains.

'There's a tea tray over in the window, dear, and some of that nasty long-life milk but if you want the proper stuff you come down to the kitchen and help yourself.'

'I'm sure I'll be very comfortable here.' Lily scanned the room again, deciding cat swinging wouldn't be on the agenda.

'You get settled in dear and then come back down for a cup of tea.' Betty smiled and left her to it.

Lily had come to Britain to find chefs for her new television programme, but she suspected that she might just discover more about herself too.

Lily slathered her second scone with more of Betty's wonderful home-made strawberry jam and thick Cornish clotted cream. 'These are delicious. Would you mind sharing the recipe with me?'

Betty chuckled and shook her head. 'Recipe? I make them up until the mixture feels right, dearie.'

Lily understood because she did most of her own cooking the same way. The soft, almost biscuit like cakes didn't resemble any scones she'd eaten in the States. 'Can I watch you make them sometime?'

The woman's gentle laugh showed that she thought Lily was a touch strange. 'Of course you can. You'm a bit of a cook, then?'

'Yeah. I've got my own catering business, and I

do some television work.' Patrick would cringe to hear her playing down her reputation but she didn't care what he thought anymore. Lily's name meant nothing to these people and that was something of a welcome relief.

'Oh, dear, I'll be afraid to cook for you now.' Betty frowned.

'Please don't say that.' Lily switched on her famous *Luscious Lily* smile – the kind to send ratings sky high, especially when combined with a low cut sparkly pink T-shirt. 'I'm always on the look out for new recipes and love nothing better than eating.' It was the absolute truth and the simple reason why she'd learnt to cook in the first place – that and a fear of being condemned to eat her mother's out-of-the-box Hamburger Helper and canned peas until she left home. 'That's why I'm here.'

'To eat?' Betty sounded puzzled.

'Sort of. I'll take a few days to recover from the journey and then I'll start by checking out some Cornish restaurants I've heard about. After that I'm planning to tour around the country some.' Lily's brain raced as she recalculated. 'I'd planned to use public transportation but I gather from the taxi driver it might not be straightforward so I'm having second thoughts.'

'It won't be easy, my dear, especially if you're carrying much.'

Lily smiled at the polite reference to her large amount of luggage. There'd barely been room to stack it all in the small bedroom.

7

'I don't much fancy driving on the wrong side of the road either. You don't know of anyone who might be interested in maybe a month's work driving me around, I suppose?'

'I might,' Betty replied. 'My friend's son left the Army recently. He's . . . not very chatty but he's reliable.'

'Would you mind giving him a call?'

Betty's brow furrowed. 'I'll ring his mum first and see what she thinks.'

Lily picked up on something unsaid, but was pretty sure Betty wouldn't hook her up with any weirdo. 'Thanks.' She kept her seat as her landlady got up and went out into the hall, closing the door behind her. She itched to creep across and listen but it wouldn't do to be caught out. Lily caught the hum of low conversation then the sound of the phone being hung up.

Betty came back in. 'He'll meet you tonight, seven o'clock down at the Shark's Fin.'

'Where's that?'

'It's the pub down the bottom of the hill.' Betty smiled.

'Does this man have a name?'

''Course he do. Kenan Rowse.'

Lily smirked. 'Whatever kind of name's that?'

'A good Cornish one.' Betty's sharp tone indicated that she didn't appreciate the disparaging comment.

'Sorry. It's an unusual name, I've never heard it before.' Lily tried to back-pedal.

8

'Hmm. Don't suppose you have it over there.'

'How will I recognise him?' She didn't intend to wander around the whole pub asking for this unknown man.

'He'll know you. I described you over the phone. It shouldn't be hard.' Betty's eyes twinkled and Lily could just imagine what had been said.

'I'd better go up and change.' This was work so Mr Kenan Rowse would get *Luscious Lily* full-bore on tonight.

CHAPTER 2

Kenan's beer glass slipped from his hand and he managed to catch it with two fingers and set it down on the table. His vision filled with a mass of shining red curls resting on creamy shoulders dusted with freckles. Kenan's brain registered a short, bright orange dress clinging to every curve and something deep inside him tightened. On automatic pilot he stood up and caught her eye, giving a quick nod of acknowledgment. The woman sashayed across the room and every man in the place followed her progress with their eyes. Next thing she stood right in front of him and a dangerous musky perfume tickled his senses.

'Kenan Rowse, I assume?' Her smooth honeyed drawl wrapped around his brain and he wished himself safely back in a foxhole in Afghanistan.

'Mr Rowse?'

He snapped out of his trance. 'Yes. Sorry. I was miles away.' Kenan shot out his hand and as she gave it a firm shake his fingers rubbed against a myriad of small calluses and scars. 'Join me.'

Lily dropped into the nearest chair, crossing one

long elegant leg over the other, and he fought not to stare. He met her inquisitive sapphire eyes and wondered why she was frowning. Perhaps she was waiting for him to have some manners, offer her a drink, and make conversation like a normal person? 'You must be Lily Redman.'

'Boy, you're a smart one,' she jibed. 'Go to the top of the class.' She quickly surveyed the room before fixing her attention back on him. 'You gonna offer me a drink or do I buy my own?'

'Sorry,' Kenan muttered. 'What can I get you?'

'Rum and Coke with plenty of ice, not the couple of pathetic cubes I hear y'all consider enough.' She tossed her head and the dramatic halo of curls flew around before settling back down.

'Certainly.' He already hated the idea of being a lackey for this disturbing woman but needed to get out from under his parents' feet. They'd put up with him for six months now and their patience was wearing thin, along with his own. Until he decided what to do with the rest of his life this temporary job was better than nothing.

Up at the bar he glared at Dave Winter, making it clear he'd better not ask any dumb questions about Lily. With the efficient village grapevine working its usual magic, no doubt everyone in the village already knew who she was. Kenan made his way back to the table and set the glass down in front of her. 'There you are.' He almost added – don't choke on the ice cubes – but didn't do sarcastic humour or any other sort these days.

'Thanks.' She took a deep swallow before breaking into a satisfied smile. 'Boy, I needed that.'

He sat in silence as she finished it off, and set down the empty glass.

'So, would you care to hear what I've got planned?' she asked.

Kenan grunted.

'We won't wear ourselves out talking that's for sure,' she jested, and the corners of her glossy orange lips turned up in a tempting smile.

'I was told you're after a driver not a conversationalist,' he challenged and her bright blue eyes twinkled right back at him.

'So you can speak more than two words? I was beginning to wonder.'

He deliberately didn't rise to her bait.

'I'm a chef.'

'That explains your hands.' Kenan wanted to bite off his tongue. Keeping things impersonal was his number one rule these days.

'You're smart.'

He wasn't sure Lily intended it to be a point in his favour and felt a touch guilty as she drew her hands back down to her lap.

'I run my own catering business in Nashville, Tennessee and I've got a nationally syndicated TV show called *Luscious Lily*. I'm putting together ideas for a new show called *Celebrity Chef Swap*, which will feature renowned British chefs swapping kitchens with ones in the States. I'll purposely match people with very different styles of working so it should make for interesting viewing. After I get over the jet lag, I want to start by meeting up with a couple of chefs in Cornwall who've agreed to talk to me: Luc Pascal at the Bountiful restaurant in Fowey and Fiona Madden at the Water's Edge in Charlestown. I've also made tentative plans to go to Keswick in the Lake District, Edinburgh, Scotland, and Cardiff in Wales, too. I need someone to drive, deal with the travel arrangements, and luggage. I plan to be here for a month. Think you could manage?'

He'd never heard anyone talk for so long without apparently drawing breath. 'Yes.'

'Yes? That's all you've got to say?'

'You spelled out the details of the job and asked if I could do it. I said yes. What more do you want?' he snapped.

'Nothing, I guess.' She succinctly listed the pay and hours and a few more details, but he kept his response to a brief nod. 'So, you comin' on board?'

'Yes. When do we start?'

She nibbled at her lip and Kenan resented the fact that he found the childish trait endearing. It hinted at an unexpected vulnerability and made him wonder about the woman underneath the flashy outer persona. 'Today's Saturday, how about Monday?'

'Fine. Have a list ready for me of all your planned stops and I'll get an itinerary put together,' he quickly replied.

'I'm sure you will, down to the last minute I'm guessing.'

13

He didn't comment, pretty sure she hadn't intended him to.

'My round. Isn't that what you Brits say?' Lily picked up her glass. 'What're you drinking?'

'Pint of Tribute.' He pushed his glass across the table. 'Thanks.'

'You're welcome.' Lily stood up and headed for the bar, her hips swaying far too temptingly. The last thing he intended was to dally with his new employer but . . . *Bad idea. Forget it*. He didn't do relationships with women these days in any shape or form, and for bloody good reasons. *Remember them*.

While she stood and waited for their drinks Lily pulled her dress down slightly, which did nothing for the miniscule length but sent Kenan's heart rate soaring. Unexpectedly she glanced back over her shoulder and caught him gawking. Her blatant smirk made the heat rise in Kenan's neck and he jerked away to stare out of the window.

'Let's toast our road trip,' she said, as she returned with the drinks.

Kenan steeled himself to turn back around and meet her gaze. She raised her glass and reluctantly he picked up his pint, leaning it towards her. Lily chinked her glass against his and flashed another of the brilliant smiles she used like a heat-seeking missile homing in on its target.

Kenan leaned closer, drawn by her delicious warm scent. Of its own accord his finger reached towards the fiery red curls, and the pulse throbbed harder

14

in her long, elegant neck. A pink flush crept up to stain her creamy, freckled skin making her look even more lovely.

Kenan withdrew his hand and pressed his fingers deep into his thigh. He couldn't do this, he mustn't. His ex-wife had ripped out his heart, stamped on it and consigned it to the dustbin. 'If you'll excuse me, I need to leave.' He stood up before she could reply, desperate to get away.

'Okay.' A touch of puzzlement dimmed her deep blue eyes and before he could move away she rested her hand on his bare forearm. Kenan could've sworn her fingers burnt through his skin. 'You sure you're all right?'

The concern resonating through her low, soft voice almost broke through his reserve, but at the last second Kenan came to his senses. 'Perfectly.'

'Okay. Well, I guess I'll go too, it's been a long day.' She gathered up her oversized orange bag and slung it over one shoulder.

He stood back and remembered his manners to let her walk out of the bar in front of him. Kenan tried to drag his eyes away from Lily Redman's neat curved backside encased in tight shiny orange silk, but he wasn't a saint. His jeans became uncomfortably tight and he struggled to banish thoughts he'd no right to have. A month alone in a car with this woman? No way would he survive unscathed.

They stepped outside into the street and the cool air brought him to his senses.

Lily shivered and, without thinking, Kenan slid an arm around her shoulder. She stared up at him, his own shock mirrored in her eyes.

'You were cold,' he explained, trying to sound practical.

'Yeah, I am but . . .'

Kenan pulled away and fought for control. 'I'll walk you home.' A cross between relief and disappointment slid over her extraordinarily expressive face.

'There's no need.'

'You're not going up the hill alone,' he retorted.

'Now look here, pal.' Her voice held an unexpected edge of steel. 'You're working for me. End of story. You aren't responsible for me. St Dinas isn't New York, and I've survived walking there alone. Back off.'

He tossed his hands up in the air and almost cracked a smile. 'You're the boss.'

'Exactly,' she snapped back. 'Be at Cliff House Monday morning at nine to pick me up. Any questions?'

Kenan had about a million but for now he resorted to shaking his head and walking away.

CHAPTER 3

'Kenan's here,' Betty shouted up the stairs. Lily cursed at the pile of abandoned clothes strewn all over her bed. She should have known her ex-military escort would be on time. 'Give him a cup of tea and say I'll be down in . . . ten minutes,' she called back with a tired sigh. Today was a short trip out to meet the first possible candidate for the *Celebrity Chef Swap* show. She figured the dour Kenan could take her sightseeing afterwards for the rest of the day. He'd probably rather shoot himself in the knee, but she was the one paying so it was tough.

Luc Pascal was French and a notorious womaniser so she'd play up *Luscious Lily* to the hilt. She tugged on a neon pink T-shirt, adding a pair of slim dark jeans and her signature pink stilettos. Lily rifled through her jewellery and selected pink dangly earrings and an armful of glittery bracelets. She added a pink diamond pendant on a chain, adjusting it to the perfect length to rest in the vee of her generous cleavage. One quick check in the mirror, a fluff of her hair, a slick of glossy pink lipstick and she was ready.

'Coming.' She ran down the stairs and tumbled to a halt an inch before she'd have landed right on top of Kenan Rowse's large feet, clad in black shoes so highly polished she could have applied her make-up in them. 'Oh, you're here. I thought Betty would be plying you with food.'

'Not necessary,' he answered with a hint of impatience. 'What needs to go out to the car?'

'Just these.' She thrust her iPad bag and camera plus a pink bag in his direction, keeping hold of her large pink tote bag. He snatched them from her hands, turned on his heels and headed out the door. Lily guessed he meant for her to follow.

Betty watched from the kitchen door and Lily got the distinct impression they were under surveillance. 'I won't need dinner tonight, thanks. Have a nice day.' She strode off and closed the front door behind her.

Lily stopped and sucked in a welcome breath of fresh, salty air.

'Ready?' Kenan's deep voice, tinged with the hint of what she recognised now as a Cornish accent, interrupted her pleasant thoughts. Ramrod-straight, legs spread, arms folded across his broad chest, he held open the passenger door of a gleaming black SUV.

'Very nice.' She eyed up the vehicle first, and then him, but his face never lost its impassive stare. The flash of interest she'd picked up on last night was well under control this morning. 'Is it yours?'

'No, I stole it to run you around the country in. Of course it's mine,' he retorted.

'Sorry.' She needed to mind her own business. He was her employee. End of story. 'Let's get this show on the road.' Lily avoided his impenetrable grey eyes and hopped up into the car, tucking her bag under her feet. He slammed her door shut and walked around to slide into the driver's seat.

'Don't you have a GPS?' she asked, not seeing one of the gadgets essential to her survival.

'Don't need one. Fowey first, right?'

'Yeah.' No doubt he could find his way in a snowstorm, blindfolded, in a place he'd never been before. She'd heard such people existed and should've known Kenan Rowse would fit the bill.

For the next half hour she clutched onto the door handle and prayed. Lily closed her eyes as he deftly negotiated narrow lanes, squeezed past a bus pulled over to one side to pick up passengers, and generally scared her half to death. The view along the rugged coastline was amazing when she was brave enough to risk a look.

Lily sneaked a glance at Kenan and caught the hint of a smile lurking around his stern mouth. 'Having fun are you?' The brief flash of humour disappeared and she wished she'd kept quiet. 'Are we nearly there?'

'Yep. Bountiful is around the next corner, right on the cliff edge.'

'I expect you're wondering why I particularly wanted to come here?' she probed.

'You want lunch?'

Lily cracked a wide smile. 'You are so literal.'

Kenan shrugged and returned to concentrating on the road.

'Yeah, I want lunch, but I'm here because of Luc Pascal. He's the—'

'Michelin starred chef. Expatriate Frenchman, converted to a lover of all things Cornish where food is concerned. His signature dish is a superb fish pie according to his website.'

Lily gaped in shock and couldn't say another word.

Kenan flicked the indicator on and steered the car off onto a narrow gravel road.

'You and I are going to talk one day even if I have to tie you down.' She should've guessed this intense man would treat their outing like a military mission and have done his homework.

'Not going to happen. It wasn't in the job description.' He pulled the car into an empty spot outside the front door.

She undid her seat belt and inched closer, watching his sharp, well-defined jaw clench into a rigid line. Lily crept one finger along his arm, putting a dent in his starched white shirt, and his muscles tensed as his broad hands gripped the steering wheel. 'We'll see about that.' Kenan's noisy deep breath sent a shaft of desire coursing through her body. Lily mentally counted to ten before moving away. 'Bring my iPad bag and camera, please.' What was she playing at?

He didn't answer, flung open his door, grabbed her things from the boot and waited for her to get out before locking up.

'Ah, *chérie*, at last I get to meet the famous *Luscious Lily*.' A tall, heavyset man in chef's whites swept out from the dining room. He tossed a strand of thick blond hair out of the way and bent over Lily's hand, kissing it enthusiastically.

'I'm the one who's honoured, Chef Pascal,' Lily insisted with a bright smile, discreetly retrieving her hand and putting it down by her side out of reach. 'When we spoke on the phone I was surprised you'd even heard of me. I haven't broken into the UK market yet.'

'Oh, I keep my pulse on what's going on,' he said with a leer and her heart sunk.

'How about we go inside to talk about my idea?' Lily suggested.

'Ah, you Americans. Always in a hurry. Today you are my guest. First we will enjoy a leisurely lunch.' He rested his hand low on the curve of her back and gently nudged her forward.

She glanced back over her shoulder at Kenan. 'Join us.'

'You bring a bodyguard with you, Lily? I am not dangerous.' He flashed a wolfish smile.

'Kenan's my driver and assistant.' *Assistant? Where did that come from?*

'He could eat in the kitchen with the staff while we get to know each other better.' Pascal's hand

21

slid further down Lily's back, resting on the curve of her backside. At a guess she'd say Kenan was this close to swatting the chef's plump white fingers away.

'Kenan needs to be with me to take notes. He's my sounding board.' *Play along with me. Come on.*

Kenan gave the semblance of an apologetic smile. 'Sorry, mate. Got to do what the boss wants.' He stepped up beside her, resting one large, reassuring hand on her shoulder

'Follow me. I've reserved the best table for us.' He tossed Kenan a dismissive glance. 'I'll have them bring another chair.'

'Thanks,' Lily murmured at her new 'assistant'. There was the vestige of a twinkle in his stern grey eyes making her darn sure he'd have the world's sexiest smile if he ever gave in to one.

She made sure to sit opposite Luc, with Kenan between them, and they settled down to read the menu. She and Luc entered into a long discussion about what to select and she bowed to his suggestions, wanting to sample the best he had to offer. The man's cooking was legendary and even if he didn't agree to be on the show this was a not-to-be-missed experience.

Lily suppressed a smile at Kenan's controlled response to the appetiser. At a wild guess she'd have to say that he'd never come across razor clams before served with crab and samphire, the sea vegetable she'd only tasted once before in Paris. His set expression and the way he bolted it down told her all she needed to know. Mr Kenan Rowse was no foodie, but she loved nothing better than changing people's perceptions of cooking and he'd be an interesting challenge. *You sure that's all you've got in mind for him?*

What Luc Pascal could do with food was truly sublime. Kenan was right about the fish pie but she'd bet anything he didn't realise it was the combination of the finest, locally sourced ingredients and an indefinable hint of French flair which made it so wonderful.

'I am guessing you did not enjoy the food, my Lily,' Luc Pascal murmured, reaching over to pat her hand. Flirting was part of breathing to him and she realised now that she'd overreacted earlier by taking him too seriously. 'I heard you were an outspoken woman, but you are on mute today?'

She mentally shook herself. 'I'm sorry. Your cooking has overwhelmed me.'

'I thought maybe the puff pastry on the fish pie was a touch overdone?' he questioned, perfectly serious.

Lily shook her head. 'It was perfect. Crisp and light on top, and delightfully soft where it met the velouté sauce. I'm sure you bought all the lobster, prawns, monkfish and scallops locally.' She smiled. 'I bet you know all the fishermen personally, and probably their families too?'

'It is the only way to make truly great food.' He cut a small sliver of cheese and popped it onto a

23

buttery homemade cracker. 'What do you think of my selection of local cheeses?'

'Amazing. I've fallen in love with this Cornish Blue.' She sliced off another piece and savoured the rich creamy flavour.

'Quite different from the more mature Stilton, isn't it? It's made to be enjoyed young.' He grinned and Lily extended the sentence in her mind – like a woman. 'Now, I'm ready to listen, *chérie*. Convince me I should be part of the – what did you call it – *Celebrity Chef Swap*?'

'I plan to take British and American chefs and put them in each other's kitchens for a week. I'll stick to English speakers so theoretically there won't be a language problem, although I kinda think putting a Scottish chef in a New York kitchen should make for interesting TV.'

Lily's heart thumped. If Luc Pascal signed on then the others would be far more keen to join in. The Frenchman's influence was wide-ranging, belied by the size of this small restaurant. With three Michelin stars, a shelf full of bestselling cookbooks, and his own training programme for young chefs, she needed him badly. He'd refused every other television offer so hers must be irresistible.

'I know you don't need the publicity, the money or the aggravation.' He agreed with a touch of amusement. 'But there's something you'd get from this show that you can't find anywhere else.'

'Enlighten me, *chérie*.' His wry smile encouraged her to keep going.

'You're a naturally curious man. If I wasn't being polite I'd call you nosey.' Now his smile turned into a full-on grin. 'You'd love nothing better than having free rein to poke around in another chef's kitchen. You are also – excuse my American bluntness – arrogant about how things should be done. You'll relish being able to steer someone else's staff in *your* direction.'

Luc burst into loud, unrestrained laughter. 'Ah, Lily, you are the very devil.'

She frowned and nibbled at her lip, a nervous habit she detested but never had grown out of.

'That is a compliment, *chérie*. You've done your homework and found out my weak spot. You should be a general in the army. You'd win every battle.'

Lily crossed her fingers under the table.

'I can't resist you, my dear. Give the details to my agent and we'll hammer it out.' He held out his hand. 'Shake on it, my *Luscious Lily*. I do believe this might be fun.'

Before she could react he seized hold of her hand and brought it to his lips. Lily caught sight of Kenan's rigid face and suppressed a giggle knowing her mother would approve of his protective attitude. She'd been furious when Lily dumped Patrick. The fact he was unfaithful and controlling could apparently be excused because he was a handsome man with a good job and plenty of money. Lily guessed her mother's reasoning came from her own struggle after Josh Harding ran off

25

leaving her pregnant and penniless, but she wasn't her mother. She'd take care of herself and Kenan could keep his outdated ways to himself.

'I'm thrilled we'll be working together. Thank you so much. I'm guessin' we'd better be going, don't you, Kenan?' He grunted and stood to join her.

Kenan extended his hand to the Frenchman. 'Thank you, sir. Miss Redman needs to get to her next appointment.' He steered her outside and in five minutes she was in the car with her seat belt buckled. Lily glanced over at Kenan's face, dark as thunder, and waited.

CHAPTER 4

'Where next?' He refused to look directly at her, needing to get under control emotions he resented having in the first place.

'Apparently I've some urgent appointment. You don't want to discuss what happened back there?' Lily's drawl thickened to the consistency of rich, golden syrup.

'No,' he snapped.

'Guess I need a crowbar to get anything out of you.'

He held onto his silence, the only protection against Lily's constant probing.

'I'll give up for now,' she conceded, but Kenan wasn't stupid enough to believe it was anything more than a temporary reprieve. This woman had the word relentless running all the way through her like a stick of rock.

'There's an organic farm and market shop near here at—'

'Burton's. At Penarth,' he asserted. 'We can be there in about fifteen minutes.'

'Don't tell me – you know the owner?' she teased.

Kenan shrugged. 'Pete Trewarren and I were at school together. He and his wife Evelyn took over her old family property about ten years ago.' He dared a quick glance, meeting her inquisitive stare. 'It's a working farm and it'll be muddy after yesterday's rain. You'll mess up those pretty shoes.' He gestured towards the high-heeled pink things showing off her delicate ankles and tiny feet.

'You put my other pink bag in the trunk, didn't you?'

'Yes, it's in the boot.'

Lily snorted. 'Oh, excuse me,' she exaggerated her drawl, pulling out the words like stretchy toffee. 'Better use the Queen's English or I'll be locked up in the Tower.' She ran one hand through her hair, sending the shiny curls into orbit before they settled down again. He'd swear they had a life of their own.

'Sorry,' he muttered, hating the way she turned him into a humourless jerk. Just because he *was* one these days didn't mean he cared to have it pointed out.

'No, you're not but I'll let you off this time. Inside the bag you'll find a pair of pink wellington boots. And, yes, before you laugh – I assume you know *how* to laugh – they've got my name spelled out on them in sparkly fake diamonds. Satisfied?' She smirked.

Kenan grunted. He tightened his face, determined she wouldn't find out how close he was to laughing. She'd slid under his skin and lodged there, like an annoying prickly burr, and he was fighting it big time. 'Here we are,' he stated baldly, and drove up a rough track into a courtyard fronting several old granite farm buildings. 'Sit there and I'll get your boots.' He waited for another smart-ass retort but she just smiled sweetly. Kenan wasn't fooled for a moment. He got out and fetched her bag, opened it up on the back seat and found the boots.

'Stick your feet out here.' He opened her door and grasped hold of her right foot, pulled off her shoe, and tossed it back inside. Kenan pulled on the bright pink boot, rested his fingers on the warm, smooth skin near her knee and glanced up. *Big mistake.* Lily's startled gaze drew him in and for several long breaths he couldn't move. She cleared her throat and he dropped his attention back to the task in hand.

He repeated the process with the other foot, minus the lingering touch. Standing up he went to the back of the car again and stood for a minute to rest his trembling hands on the open door. Back to steadiness he picked up her camera bag and returned to face her.

'There you go.'

'Thanks.' She seized it from his hands with only a sidelong glance.

Was it good that she was equally affected or did it make things worse? He rather thought, worse. Kenan spotted Pete ambling across the farmyard towards them and let out a long exhalation, grateful for the interruption.

'All right, mate. How's it going?' They shook hands and Kenan gestured towards Lily.

'This is Lily Redman. She's here from America.'

She stuck out her hand and flashed Pete a beguiling smile. Kenan watched his friend succumb to her charms in about two seconds. What was it about him and women who could bewitch any man in sight? Surely he'd been through enough with his perennially unfaithful ex-wife to have learned his lesson on that score?

'I'm a chef and I'm here exploring ideas for a new TV show. Mr Rowse is working for me as a Jack-of-all-trades, aren't you?' She flashed her sweetest smile at Kenan without waiting for a reply. 'I want to get a feel for the organic food movement here, purely for my own satisfaction.'

'It'll be a pleasure to show you around.' Pete glanced down at her legs. 'Nice boots. I'll have to get the wife a pair. She's always complaining that she lives in ugly green rubber boots,' Pete joked.

'You tell me her size and I'll send a pair over when I'm back in Nashville.'

'Nashville?' Pete's voice rose. 'Is that where you're from?'

'Yeah, I grew up there,' she replied. 'I worked in New York for a while but went back soon as I could.'

'The wife and I are both big country music fans,' Pete declared. 'We'd love to go there for a holiday if we weren't tied to this place. Don't suppose you know Vince Gill?'

'Yeah, I've catered several parties for him and Amy.'

Pete's broad, ruddy face lit up and Kenan knew she'd scored another fan.

'Keith Urban lives down the road from me too, in Leiper's Fork.'

'He's the wife's favourite,' Pete exclaimed. 'After you've had a look around you'll have to come meet her.'

Lily grinned and threw Kenan a satisfied smirk. He didn't answer just followed along in their wake. Pete was one of the few old friends he still hung out with and he wasn't sure of the wisdom of exposing him to Lily. If he wasn't careful she'd winkle his life story out of Pete before the tea had a chance to get cold in the cup.

'We supply a lot of hotels and restaurants. If you come into the packing shed they're putting together the boxes to go out today,' Pete explained, leading the way into the long, low building. 'Salad leaves, tomatoes, courgettes, peppers, new potatoes and cucumbers.' Pete started to fill a box while he talked. The long wooden trestle table was covered with various sized boxes being filled by a handful of seasonal workers. 'There's spinach, peas and beans too for some of them.'

'Everything looks amazing.' Lily grabbed a handful of pea pods, opened one and popped a couple of peas into her mouth. 'Oh, my, that's good. Really sweet.'

'Better than any of the mass-produced junk,' Pete asserted.

'Certainly is.' Lily munched away happily. She turned and thrust a pod in Kenan's direction. 'Try it. They're like candy.'

He couldn't refuse without being churlish so followed orders, biting into the sweet crunchy vegetable.

'You like them?' she persisted.

'Yes. Fine.'

'Don't over enthuse, will you?' Her fiery blue eyes challenged him and Kenan caught Pete scrutinising them both.

'Give over, Lily, they're peas. What do you expect me to say?'

'Don't you care about where your food comes from?' she probed.

'Never given it much thought.' Kenan shrugged. 'If there's food available when I'm hungry, that works for me. I don't see what all the fuss is about.'

She shook her head sadly, and the devilish twinkle returned to her eyes. 'I'll make you understand one day. You see if I don't.'

Kenan folded his arms and met her challenging stare head on.

'You can come see the fields or have tea. Take your pick,' Pete intervened.

'I vote for tea. It might cheer up my companion,' Lily said with a mocking laugh.

Kenan kept his mouth shut and shoved his hands in his pockets.

'I doubt it will, my dear. He's not much fun these days.' Pete good-humouredly poked Kenan's arm. 'You've had a tough time, haven't you, mate?'

He fixed his friend with a long hard stare. 'No more than a lot of others.'

'Nothin' wrong with admitting things haven't been a barrel of laughs for you recently, you stubborn so and so. There was all that mess with Olivia and then Afghanistan . . .'

'That's the past,' Kenan insisted, needing the conversation to end right there. Thankfully Pete got the hint and shut up, but Lily had stood there drinking in every word. He'd be for the high jump later.

'Right. Tea. Come this way.' Pete ushered Lily in the direction of the farmhouse and Kenan trailed along in their wake.

Evelyn, her red striped apron dusted with flour, came to the door smiling and encouraged them to come in. The comfortable, untidy room, with its plain country furniture and fresh baking spread out on the table, seemed to mock him and his empty life. A shaft of envy skewered Kenan and he dropped down into the nearest chair without saying anymore than a gruff hello.

The conversation flowed around him jumping from the problems of farming in Cornwall to Lily's take on the latest country music gossip. Kenan tried to choke down a scone but after ten minutes he couldn't take any more. He pushed back his chair and stood up. 'I'm going to take a walk around. Stay as long as you like.' He gave Lily a nod and waited for a snappy reply but only received a pitying glance. *Make me feel worse why don't you, woman?*

He strode outside and stalked off towards the fields, not slowing down until he was well out of sight of the farmhouse. He leaned on the fence and stared out over the timeless landscape spread in front of him. The sight of the neat, ploughed earth and lush vegetables growing in the summer warmth eased whatever was gnawing at his insides. After a few minutes he began to think he might manage to get through the rest of the day.

Lily made her excuses to Evelyn and Pete by saying they needed to be getting back to St Dinas. 'I've got to make some calls to the States for work.'

'Come back anytime. We'd love to hear more about Nashville,' Evelyn said with a friendly smile.

'I'd love to and I promise to get you some lady-like boots.' Lily turned her leg, showing them off again, rewarded by a grin from her new friend. 'Thanks again.'

She made her escape and set off to find Kenan. He'd looked terrible earlier, haggard and utterly miserable, and the curious side of Lily wanted to know why. It wasn't hard to track him down, leaning in over a gate and staring into the distance, but at the last second she hesitated. Was his private life any of her business?

'You okay?' she asked, and he was startled,

jerking around with a fierce, dark glare. 'In case you're worried, Pete and Evelyn didn't tell me anything.' Lily met his gaze straight on, struggling not to tremble under the magnetism of his steel grey eyes. 'Of course, if you want to share anything I'll listen.'

'I don't. I'm not into the whole soul-baring business everyone's so damn keen on these days. Afghanistan isn't for your ears. Maybe I'll talk about it when I'm an old man.' He shrugged. 'As for Olivia. She's my ex-wife. Let's just say it was a nasty divorce and leave it at that.'

'I didn't know you'd been married.'

'No reason why you should. You employed me for a job. You're not writing my biography.'

His sarcasm made her wince, but she was pretty certain it was nothing more than a cover-up. 'It would be a pretty short book,' Lily teased. The corner of his mouth twitched meaning she'd almost got him to smile. One point to her. But then with slow deliberation he reached out his hand to rest it against her cheek. Lily leaned into the warmth of Kenan's touch as his sure, firm fingers stroked idly over her skin. A quiet groan escaped the back of his throat and she tilted her face to expose herself to his intense stare sending her senses into overdrive.

Kenan's fingers dropped away and his large, sure hands inched down to her waist, fitting into her curves, and he eased her up against his lean, hard body.

Lily's breathing came in short puffs and a flare of heat rushed up her skin setting it on fire. He lowered his head so close to her mouth that she caught the scent of the strawberry jam they'd eaten on his warm breath. Reaching up she clasped her arms loosely around the back of his neck and raised up on the toes of her boots ready to be kissed, her heart racing.

'Damn it, Lily.' Kenan pushed her away and she almost stumbled on the rough ground before managing to catch her balance.

'What the hell . . .' She straightened up, glaring at him.

'Sorry. I don't know what came over me. My behaviour was completely out of line.' He stared down at his feet, as though they were the most interesting things on the planet. 'We'd better go. I promise there won't be a repeat of that.'

'Why not? Didn't you want to kiss me?' The question tumbled out and his face turned to stone. There'd be no truthful answer but the perverse side of her hadn't been able to resist asking anyway.

'We're leaving now.' He strode off, not checking back to see if she followed.

CHAPTER 5

Lily didn't rush to join him. Her breathing slowed back down and rational brain cells crept back into her head. She'd broken her longstanding rule never to mix business with pleasure by getting involved with Patrick and should have learned her lesson. On the plane over here she'd promised herself not to get involved with any man for a very long time. Three days couldn't be defined as long in anyone's book.

But something about Kenan's hard narrow face, blade-sharp cheekbones, and piercing grey eyes grabbed her from day one, and wouldn't let go. There was no hint of softness about the man but she'd studied his generously shaped mouth and guessed he'd be a devastating kisser. She'd almost got to find out until he freaked out on her. But there was something else, something indefinable that went beyond simple physical attraction. There were layers to this man that she wanted to peel back in order to discover the core of him. If he had his way she'd never find out what made him tick but the challenge was irresistible.

She strolled back across the courtyard and found

Kenan waiting with the car door open, his granite features resembling the presidents carved into Mount Rushmore. *Right.* She'd be cool and professional too. 'I'd like to return to Cliff House. We've done enough for one day.' *Understatement.* 'Tomorrow we'll do lunch at Water's Edge in Charlestown, plus I want to check out the Eden Project I've heard so much about. First thing on Wednesday arrive ready to take off for a week. I'll print off the list of appointments later so you can book our accommodations and plan the route.'

His implacable expression didn't shift. 'No problem.'

She got into the car and he silently removed her boots, leaving her to slip her shoes back on herself. Neither spoke all the way back to St Dinas but by the time they arrived at Cliff House Lily almost burst from the effort. Silence wasn't a natural state for most Southern women, taught from childhood to initiate polite conversation and put people at ease. Her mother would have called her out for being rude but limits were limits, and she'd reached hers for today.

She threw open the door and stepped out before he could do his polite chauffeur thing. He didn't comment, only got out himself and retrieved all her bags from the world-famous boot. Lily tried to take them from his hands but he ignored her and stomped off into the house leaving her to tag along behind like an irritating little girl who wouldn't leave her older brother alone. She couldn't easily catch up in her standard six-inch stilettos. If she stayed here much longer Lily might have to resort to comfortable shoes.

'What time tomorrow?' he called back brusquely over his shoulder.

Wow three words. Lily bit her tongue on snapping out a scathing reply. She'd no right to complain. 'Ten is early enough.'

'Right.' Kenan headed for the front door and opened it with one hand while he managed her bags with the other.

'There you are, my dears.' Betty Tremayne bustled out from her kitchen. 'Your mother's been trying to get a hold of you, Kenan.' A deep frown settled on her forehead. 'She says Olivia turned up today and—'

'I'm heading there now,' he cut her off and an instant rush of heat flamed the older woman's face. Lily seriously considered smacking him for being so rude. 'Good night.' He nodded to them both and virtually ran from the house.

'It's all right, love. No harm done. He's a good boy at heart.' Betty wiped her flour-covered hands on her apron. 'How about a nice cup of tea?'

About to say she couldn't eat or drink another thing, Lily mentally kicked herself. She was being handed the chance to find out more about Kenan on a silver platter. 'Sure. That'd be good.' Lily abandoned her bags in a heap to one side of the stairs and followed Betty. She was an expert at sniffing out things. Her mother always said she'd do well as a CIA agent – her sharp brain and smooth tongue could achieve more than all the fancy spy equipment going.

'What've you been baking?' Lily asked artlessly, and peered at the cooling racks full of warm, fragrant cooking spread all over the counters. Betty smiled, and for a second she almost felt guilty. It soon passed and she settled in to pick her land-lady's brain.

Kenan's nerves were strung tighter than a guitar string. The interlude with Lily had left him on edge, wondering how he'd cope for a week with the woman, let alone any longer. Why had Olivia turned up to cause trouble again? When they divorced he'd given in to her wishes, so why wouldn't she leave him in peace? She'd convinced him that it would be less unsettling for Mandy if he didn't pop in and out of his daughter's life at irregular intervals and so he'd reluctantly stayed away. Olivia used the fact that he'd had some anger issues during his time in the Army to imply he wouldn't be a good father. She'd probably been right but it had hurt like hell every single day. Olivia's unfaithful behaviour had pushed him close to the edge. If Mandy hadn't interrupted them arguing one day he couldn't be sure what he might or might not have done and Olivia had used that against him. She sent the agreed upon photos and updates on Mandy twice a year but, apart from sending child support, it had been their only contact for nearly six years. Facing his ex-wife again was the last thing he needed today. Kenan rubbed at his forehead, wishing the burgeoning headache would go away.

He trudged up the path to his parents' house and sucked in a deep breath before unlocking and opening the door.

'There you are, son. We weren't sure what to do.' His father's face was grey with worry. Kenan stepped towards the living room, but his father grabbed his arm. 'Not yet. We need to talk before you go in there. Go in the kitchen a minute.'

A knot formed in Kenan's stomach as he obeyed and headed down through the hall and into the sunny room. He walked over to the large, open window and fixed his gaze on the back garden. In Afghanistan he'd dreamed of this – the lush green grass and vibrant summer flowers. It had comforted him to imagine his parents sitting out on the small patio, enjoying the warm evening air. He waited a minute before turning back around. 'All right. Tell me the worst.'

His father shuffled from one foot to the other, went over to turn the kettle on and couldn't meet Kenan's eyes.

'Come on, Dad. Spit it out.'

William Rowse sighed and set the mugs he was holding back down on the counter. 'Olivia arrived here in a taxi just after lunch . . . with Mandy. She's grown so much, Kenan. We couldn't believe it was our little girl after all this time,' his voice

41

cracked and he ineffectually wiped at his moist eyes.

'Mandy?' The name stuck in Kenan's throat. He hated having caused his parents so much pain because of the mess he'd made of his life.

'Your mother fed them and then Olivia sent Mandy out in the garden to play. Olivia said she felt bad for keeping the kiddy from seeing us and would we like to have her to stay for a few days?' He cleared his throat and fiddled with the sleeve of his shirt. ''Course your Mum was over the moon.'

'And you weren't?' Kenan asked, not quite understanding what his father was getting at.

'Don't get me wrong, Son, but I don't believe Olivia's doing this out of the kindness of her heart. She's up to something.' He rooted around in his pocket, pulling out a scrappy piece of paper and holding it out to Kenan. 'She said to give this to you.'

Kenan scanned the few brief lines and anger rolled through his body. He clenched his fist to avoid punching it through the nearest wall.

'Take it easy.' His father's steady voice resonated between them. 'The girl's not to blame.'

'I didn't say she was but I can't believe Olivia would dump her this way. Why didn't she at least call first? What does she think I'm going to do with Mandy when the poor kid doesn't even know me?' Kenan's long-buried pain exploded.

'Take care of her? She *is* your daughter.' His father's stern tone shook Kenan.

'I know that. It's complicated and I don't expect you to understand, but at the time it made sense for her to be solely with Olivia. Girls need a mother.' He'd never shared the full story with his parents, and didn't intend to now. He saw Olivia's betrayal of him as partly his own fault for not being the husband she deserved. She had used his uncertain temper against him and he'd been too mired in self-hatred to fight her.

'We'll manage between us, and I don't think it'll be for long. You can't put it all on your mother though. You know her heart's dodgy and I've taken enough time off work recently.' His father's voice dropped. 'Mandy's waiting to see you. We showed her some photos because she couldn't remember what you look like.' Unspoken disapproval hung in the air. 'She's beautiful. I can't believe she's eight.'

Nor can I. He'd never forget holding his tiny, perfect daughter for the first time. He'd believed they could be a real family, but it had unravelled in two short years. 'All right, let's get this over with.'

'That's no way to talk about—'

'Dad, drop it, okay. I didn't mean it that way. She'll probably scream or cry and I won't bloody well know what to do.' Kenan pushed past and walked towards the living room. He stopped outside for a second listening to a girl's high-pitched voice chattering away to his mother. Before he could lose his nerve Kenan swung open the door and stopped dead in his tracks.

'Daddy?' A tiny girl with a blonde ponytail and

43

huge blue eyes stared at him, and Kenan's heart broke.

'These are delicious.' Lily took another of the small cakes from the plate and bit into the light sponge.

'It's only a butterfly bun, my dear, nothing special,' Betty protested with a pleased expression.

Lily examined the cake again, loving how the top was arranged like butterfly wings on a spoonful of delicious butter cream. 'This is another thing you've got to teach me to make.' Her mind raced imagining the different flavour combinations she could put together – apricot cake and almond cream, German chocolate cake with coconut cream – the possibilities were endless. Everyone was doing cupcakes these days, but this was something unusual. She sipped her tea and wondered how best to turn the conversation towards Kenan.

'He's a private man and I'm not talking about him behind his back,' Betty stated firmly and a rush of heat lit up Lily's face. 'I like having you here, my dear, and I'm some glad you're helping Kenan out with a little job. He needs a break but how much he wants to share about his past is up to him.'

Lily couldn't quite meet Betty's shrewd eyes. 'Sorry, I didn't mean to pry. I guess I'm a people person.' She'd try another tack. 'We went to Pete Trewarren's farm this afternoon.' Lily chattered casually about the wonderful vegetables, which led onto the fact they'd had tea in the farmhouse.

'Evelyn's a good woman and a wonderful cook,' Betty said.

'She sure is. I'd never had sausage rolls before and her pastry is awesome.' She decided to take a chance and put out another feeler for information. 'They mentioned Kenan's ex-wife and how he'd had a rough experience in the war.'

Betty's lips pursed and Lily crossed her fingers under the table and waited to be told off. 'It's no secret, I suppose. We all know he saw things no one should and was lucky to come home in one piece.' She looked thoughtful. 'I'm not sure he always feels that way. He's probably got that thing you hear about in the news all the time.'

'PTSD?'

'That's right. 'Course they used to call it "shell shock" back in the Great War but it's all the same, isn't it?' She frowned and shook her head. 'I know they help them more these days, but Kenan's not the type to talk to some doctor, is he?'

Lily certainly couldn't imagine Kenan spilling his guts to a psychiatrist or letting himself be drugged up with antidepressants. He'd push through it and hope to come out the other side. 'Nope, he isn't.' Lily sipped her tea and forced herself to be patient. It didn't take long.

'His marriage wasn't a good one and the divorce was messy. Olivia weren't a good wife to him. Pretty girl but hard as nails. Kenan got taken in by her, you know what men are like. Turned heads she did. Too many, if you get my meaning.' Betty broke into a smile and wagged her finger at Lily. 'You'm a devious one. I said I weren't going to talk about Kenan and look at me. Get on with you and let me clear up. Will you eat a bite of supper with me later? I made a crab quiche earlier to have with some salad from the garden.'

Lily wasn't sure she could eat another thing today but there was no getting out of it politely. 'That'd be great. I've got some work to do if the Internet's working.'

'It were all right earlier. I talked to my daughter in New Zealand on Skype,' Betty said proudly. 'We'll have supper about eight, if that's all right?'

'Perfect, and thanks again.' Lily ran out and scooped up her things from the hall before running upstairs. She'd made more progress on the Kenan investigation than she could've hoped for. If he wouldn't open up himself she'd find other ways. Lily refused to delve too deeply into why she was so determined to find out more about her temporary driver or why she found him so devastatingly attractive.

First thing Lily did when she got to the bedroom was turn on her phone and plug it in to recharge. She then switched on her iPad and waited for it to open up so that she could check emails. Her cellphone immediately beeped with a new text message.

Urgent. Need to meet tonight. Possible change of plans for tomorrow. Kenan.

Irritated, she texted right back. *Shark's Fin. Nine p.m. Lily.* He'd better not screw around and bail out on her. Kenan Rowse would discover she wasn't a woman to be messed with.

CHAPTER 6

'Mandy's gone off to sleep. What're you going to do about this American woman?'

Kenan glanced up from nursing his cold cup of coffee and met his mother's worried gaze. 'Don't know, Mum. I'm meeting her down the Shark's Fin later.' He shrugged. 'I'll probably have to quit the job. I can't let Mandy down and who knows when Olivia will decide to swan back in?'

'I'm sure we could manage for a few days. I love having the little sweetheart here. I've missed her something awful.' She gave a heavy sigh and tears brimmed in her eyes.

'You aren't well enough,' his father interrupted. 'You know the doctor said you weren't to overdo it.'

'But the boy needs to work. You said so yourself,' she persisted.

Kenan needed to step in before this disintegrated into another of the circular discussions they'd got mired in on a regular basis since he returned home. He'd only ever intended this as a breathing space to sort out what to do with the rest of his life, but it had dragged on longer than

48

he'd hoped. Lily's arrival gave him the perfect temporary escape lifeline and he hated having to abandon the chance to get away.

'Dad's right. I'll see what Lily has to say and we'll talk later, okay? I know you want to spend time with Mandy, but I can't have you being totally responsible. I'd never forgive myself if you got sick again.' Kenan hated to remember how awful his Mum looked in the hospital, convinced the stress he'd caused had sent her there in the first place. 'End of story, Mum.' He caught approval in his Dad's face, something he didn't often see there and guessed he'd said the right thing for once.

He stood up and took his dirty cup over to rinse out. 'I'll be off soon. Thanks again for everything.' Kenan couldn't look at them and left before his mother could do anything like hug him.

Kenan nursed a pint of Tribute and considered how little he could get away with telling Lily.

'Somebody died?' Lily's soft drawl startled him from his musings. 'You have to be the most miserable man I've ever met,' she teased and dropped into the chair next to him, flashing one of her gut-wrenching smiles.

What did she know about him? Nothing, and he intended keeping it that way for his own sanity. 'Good evening, Lily. May I get you a drink?' He struggled to be polite. The idea of asking her a favour stuck in his throat.

'Like that, is it?' She rested her hand on his arm,

warming the skin on contact and he fought against reacting. 'My usual will do fine. Thank you so much, my ultra suave escort,' Lily joked with a dramatic eye-roll.

'Do you have to call me that? I'm not a damn gigolo,' Kenan protested.

'Don't worry, no one would ever mistake you for one of *those*.' Her sapphire-blue eyes flashed with mischief. 'You *are* good-looking in a macho sort of way, but charm and smooth manners are essential for gigolos so you shouldn't bother applying for the job.'

He didn't reply but stood up to fetch her a drink as ordered. As he brushed past her Kenan got an unneeded blast of spicy perfume. The damn woman must've filled one complete suitcase with the stuff and was using a different one every day as her own particular form of torture. He escaped to the bar, noticing on the way over how much attention she was receiving again from all the men in the room. Not that he blamed them. Tonight's scarlet miniskirt, white silky top, and yards of toned legs finished off by high-heeled red sandals didn't exactly fade into the background.

'There you go, mate. You'm a lucky man tonight.' The barman gave Kenan a knowing wink and nodded towards Lily.

'I'm working for her. Driving her around the place. Nothing more,' he growled. The last thing he needed was that sort of talk spreading around the village. Grabbing the rum and Coke, loaded with enough ice to satisfy a polar bear, he made his way back to the corner and prepared to get it over with.

'Thanks.' She took the glass from his hand and for a split-second they touched and a surge of unwanted desire surged through his body.

'Okay, big boy, what's up? You asked to meet and I'm pretty sure it wasn't because you've a sudden longing for my company.'

Kenan knocked back the rest of his beer. 'It's personal, and I'm not good at that stuff.'

'Yeah, I'm guessing the British Army's bad at the whole opening up and sharing thing.' Lily gave a wry smile. 'Don't worry. I won't bite.'

He gritted his teeth and ploughed on. 'My marriage didn't last long – it was all over in less than three years.' Kenan dropped his gaze away finding it easier not to meet her sympathetic curiosity head on. 'We had a beautiful daughter together. Mandy's eight now and, for various reasons, I hadn't seen her in a while.' He cleared his throat and forced himself to glance back up. 'Yesterday afternoon my ex-wife turned up with Mandy. Olivia . . .' his voice faded and Kenan stumbled over what to say next.

'Go on,' Lily's soothing voice trickled over him and he sucked in a deep breath.

'Olivia asked my parents if they'd like to have Mandy to stay for a few days. She gave them a note to pass on to me.' Kenan searched through his wallet and handed over the crumpled sheet of paper.

'You sure you want me to read this?' Lily asked.

He nodded and scrutinised her expression as she scanned the few brief lines. By now he knew them by heart.

I'll be back for her soon. It's your turn. This is my London address if there are any problems. Olivia.

'There's a lot I could ask but the obvious one is – why are you sharing all this?' Lily sounded puzzled.

'Why the hell do you think?' He couldn't control his exasperation. 'I can hardly go off with you and leave Mandy with my parents. She doesn't know them anymore than she does me, plus my Dad's working and Mum's health isn't great.'

Lily rested her warm hand on top of his. 'I get it. I'm not dumb.' He saw the wheels racing around in her head and waited. Some bizarre idea was about to emerge. The woman was full of them. 'It's simple. She can come with us.'

'You're mad,' Kenan stated bluntly, but she only bestowed another kind smile in his direction. She appeared to take no notice of the surly manners he used to keep everyone else at bay and he wasn't sure how it made him feel. Exposed was the word that sprang to mind.

'I think we've established that fact. What's the problem? The car's big enough.'

He yanked his hand away, unable to think straight with her touching him. 'I don't want your sympathy. You need someone free to work with no restrictions and I can't do that with Mandy to take care of.' He shoved one hand up through his close-cropped hair.

Lily leaned back and crossed her arms, tightening the shiny white material across her full breasts and driving him half-crazy. 'Look, you need the job and I need help. I don't have time to find someone else and we work together . . . okay.'

The woman was certifiably mad. The unwanted desire ricocheting between them didn't need fuelling, exactly what she seemed determined to do.

'You sure as heck had to be adaptable in the military so consider this another assignment,' she dared him. 'I'd bet anything you tackled whatever they threw at you. You're obviously a born leader because you're always trying to boss me around.'

And we both know what a waste of effort that is. You're worse than a steamroller on steroids.

She prodded him hard in the ribs.

'What did you do that for?' Kenan complained.

'A reaction. What were you muttering to yourself?' Before he could answer she carried blithely on. 'Maybe it was something on the lines of – who's the bossy one?'

Kenan enjoyed the sparring between them more than he should, but wasn't about to admit anything to her. 'Before I even consider your suggestion you need to meet Mandy. You might think she's a brat and she might hate you on sight.'

'Is she a brat?' Lily joked.

'Of course not,' Kenan reacted in one second.

'She's bright, funny and the prettiest little girl you've seen in your whole life.'

'Not that you're prejudiced, of course.'

'You're teasing me again.' He relaxed back into the seat, spreading out his hands on the table.

'Yeah, not good with it are you?'

'Sorry.' The rarely used word dragged from the back of his throat. 'It's not something I say often, so make the most of it.'

'I'd never have guessed,' she jibed, glancing at her watch. 'It's too late for me to come over tonight. Tell you what – we'll continue as planned with our visit to Water's Edge at Charlestown tomorrow. We'll see how it goes and if things are okay, we'll pack up and leave on Thursday.'

'And if not?' Kenan persisted.

'We'll deal with it then. Don't anticipate problems.'

'You told me to use my military training and anticipating problems is as essential as working out possible solutions. I'll come up with a Plan B,' he declared.

'I'll bet you will,' Lily said with a chuckle. 'Probably C, D and E as well.' She gathered up her large, pink leather tote and stood up. 'I'd better go. I've got things to do, plus if I don't call my mother soon she'll be on the next plane over.'

'I'll give you a lift.' He stood as well and quickly glanced down at her shoes. 'I don't know how you made it down here but you'll sprain your ankles climbing back up the hill in those things.'

'Thanks. I could argue but I'll concede you're right – for once.' Lily smirked. 'Don't expect to hear that again anytime soon though either – it's rather like one of your apologies.'

'Wouldn't dare.' Kenan cut an exaggerated salute and without thinking tucked her hand through the crook of his elbow, steering them out through the crowded pub.

Back outside he pulled her across the road to the harbour wall. 'Come and see the view.' Kenan stood Lily in front of him and shoved his hands into his pockets because if he didn't he'd be tempted to slide his arms around her narrow waist and ease her back against him. He knew too well how damn good that would feel. 'Lovely isn't it?' He murmured half to himself, gazing out across the ink-black sea. Reflections from the multicoloured lights strung up around the harbour danced over the quiet waves.

'I used to dream of this in Afghanistan. I could picture every detail. Didn't matter if it was a hundred and twenty degrees and in the middle of a sandstorm, in my head I was here.'

'How long were you there?' Her quiet voice drifted in the still air.

'A year the first two times and about nine months the last go around.' Without having to meet her inquisitive eyes the words tumbled out. 'The last one should have been a full year but I got caught up in an incident.' Her silence drew him on. 'I let my mates down and one died.' He'd never said the words out loud before to someone who knew nothing of his past. Lily tried to respond but he cut her off. 'Don't pacify me. It won't work.' The crushing video replayed in his head every day.

Lily turned to face him and slid her hands up to reach around the back of his neck. Her slim, strong fingers toyed with his hair, making him shiver. As her clear blue eyes penetrated deep into him, Kenan lost the ability to breathe. 'I've never been one for platitudes and I'm guessing you've heard them all anyway. All I'll say is – if you don't live your life to the full it's the ultimate insult to your comrade.' She pressed a soft kiss into his cheek. 'End of advice for the night.'

'Good.' Her glossy red lips glowed in the moonlight tempting him beyond belief. His whole body ached with need for her and Kenan struggled to remember why this was a lousy idea. 'Lily, we shouldn't . . .' She trailed her hands slowly down over his spine turning him to jelly.

'Kenan, haven't you ever done anything you shouldn't before now?' He caught the hint of throaty laughter in her voice.

With a heavy sigh he forced himself to ease away. 'Oh, Lily. I've got to go. They're expecting me back home.'

'Are you always so sensible?' she complained.

'Yes. I'm well known for it, but you're tempting me to break the rules,' he murmured.

'One day we're going to break them together. I know it and so do you.'

He couldn't answer, unable to either admit the truth or lie. 'Come on. My car's around the corner.' Kenan draped his arm around her shoulder. 'I'll take you home and if you behave I'll give you a chaste good night kiss.'

'I suppose it's the best offer I'm goin' to get.'

This was out and out insane. He hadn't been this drawn to a woman since . . . well, never.

This wasn't featured in any military training manual he'd ever come across and Kenan had a strong suspicion he was in deep trouble.

CHAPTER 7

'Hi, Mom.' Lily held the phone away from her ear after being almost deafened by her mother's loud squeal. 'Yeah, I'm real sorry I didn't call before but I've been kinda busy. I did text when I got here. I don't need the guilt trip, okay?'

'How're you gettin' around? Please don't tell me you're driving on the wrong side of the road in some undersized excuse for a car?' Tricia Redman persisted.

'My landlady hooked me up with a good guy to drive me around and organise things,' Lily rushed straight on before she got the standard 'beware of strange men' lecture. 'He's ex-army and straight as they come. Very reliable and sensible.' *Except where it comes to me.* Her mother didn't need to hear that piece of the story.

'Hmm, well I guess it'll be okay.' Her mom hesitated, 'I don't suppose you've heard from Patrick?'

'No, why should I? I fired him as my business manager, remember? I want nothing more to do with him, apart from when I'm forced to see him at the network.' Her mother's awkward silence opened an empty pit in Lily's gut. 'You've talked to him, haven't you?'

'Oh, Lily, sweetheart. I—'

'What was the last thing I said when I left?' A rush of anger spiralled up through her head.

'Not to speak to him,' her mom muttered, 'but he called and was so sweet an' all asking after you.'

Lily counted to ten on her fingers before she calmed enough to speak again. 'He's always *sweet* . . . sweet is Patrick's specialty. People fall for it and trust him but most live to regret it.' *Like me.*

'Well, sweetheart, he asked how I was doing and we chatted a while.'

'And?' Lily mentally pinned her mother to the wall.

'Don't be this way, Lily Elizabeth. I didn't mean any harm. Patrick assured me he regretted the way you'd parted. He wants to make up with you, honey.'

'Of course he does. I'm the goose who's laying golden eggs as far as he's concerned. Never once did he apologise for fu—'

'Mind your language, young lady,' Tricia cut her off and Lily bit her tongue hard enough to draw blood.

'He knew I was coming over here to do research for the show but I purposely didn't give him any details. Please tell me you haven't mentioned exactly where I am?' She crossed her fingers without much hope. Her mother always was a sucker for Patrick's smooth Irish charm plus his sizeable bank account and position as a big name on the Cooking Network. Maybe she shouldn't be too harsh. After all she'd fallen for it all herself and at the beginning it had been wonderful. To find an intelligent, good-looking man whose passion for food equalled her own had seemed a match made in heaven.

'I might've done.' Tricia's voice had taken on a defensive edge.

'In other words – yes?' Lily sighed.

'Yes. Are you satisfied?'

'No and I'm sorry if I was mean, but I've got to protect myself,' Lily asserted.

'He'd never hurt you.'

'Right.' Lily rubbed at the tired ache spreading up her temples. Her mother didn't know half of what she'd put up with from Patrick one way and another. He'd controlled her professionally and personally for far too long and she'd been naive enough to let him. 'Look, I gotta go. It's late here. I'll call again soon. Bye, Mom.' She slammed the phone shut and tossed it on her bed.

Another problem to keep her awake tonight.

Kenan's eyes struggled open, fighting against the leaden tiredness pulling at his whole body. From two o'clock onwards he'd been haunted by his usual nightmares. Images of Kalinah's innocent smiling face before they dissolved into endless piercing screams replayed in a never-ending loop.

'Daddy.' A shrill voice broke through his mental fog and he pulled himself up to sitting. 'Granny says you have to come right now and eat breakfast. She's cooking runny eggs the way I like them and bacon with all the nasty fat cut off.'

His stomach roiled. A gallon of strong black coffee was his weapon of choice in the fight to face the morning. Kenan focused on his beautiful, solemn-faced daughter studying him from the doorway and tried to smile. 'Hey, Mandy. Do you want to come and give me a hug?'

Her big blue eyes, the image of Olivia's, widened, and she nibbled at a fingernail, deep in thought. Without answering she crossed the room in tiny hesitant steps and stood by the side of the bed.

Kenan lay still, not wanting to move quickly and scare her. It hurt like hell to realise she wasn't sure of him, but what did he expect after six years? He'd missed so much and would never make up for that if he lived to a hundred. 'Jump up here.' Kenan patted the covers and held his breath.

'I'm hungry.' She didn't move, studying him some more. 'Granny said you're a slug. Why'd she say that? They're slimy and gross. You don't look like one to me.'

'She was having fun with you, sweetheart. I promise I'm not a slug. Daddy needs to go to the bathroom before I come downstairs. You run along.'

'You need to pee, Daddy?'

Her artless comment had him choking back a

61

laugh. 'Yes, poppet.' Kenan reached towards her long, silky hair but she pushed his hand away and stepped back placing her hands on non-existent hips and glaring right at him. 'Granny already combed my hair. Do not mess it up.'

She stalked from the room and thumped away down the stairs. For a second the image of Mandy and Lily getting together filled his brain and he sighed. Boy, was he ever in trouble.

Kenan dragged out of bed and made his way to the shower. He set the water to icy cold and jumped in, desperate to sharpen his wits. He couldn't afford to get being a father wrong a second time. After several bone-chilling minutes he shut off the water and grabbed his towel, giving his body a brisk rub dry. Kenan quickly pulled on his clothes and ran a comb over his hair. This was set to be a very long day.

'What's this?' Betty gave the loaded plate Lily placed in front of her a suspicious prod.

'French toast with bacon and strawberries. I woke up early and . . .' her voice trailed into silence. She shouldn't have assumed it was all right to take over her landlady's kitchen, but she hadn't been able to sleep and cooking always worked as therapy when she was worried. It had been a real challenge working in the smallest space she'd cooked in for ages with none of the modern conveniences she took for granted these days like a dishwasher or garbage disposal. She'd found out why Betty went shopping most days when she discovered the tiny under-the-counter refrigerator couldn't even fit four pints of milk standing upright. 'I'm sorry if you—'

'Don't be daft, my 'andsome, I'm some 'appy. No one ever cooks for me. This must've taken ages.' Betty beamed.

Lily pressed her arms to her sides to avoid making a fool of herself and giving her landlady a hug. 'It's not hard but takes a while to fix. I've done the basic recipe many times but changed it around a bit today so you're my guinea pig. I swapped the orange zest for lemon and you didn't have honey so I tried out your golden syrup. It's pretty good stuff.'

Betty cut a piece and popped it into her mouth. Lily watched anxiously and waited for the verdict.

'That's some good I must say.'

'You can pour warm syrup over it too,' Lily suggested, stifling a laugh as Betty screwed up her face.

'I don't think so, dear. Next thing you'll be telling me to put it on my bacon.' She chuckled. Lily loved how different people were the world over when it came to the food they would or wouldn't eat. Tradition and habit had a lot to answer for.

'We do eat it that way but I wouldn't dare suggest that to any decent English person. Before I came I was warned y'all don't like things too sweet. They said it was as a consequence of the war and sugar rationing?'

'I suppose that's right.' Betty glanced over at Lily's untouched plate. 'Aren't you eating any? It's not like you.'

Lily tried to respond to her landlady's warm smile, but the nerves in her stomach won out. 'I'll be eating a big lunch later so I'm saving my appetite.' She checked her watch. Only thirty minutes and they'd be here. 'I've cleared up so you shouldn't have any dishes apart from your own plate. I hope that's okay?'

'Of course, dear, you run along.'

'I'll get my things together before Mr Punctual arrives.' Lily got up and headed for the door, hesitating at the last moment and glancing back at Betty. 'Did you know he's bringing his daughter with him today?'

'Eileen, his mum, rang me yesterday. Some bothered up she was with the little girl turning up out of the blue. She needed to borrow a few of the books and toys I keep here for my own grandchildren when they visit. I took them down to her and met little Mandy.'

'What's she like?'

'Pretty little thing. Seemed happy with her Gran, but sat ever so quiet and well-behaved while we talked. You're a sweet girl so just be your usual kind self and you can't go wrong.'

'I'm overthinking it, aren't I?' Lily said ruefully. 'Thanks. Y'all are so good to me.' She ran out into the hall and took the stairs two at a time.

Lily opened the closet door and stared at the

contents. For once she was unsure about what to pick. Fiona Madden at the Water's Edge had a reputation for being difficult and demanding – one of the reasons she'd made Lily's shortlist. She wasn't a man to be swayed by a clingy low-cut top or killer heels, plus Lily needed to remember that she'd be under the scrutiny of an eight-year-old girl. She threw a handful of tops on the bed and picked out the simplest, loosest one. Lily slipped on the cotton-candy pink shirt and did up a couple more buttons than usual. She pulled on a pair of khakis and abandoned her typical stilettos for soft cerise leather ballet flats. Very restrained for her these days. When Patrick first spotted her as a young chef making her name in local television, he'd moulded her into *Luscious Lily* as a marketing tool. It had proved a huge success and kick-started her career, but recently she'd got tired of the whole facade. So many mornings these days she woke up and longed to go out without make-up and dress more simply.

Lily considered tying her hair back but immediately tossed out the idea. The mass of wild red curls was her trademark and she'd grown to love it. She'd hated her hair as a child and endured endless teasing and name-calling in school, frequently coming home in tears. One of the good things Patrick did for her was convincing Lily that her hair was an asset and set her apart. He'd taught her to use it shamelessly as part of her appeal.

'They're here,' Betty called up.

65

'Damn.' She'd planned to be waiting on Kenan for once but should've known he'd catch her out. 'Five minutes,' Lily yelled back. She put on a slick of glossy pink lipstick and shook her head to fluff up her hair some more. Okay, iPad, camera, purse, sunglasses – she was all set, apart from the butterflies zooming around in her stomach.

Lily took several deep steadying breaths and left the safety of her room. The second she reached the top of the stairs two pairs of eyes stared up at her. One set belonged to a cute, blonde girl in a yellow dress and the other were Kenan's – steady and unreadable this morning. She swallowed hard and plastered on a bright smile.

'Mandy, this is Miss Lily, say hello,' he said encouragingly, but the kid didn't speak, just continued to stare. 'Lily, come and meet my daughter.'

She heard the plea in his voice and guessed he was floundering.

Lily ran down the last couple of stairs and crouched down in front of Mandy. 'Kenan, you didn't tell me she was a princess.'

A wary smile touched the edges of the girl's pretty blue eyes.

'Uh, didn't I?'

Lily picked up a strand of Mandy's hair. 'No, but she must be. Princesses in storybooks always have long blonde hair and blue eyes. Yes, definitely a princess.'

'Don't be silly.' Mandy giggled. 'I'm Amanda Jane Bellingham.'

Lily caught Kenan's quick intake of breath and guessed he hadn't known that his daughter didn't share his name. 'I'll keep your secret,' she stage-whispered. 'I don't blame you. A lot of princesses pretend to be ordinary little girls.'

Mandy beamed and reached out to touch Lily's hair. 'Your hair's pretty, too. I think you look like a princess too but you talk funny, so I don't know if you can be one.'

Kenan's brow furrowed, plainly ready to tell her off for bad manners. Lily threw him a quick, sharp glance and he shut up.

'Thanks, sweetheart. I'm from America and we do speak kinda different. We aren't lucky enough to have any princesses either.' She shrugged and stood back up. 'It's tough luck but I'll just have to get to know you instead.'

Kenan gestured towards her bags. 'I'll stow those in the car if you're ready?'

'Sure. Thanks.' She glanced back at Mandy. 'Your Daddy's a good packhorse.'

Mandy laughed and bounced up and down on her heels.

'Lead on, cowboy,' Lily instructed Kenan with a big smile.

'He's not a cowboy, Miss Lily,' Mandy said very earnestly.

'I know but we'll pretend with him too. He fancies himself on a horse wearing a big black ten gallon hat and silver spurs.' She couldn't resist grinning at him and he managed a half-smile in return.

'Time to round up and head on out,' he drawled in a fake Texas accent. Taking the bags from a dumbstruck Lily, he gave her a sly wink and strode off towards the door.

Wow. How could the man turn her inside out with one hint of playfulness? Boy, was Lily ever in huge trouble. While he'd stayed dour and serious she could talk herself into resisting him, but now? Before she could think too much about the change she rested a hand on Mandy's shoulder. 'We'd better go. Mustn't keep the wagon driver waiting.'

'You're silly,' Mandy said with a giggle. 'Daddy has a big black car. Come on.' She reached out and Lily's throat tightened as she took hold of the little girl's soft hand.

'You're right. Let's go and have fun.'

CHAPTER 8

Kenan parked the car at the top of the hill leading down into Charlestown and killed the engine. 'Right, ladies, we're here.'

'I bet you're ready to get out? I know I am,' Lily asked Mandy, as she undid her own seat belt and flung open the door.

Before Kenan knew it, Mandy had jumped out too and was hopping impatiently up and down on one leg. Kenan gritted his teeth and got out to join them.

'Can I run down to the beach, Daddy?' Mandy tugged on his hand.

'We'll stay together until we get there and then you can run around as much as you like,' he said firmly, and Mandy screwed up her face.

'Your Dad's right,' Lily said with a secretive smile. 'There are lots of cars and people here.' She lowered her voice and glanced furtively around. 'We've got to protect the princess from harm.'

'Okay.' Mandy beamed and seized Lily's hand too.

Kenan couldn't let go without being churlish so the three of them started off down the steep hill.

It crossed his mind that people seeing them would assume they were a family and wasn't at all sure how he felt about that.

'Oh my God, this is the cutest place I've ever seen.' Lily's enthusiasm drew him in and he couldn't help looking around them. 'They're like dolls houses aren't they?' She gestured towards the small pastel-painted fishermen's cottages lining each side of the road, all decorated with hanging baskets awash with bright summer flowers. 'If I copied this idea in Nashville they'd shrivel up in the heat.'

Kenan gave in to a wry smile. 'That's not usually a problem here. They might be drowned out with too much rain but they'll take as much sun as Cornwall can dredge up.' He pointed over to the right where several old-style tall ships nestled in the inner harbour. 'Those have been featured in lots of historical films and TV programmes.'

'They're beautiful. Are you allowed onboard to have a look around?' Lily asked, stopping by the iron railings and peering down.

'Yes, but we don't have time today.'

'Spoilsport.' Lily sighed and they carried on walking. Every few steps she slowed down to gaze longingly into the open doors of all the gift and craft shops they passed.

'We'll come back and check them out another time,' Kenan promised, thinking all the while he was dooming himself to more trouble. 'I'm sure Mandy can be bribed with the promise of a princess necklace?'

'Yeah, always works for me,' Lily replied with a chuckle.

'I'll remember that.' He raked her with his gaze and a flush of heat tinted her pretty skin.

'I bet you will,' she whispered. Lily turned away and bent down to talk to Mandy. 'Do you like the sea, Princess? Where I live we've only got lakes and it's not the same.'

'There's an indoor swimming pool near where I live with Mummy. I've only been to the beach two times before.' She eyed the water nervously and went quiet.

Kenan wished she hadn't been reminded of home and her mother. 'Come on, girls.' He steered them all towards the tiny beach. 'Let's stake a claim to that rock.' He pointed towards a smooth, flat rock at the bottom of the small slipway. 'Mandy, how about I help you take your shoes off, and you can play in the sand?'

'I'm not a baby, Daddy. I'm eight. I can take my own shoes off.' She sat down on the rock and bent over to remove her black school shoes and white ankle socks. Then she turned back to Kenan with a puzzled frown. 'What am I supposed to play with?'

He reached behind his back for a plastic carrier bag he'd brought from the car and held out a red plastic bucket and small spade. 'Your Gran told me to bring these.'

Mandy beamed and snatched them from his hands. 'Thanks.' She smacked a kiss on his forehead and Kenan quickly put a hand on her thin arm to stop her running off.

'Hang on. You can't go in the water today, sweetheart, because you need to stay dry for lunch. I'm sorry. I promise I'll bring you another day.' He hoped she'd be here long enough for him to keep this promise. 'Remember to stay where you can see us,' he said firmly. The sudden responsibility petrified him. If he screwed up, Olivia would never let him see Mandy again and rightly so.

'Yes, Daddy.' Mandy walked away, one slow step at a time, stopping to wriggle her toes and check out the sand as she went.

'She's your daughter all right,' Lily observed.

'Cautious and careful, you mean?'

'Yeah. That's not a bad thing if you don't take it to extremes.' Lily put the thought out there and he struggled to find an answer.

'Sometimes it can save your life. Of course, you have to know when to take chances too.' He splayed out his hand on the damp rock, inches away from hers, desperate to touch her again, while knowing that he mustn't. 'I used to have a better balance, but . . .'

'You'll get it back.' Lily's sympathy made his throat tighten.

'Maybe.' Kenan wasn't so sure but wasn't about to continue this conversation now. 'Anyway, enough about me. What should I know before we get to this appointment so I don't put my size twelve feet right in it?' He kept glancing over at

Mandy playing contentedly a little way in front of them.

'I'm guessing you've seen Fiona Madden on TV?'

'Hardly,' he answered with a disparaging shake of his head. 'I hardly watch any TV these days and I've never voluntarily seen a cookery programme.' Kenan shrugged. 'Sorry. Food's not really my thing.'

She stared at him as though he'd grown a second head. 'You eat, don't you?'

'Of course, but I'm not that fussed what it is. Mum's always been a plain, ordinary cook and in the Army you took what you could get when you could. No offence, but I've never understood why people get so worked up about food. Seems to be a craze these days.'

Lily's eyes narrowed and she nibbled at her lip. She was framing up to say something. Kenan prepared for a scathing retort to be thrown his way but instead received a pitying smile.

'As I've said before, I do believe I'll make it my mission to educate you while I'm here. Nurturing people by feeding them is such a fundamental thing. You wait until I cook for you.'

'I'm a lost cause, Lily, don't waste your time.' Kenan's gruff reply wiped away her happy smile. He hadn't meant to be so brusque but she needed to understand where they stood. Food was only an outer symbol of the differences between them.

'We'll see.' Lily appeared to concede, but he knew

he'd only got a temporary reprieve from her machinations. 'Getting back to Fiona Madden. A lot of men find her attractive, in an uptight schoolteacher sort of way. She's very disciplined and believes in strict order in her kitchen.' Kenan savoured the play of emotions across her face, from stern to curious and back again. 'It'd be a real doozy and terrific television to put her in Martin Farrell's kitchen.'

'Who's he when he's at home?' The conversation was losing Kenan.

'A very flamboyant Hollywood celebrity chef. Over the top in his dress, manner and the way he works. He yells, throws things and expects his staff to give as good as they get.' She suddenly picked up his right hand and toyed with his fingers. Her warmth flooded through his skin and set his blood on fire. 'Fiona would hate to be in his kitchen and he'd turn hers upside down.'

'You're wicked,' he muttered.

Lily tossed her hair back and leaned in closer so that he smelt today's perfume, something light and floral he guessed in deference to Fiona Madden's more conservative sensibilities. 'I try.'

I bet you do. 'How will you persuade her? I'd have thought it'd be her idea of hell,' Kenan added, with more than a touch of sarcasm.

'Let me run my idea by you and see what you think. I'll suggest to Fiona that Farrell's staff need her to sort them out. Surely she won't be able to resist the lure of showing others the benefit of her system?'

Kenan wasn't convinced. 'Wouldn't she hate the idea of this Farrell chap messing around in her kitchen?'

'That could be my stumbling block, but . . .' Lily flashed a brilliant smile and teased a long, warm finger down his cheek, sending shivers through Kenan. He half-turned to face her, while keeping Mandy in view out of the corner of one eye. 'That's where you come in.'

'Me?' Kenan shook his head. 'Oh, no, you're not dragging me into this. You've picked the wrong person. I'm not interested in food plus I'm not the talkative salesman type. You hired me to drive and haul your bags around. End of story.'

'Oh, come on. It'll be fun,' she wheedled, fluttering her eyelashes. 'You're the perfect foil for me. I'll lay on the Southern charm, while you appeal to her desire to make everyone conform to her system. You can present it as the perfect opportunity for her to spread the word, as it were,' she suggested.

'All this is on purpose, isn't it?' He gestured down over her outfit. 'You've tamed *Luscious Lily* so as not to scare Fiona Madden off?' He'd speculated before today how much of Lily's alter-ego was put on and had come to the conclusion that she'd created *Luscious Lily* as a marketing ploy. He was curious to get to see the real Lily underneath all the glitz. At a guess, Kenan was pretty sure she'd be even more dangerous.

'You're too smart for your own good,' she said

and studied him hard. 'One day I might tell you more about *Luscious Lily* . . . or not.'

'You will,' he said succinctly, checking his watch and Mandy at the same time. 'We'd better get going.'

Kenan slid off the rock and made his way over to his daughter, crouching down beside her. 'It's time to leave, sweetheart.'

'Oh, Daddy, I don't want to go.' Mandy's face crumpled and he prayed she wouldn't cry. He couldn't handle crying women whether they were eight or eighty.

'Sorry. We'll go now and have a nice lunch.' She didn't look convinced and Kenan couldn't blame her. He'd much rather get a decent plate of fish and chips somewhere instead of fancy bits and pieces that would leave him still hungry afterwards. Mandy stood up and took his hand, obviously resigned to her fate.

Lily was ready and waiting for them. 'You need to wash your hands before lunch, young lady. Goodness, I sound like my mother.' She laughed over at Kenan before glancing back at Mandy. 'I saw some restrooms on the way down. We ladies can go in together and freshen up.'

He hadn't thought about that side of things. How did other single dads manage?

'What's a restroom?' Mandy wrinkled up her nose.

'You call it a loo or a toilet, honey.' Lily chuckled. 'Back home where I come from, we call it a restroom.'

'That's silly. When you want to rest you go to bed,' Mandy stated very decisively.

'She makes sense,' Kenan insisted, managing to stifle a laugh.

'That's enough nonsense, the pair of you.' Lily seized Mandy's hand and started to walk back up the hill, taking for granted that Kenan would follow.

Kenan stopped outside the front door of the Water's Edge restaurant. 'Remember what I said, Mandy. Good manners please. Only speak if someone speaks to you. If you don't like the food just leave it – don't make a fuss.' He raised an eyebrow at Lily. 'I hope this'll be all right. I'm not used to working this way.'

'Me neither but we'll be fine. Princesses always have perfect manners, don't they Mandy?' Lily insisted.

'Of course.' Mandy looked very smug.

Kenan took hold of Mandy's hand. Lily met his reassuring nod, put on her best *Luscious Lily* smile, and threw open the restaurant door.

CHAPTER 9

'Kenan Rowse, my assistant while I'm over here, and his daughter, Mandy.' Lily avoided catching his eye as Fiona Madden, sour-faced and immaculate in her chef's whites, sized them all up over the top of her half-glasses.

'I've arranged for you to be served my tasting menu. I won't be joining you because I need to be in the kitchen for the lunch service. When we're over the busiest time I'll call you back and you can see how I run things. Then we'll talk about this idea of yours.' Fiona was sharp and concise. 'Follow me.'

She showed them to a table near the kitchen door and strode off, her staff clearing out of the way as if she was Moses parting the Red Sea.

'Wow! She's not interested in impressing me, is she? I'd never seat favoured guests at the worst table in the restaurant.' Lily glanced around the room, noting the understated décor and air of calm elegance.

'Let's sit down and enjoy a free meal.' Kenan gave in to a wry smile. 'At least I assume she won't give us a bill when we're done?'

'She'd better not.' Lily's face burned with indignation.

'Sit there, Mandy, love.' He settled his daughter and gestured to Lily to join them. 'Come on. Get over yourself.'

'How dare . . .'

Kenan fixed her with a hard stare and she gave in. Later she'd make sure that he knew who was in charge when they were working.

'Daddy, can I have chicken nuggets, please?' Mandy pleaded.

'I doubt it.' Kenan's dry tone of voice implied he'd prefer them too.

The waiter approached with their first course, the salmon mousse Fiona Madden was best known for, and Lily dived into work mode. With her camera out and her iPad ready to make notes, she tasted and dissected Fiona Madden's food. 'Isn't this amazing, Kenan? She must've used a bain-marie, otherwise this wouldn't be as soft.' She waited for an answer but only received a mystified shrug. 'Okay, just eat, and I'll worry about the details.'

'Great idea.'

Lily didn't miss the touch of irony as she concentrated on the food and tried to ignore him, though she was constantly aware of his dark, steady gaze resting on her.

'Daddy, what's this?' Mandy whispered, poking at the single scallop arranged on top of a smudge of pesto.

'Fish. Like a fish finger without the crunchy bits,' Kenan explained.

'But I like the crunchy bits, Daddy.'

'Me too, poppet.' He quickly ate his own and came close to smiling. 'It's good. Try it.'

Lily caught his eye and nodded her approval, amused as a tinge of heat coloured his skin. 'Good girl, Mandy.' She smiled as the little girl cut the scallop in half and popped a piece in her mouth before chewing very thoughtfully and swallowing.

'It's okay, but I don't want any more.' Very politely she pushed the plate away and folded her hands in her lap.

The waitress cleared away their plates before placing a shot glass in front of each of them. 'The soup taster is parsnip and coriander. Enjoy.' She left and Kenan glanced at Lily, his eyebrow raised in disbelief.

'They're calling this soup?' He knocked back the single mouthful and shook his head.

'It's only supposed to stimulate the palate and leave you wanting more,' Lily explained.

'It does that all right,' Kenan proclaimed, full of irony. 'You want Daddy to eat yours?' he asked and Mandy nodded, so he downed it in one gulp.

Lily tried to concentrate and updated her notes as the next course arrived. Glancing up she was relieved to see a miniature, but recognisable filet mignon. 'Do you like steak, Mandy?'

'I think so.' She didn't look sure and Kenan

reached across to cut the meat for her. 'Uh, nasty, it's bleeding, Daddy.'

'Shush, sweetheart,' Kenan muttered. 'I'll eat it.' He quickly ate both portions and gave Lily a scathing look. 'Good thing the portions are small or I'd be stuffed by the time we get through this.'

She glanced at the menu. 'Next is a rocket and cucumber salad and then a grape sorbet. Those should be safe enough for you both. Then if you're a good little princess you'll get three yummy desserts all at the same time,' Lily coaxed.

Kenan's dark eyes glimmered with amusement. 'What do I have to do to get mine?'

'Try to be open-minded about this whole experience,' she urged and he gave her a curious stare before slowly nodding.

The assiette of desserts was the biggest hit and Lily guessed both her lunch companions would cheerfully have eaten more of the delicious peach tart, elderflower ice cream and chocolate meringues.

'Are you through, Miss Redman?' Fiona presented herself at the table, arms folded, her lips in a hard unsmiling line, as if challenging Lily to unarmed combat. 'You'd better bring your . . . guests as well.' She waved vaguely in Kenan and Mandy's direction.

'Thanks. I'll just tie my hair back first,' Lily said quickly, before she got a hygiene lecture. She pulled one of her specially designed pink sparkly scrunchies from her bag and scooped her hair up out of the way. 'All set.'

They all followed Fiona into the kitchen, including a very subdued Mandy. Lily promised herself that she'd make it up to the little girl because if anyone deserved a princess necklace it was this sweetheart.

Five minutes later Lily knew Fiona Madden would be perfect for the programme. She was an autocrat through and through, with no desire to change. The kitchen was immaculate despite being at the end of a busy service and although Lily considered herself fussy where hygiene was concerned, this woman had her beat hands down.

'Please stay back there until I say otherwise. I don't wish my staff's routine to be disrupted, plus you're a contamination risk.'

'Daddy. What's con . . . what she said?' Mandy's clear voice rang out and Fiona threw a disdainful look in her direction. Lily caught Kenan's eye and they shared a half-smile as he bent down to explain.

Fiona rattled through the details of how she ran her kitchen and showed off a six-inch thick binder of rules, then fixed her sharp ice-blue eyes on Lily. 'Why don't you list your professional qualifications for me, Miss Redman? I want to make sure I'm dealing with a genuine chef and not someone who merely acts the part on the television. We see far too much of that these days and I've no patience with it.'

Lily determined not to undersell herself and launched into her standard publicity spiel. 'I'm

82

largely self-taught. At sixteen I washed dishes at the local burger joint and fell in love with being in a working kitchen. After that I did various jobs and ended up as sous chef to Pierre Le Bron in New York. He encouraged me to venture out on my own, so I returned to Tennessee and set up my own catering business. I worked for a lot of celebrity clients and got the opportunity to do some local television work. From there it developed and I now have my own nationally syndicated show that regularly hits the top of the ratings. I enjoy the opportunity to educate people but my real passion is to share my enthusiasm for cooking good, fresh food well.'

'You value yourself very highly for someone with no professional training,' Fiona scoffed. 'The show you talked about on the telephone sounds like pure entertainment with the sole purpose of humiliating the chefs involved. I can assure you it's not something I intend to be involved in. I did warn you that it would be a waste of your time coming here.'

Lily's stomach clenched into a painful knot.

'Excuse me interrupting.' Kenan's deep voice next to her shoulder startled Lily. 'Miss Redman will correct me if necessary but I'm sure humiliating *anyone* is certainly not on her agenda.' He held her gaze for a moment and she nodded, unsure what direction he was going in but playing along. 'Everybody has different leadership styles and, although it'll be presented in an entertaining way, any manager can learn from seeing how other people work.'

'Absolutely.' Lily guessed she'd better jump back in and help out. For someone who'd blown off the idea of helping earlier he'd certainly done an about face. 'I'll be the first to admit I don't know everything there is to know about running a kitchen. I'm always open to new ideas and believe anyone who isn't will stagnate.'

Fiona's cheeks flushed an unbecoming shade of purple. 'Well, of course I agree. Maybe we can find some common ground.' She glanced down at Mandy. 'I expect you're bored, young lady. Why don't you and your father go out into the garden we have for our guests? There's a slide and a couple of swings and I'm sure my assistant could find you a fresh chocolate biscuit.' She clicked her fingers and a tiny blonde woman cleaning down the counters immediately dropped what she was doing. A minute later Fiona held out a white paper bag to Mandy. 'You'll find one in there for your Daddy as well.' She gave Kenan an awkward half-twisted smile and Lily almost choked. If the woman wasn't flirting she'd eat liver every day for a month.

'Thank you, Miss Madden. We'll leave you to finish your business.' He nodded at Lily. 'Let me know when you're through.'

'Please call me Fiona. We don't stand on ceremony here,' she said coyly. Several of the cooks stopped and stared, obviously wondering what strange creature had taken over their boss's body.

84

'Uh, right. Fiona.'

Lily smelt the imaginary smoke flying up from Kenan's heels as he made a swift escape. She followed Fiona into her small perfectly organised office to the right of the kitchen and sat down, turning on her iPad. With any luck they could wrap up the deal and she would have two chefs onboard already.

Kenan slammed the car into gear and peeled out of the restaurant driveway, only taking a deep breath when he reached the main road.

'Going fast for any particular reason?' Lily teased and he bit the inside of his mouth to keep from swearing in front of Mandy. 'We'll talk about Miss Fiona Madden later,' she drawled out the other woman's name in those honeyed tones and set Kenan's nerves jangling.

'Do you still want to go to the Eden Project?' he managed to ask.

'Nope.' She shook her head. 'I think we've all had enough for one day. Why don't we go back into Charlestown and check out the shops before we head home?'

'Granny Eileen's making me a pasty for tea time,' Mandy said and Kenan caught sight of her frown in the rear-view mirror. 'What's a pasty, Daddy? I've had enough funny food today.' Her nose wrinkled in distaste.

They'd eaten some unusual things at the restaurant with nothing presented as normal food. Why anyone wanted soup in a glass was beyond him, but what did he know? He'd found Lily's obvious delight in everything intriguing but incomprehensible, exactly the way he described her in his mind. Kenan had wanted to give Mandy a big kiss at the end of the meal. She'd done a damn good job of trying most things, or at least pretending to. Kenan was proud of her. He'd give Olivia credit where it was due – she'd done a fine job bringing up their daughter.

'It's good, sweetheart. I promise you'll love it. It's sort of a pie with beef, potato and onion and you eat it in your hands.' He struggled to explain the Cornish specialty, stamping on a stab of anger as he realised she'd never eaten one before.

'Okay. She's making one for you too,' Mandy declared.

'Would you mind if I leave you to eat with Granny and Grandpa and take Miss Lily out instead? We've got work to talk about.' Was he totally brain-dead? 'Is that okay, poppet?'

'Mm. I suppose so. Grandpa Bill said he'd play Snakes and Ladders with me after tea.'

Kenan sneaked a glance at Lily and noticed the flush on her pale freckled skin, wondering if he'd put it there. 'Okay. Let's go shopping and see if we can find something suitable for a princess.'

Half an hour later he strongly considered sticking hot pokers in his eyes. It couldn't be more painful than shopping with two determined females. There were only a handful of shops in Charlestown but apparently they were fascinating. He checked his watch and sighed as Lily and Mandy discussed the merits of various pieces of clothing and jewellery.

'Mandy, your daddy's getting impatient. We have a duty to teach him not to rush a woman when she's shopping,' Lily teased, batting her eyelashes at him and stirring him up again.

'Should I get the blue or the yellow?' Mandy held up two T-shirts for his approval.

'Get them both,' Kenan growled and Lily's face lit up with a brilliant, satisfied smile.

'See, Mandy, it works every time. Men will do anything to escape a shop.' She draped a hand over his arm, her bright blue eyes shining with mischief. 'A princess necklace next and then we'll be done.'

He snapped his mouth shut and gave a curt nod. As they rifled through everything on display he watched Mandy blossom under Lily's attention, far removed from the serious child she'd been yesterday. This was worth any amount of excruciating boredom on his part. Suddenly Lily and Mandy giggled together and he wanted to stop the world.

'Here you go.' Lily thrust a handful of something shiny and pink in to his hand. 'You need to go and pay but don't look. Mandy wants to show it off to you when we get home.'

Kenan obeyed orders and passed the closed up bag to his daughter. He received a wide smile and

a tight, warm hug in return. *Totally worthwhile.*
'Come on, ladies, time to go.'

Five minutes later Mandy was fast asleep in the back seat totally worn out, but clutching her precious bag. Kenan whispered to Lily next to him, 'Are you all right with going out later?' He hadn't asked a woman out for so long he'd forgotten the protocol but somehow he didn't think issuing an invitation through his daughter was considered good manners.

'I guess.' She sounded as tentative as he felt, fuelling his uncertainty.

'It's just dinner, Lily.' Not sure who he was reassuring most, Kenan decided to leave it at that and concentrate on driving.

Mandy twirled around the room and Lily clapped her hands. 'See, I said you were a princess.' The little girl ran over and threw herself on Kenan's lap. Lily's heart raced as he did something she'd never seen before. Smile. Not an everyday kind of smile, but a huge, face-splitting grin brimming over with love and pride. The dark, serious man disappeared and this new version of Kenan wrung out her heart.

'Are these pink diamonds, milady?' Kenan asked, intently studying the garish necklace Mandy had fallen in love with on sight.

'Don't be silly, Daddy. They're not real.' Mandy giggled.

'Are you sure? Don't tell anyone. They'll never guess.'

Lily's throat tightened as he dropped a kiss on the top of his daughter's head. She met his gaze and something unexpected and special passed between them.

'Mandy, love, why don't you wash your hands ready for tea?' Eileen Rowse said as she came in. 'There's plenty if you want to join us, Lily.'

'Thanks, but Kenan and I have work plans to discuss. I think we're going to go out for something to eat.' She threw him a questioning look, hoping he'd get the hint.

'Yes, sorry, Mum.' He ruffled Mandy's hair. 'You be good and I'll be home again in time to read a story and give you a goodnight kiss. Promise.' Kenan turned to Lily. 'Are you ready?'

Lily took a deep breath and nodded.

CHAPTER 10

Kenan sat at Betty Tremayne's kitchen table, perched on the edge of a hard wooden chair, sipping tea and wondering how much longer Lily would take to get ready. She had insisted that what she'd worn today wasn't suitable for going out for dinner, although it would have done fine for what he had in mind. He'd been doomed to hear every detail of Betty's eldest daughter's divorce, how well her eldest grandson was doing at university and all about the mouldy bread she'd bought at the village shop this morning.

A waft of lemony perfume tickled his nose and Kenan steeled himself to turn around. The sight of Lily's clingy, bright turquoise excuse for a dress wrapped around her lethal curves, made the breath leave his body. She brushed aside one oversized silver hoop earring and played with the fiery red curls billowing around her smooth, bare shoulders.

'I'm ready to go when you are.' Kenan met her laughing eyes. This was Lily on full-bore and she obviously wouldn't take pity on him anytime soon.

'He's been a good boy, listening to all my tales.'

Betty's eyes shone with merriment. 'Still, I'm thinkin' he'd rather go and romance you, my dear.'

'He's lost his tongue, Betty.' Lily's slow honeyed drawl slid over his hot skin and he desperately needed fresh air.

'Come on, Kenan.' She held out her hand and he somehow managed to stand up.

He cleared his throat. 'We'll be off then.' He stood back and allowed Lily to go first. They walked out through the house and down the path to his car. His gaze slid down over her pert bottom and endless legs, ending up at tonight's death-defying shoes. Naturally they were turquoise to match the dress, and so impossibly high he'd no clue how she managed to walk in them.

'Enjoying the view?' She glanced back over one shoulder with her eyes flashing dangerously.

Kenan's few functioning brain cells took over and he pulled the car keys from his pocket. He stood by while she got in, unable to avoid watching the skimpy dress slide temptingly up her legs.

'Pervert.' She laughed in his face as he slammed her door shut before walking around to get in the driver's seat. 'Where are we going?'

'I didn't think you'd want to be stuck inside any more restaurants today, so I've got a plan.' He put on his seat belt and slipped the key in the ignition.

'I'll bet you have, soldier boy.' Lily's teasing smile froze in place and she suddenly looked sad and vulnerable.

'What's wrong?' he asked.

'I'm only . . . here for a few weeks,' she said, stumbling over her words.

'So what?' Kenan picked up her hands and gently rubbed over the smooth parts, the scars, and the calluses.

'There's no point us starting . . . anything.'

He chose his words with care. 'Correct me if I'm wrong but have I proposed marriage? Asked you to be the mother of my children? Suggested setting a wedding date?' With each sharply worded question she relaxed into his touch.

'No, you haven't.'

Kenan hardly ever explained his feelings to anyone and hadn't a clue where to start. 'You know I'm attracted to you. That's bloody obvious. But it's been so long for me and I've screwed up too many times before. I'm not a good bet, Lily. I don't know what it is about you, but I can't seem to get you out of my head. Do you think perhaps we can both stop worrying and just enjoy spending some time together for now? I'm not making any promises or asking for any in return.'

'Deal.' Lily rested her hand on his cheek. 'I want to find out what makes you tick.'

He chuckled. 'Good luck, sweetheart. No one else has ever succeeded.'

'Us Southern gals love a challenge. Bring it on.'

He couldn't resist dropping a light kiss on her forehead before settling back in the seat. 'We'd better get going before poor Betty falls out of the window trying to see what's going on.'

'So, where are we goin'?' Lily asked, as he pulled away from the kerb.

Kenan kept his expression unreadable enjoying the fact he was one up on her for once. 'Guess you'll find out when we arrive.'

Lily gave an exaggerated sigh, folded her hands in her lap and went quiet, but he knew she'd get her revenge later.

He headed towards Land's End and enjoyed the dramatic change in the landscape from the more obvious prettiness of the coast around St Dinas. Something about the rugged, scrubby land marked by abandoned mine shafts, massive granite boulders, and set off by flashes of bright yellow gorse appealed to his austere nature.

'What did they mine here?' Lily asked, peering out of the window.

'Tin mainly. It started centuries ago but by the late eighteen hundreds it was pretty much over. They couldn't compete with overseas prices so a lot of the miners emigrated over your way. The last Cornish tin mine closed about fifteen years ago.'

'It always saddens me to see a place lose its identity,' she murmured.

'Life changes. Nothing stays the same. You're old enough to know that.'

'Yeah.' Lily gave his arm a gentle squeeze. 'You've had some tough times, haven't you?'

Kenan cursed himself for allowing the conversation to drift in an unwanted direction. 'Not tonight, please. Maybe one day.' He'd no intention of spilling his guts to her or anybody, but the half-promise might quieten her for a while.

'Fine.' Her hand dropped away but he knew she'd harangue him again when least expected.

He slowed down as the roads narrowed. 'They've turned Land's End into a theme park without the hair-raising rides,' Kenan explained. 'It's ghastly. We're going to Cape Cornwall instead. You get basically the same view without the cheap tacky add-ons and the sunset there is hard to beat.'

They made their way down the rough, narrow road and Kenan guessed by her frequent sharp intakes of breath that meeting another vehicle wouldn't make her happy. As they pulled into the small car park with nothing in sight apart from a closed up caravan that sold tea and sandwiches during the day, he guessed Lily must be wondering where they would be eating.

'Right, we're here.' Kenan hopped out and ran around to open her door. As she stepped out Lily stared down at her shoes then at the rough gravel.

'You should've warned me.'

Kenan grinned. 'I suppose I should, but I love seeing you in those things. They spark off all kinds of fantasies.'

'Yeah, like spending hours in ER when I break my ankle on those rocks.' She glared and pointed towards the rough grass and rocks leading to the cliff edge.

'I was a Boy Scout and we're always prepared. Don't move.' He went to get his supplies from the boot only to return with a pair of her own flat, sunshine-yellow shoes. 'Betty sneaked these out of your room. Sorry they don't match.' He smiled and crouched down to remove her fancy shoes before slipping the others on. 'Remind you of anything? Pink wellies, maybe?'

Lily's bashful smile made him want to kiss her senseless. *How unusual. All you have to do is look at the woman to want to do that all the bloody time.*

'Right, I think we're all set. I'll get our picnic.' He set her feet gently on the ground and reluctantly let go.

'Picnic?'

Kenan left her briefly and gathered up a wicker basket, blanket and cushions from the boot. 'Okay, come on.' Lily stood up and he locked the car. 'I've got the perfect spot.'

'Why am I not surprised?' she grumbled half-heartedly, and followed along behind as he led the way along the winding path.

They walked around the far side of the rocky outcrop of land and into the sheltered hollow where he'd often spent a sleepless night staring out over the ocean.

Kenan spread out the tartan blanket he'd begged from his mother earlier and held out his hand to Lily. She gave him a gentle, knowing smile as he helped her down on the ground. It took some wriggling on her part to shift the dress enough to allow her to sit, and Kenan suppressed a grin. A gentleman would have warned a lady to dress suitably, but he wasn't that noble.

'Right, surprise time.'

Salty local ham, a creamy Cornish Blue cheese, fresh crusty bread, tangy pear chutney and bottles of Cornish cider – the man knew all the right buttons to hit for a food nut. She appreciated the care Kenan had taken, no one had ever done this for her before.

'You know, I want every detail of where you found these great foods,' Lily insisted, finishing up a bite of cheese.

'I cheated and rang up Paul and Evelyn this afternoon. They pulled it all together and can tell you where everything's from another day.'

'Don't even try to tell me you didn't enjoy it as well?' Lily was determined to get him to talk about the food they'd eaten if it killed her.

'All right, I'll admit it.' Kenan gave in to a wry smile. 'Satisfied?'

'But why did you like it?' she persisted, not able to leave it alone just yet.

He shoved a hand up through his hair, making it stand on end, and looked exasperated. 'I don't know any of the fancy words you use around other chefs to describe stuff. Simple, fresh and good – will that do? I hate pretentious in food or people,' Kenan declared.

'So do I. Think of the words I use as simply part of my job. They're a means of communication, that's all.'

Kenan shrugged. 'I suppose. Enough of food for tonight.' His gaze darkened and he reached out to stroke one thumb teasingly down over her warm cheek. 'My sweet girl.' His eyes, molten silver in the fading light, sent shivers through her blood.

A wave of shadows rippled across his face to close down his smile and he exhaled a long, heavy sigh. 'We've got a sunset to see,' he murmured and pulled her to sit between his outstretched legs with her back resting against his chest. 'Beautiful, isn't it?' Tension strummed through his roughened voice and she could only guess how much it cost him not to give in and kiss her.

Lily could only nod her head and blink back tears before staring out at the horizon, shimmering with dark golden streaks as the sun lowered to meet the sea. She knew better than to ask for an explanation. Not tonight.

Kenan lifted a handful of thick curls off her neck and pressed a kiss into her soft skin before letting her hair drop back into place. 'We'd better go,' he murmured.

'Yeah. Why are you always right?' She turned to give him a quizzical look.

'I'm far from it, Lily. The mistakes I've made would fill a book.' His hand rested against the side of her face and she leaned into his caress. 'If I ever tell you—'

'When, Kenan . . . not if,' she stated firmly. 'Come on.' Lily stood and picked up the plaid blanket to shake out the loose grass. 'There we go. You can get the rest.'

'Be careful walking, it's pretty rough. Can you see the path all right?'

'You're such an old woman at times,' she teased. 'How I've survived thirty years on this earth is a miracle.' Lily gestured towards the moonlit sky. 'See, nature has provided us with the perfect streetlight.'

'I'm sorry. Go ahead,' he conceded.

They didn't speak on the walk back but once they were in the car she rested her head on his shoulder. 'Tomorrow?' Lily trailed her fingers over his chest.

'It's up to you. You're the boss.'

'I'm going to cook for you,' she declared. It was the only way she knew to truly explain herself to him. 'Bring Mandy over for lunch tomorrow.'

'Won't Betty mind you appropriating her kitchen?' he asked with a faint smile.

'Of course not. I've won her over completely. She's already taught me how to make scones and we're doing butterfly buns next.'

'Why am I not surprised?' He laughed and started up the car, heading back down the narrow road. 'Tell me how you got to be so obsessed with food and cooking.'

She only hesitated for a few seconds before playing along with him. 'My mom was sick and told me to fix supper so I overcooked spaghetti and made a disgusting sauce from leftover Brussels sprouts and cheese from a can. Even though it was terrible it got me interested. I read every cookbook I could lay my hands on and watched all the cookery programmes on TV. I drooled over new recipes instead of spotty teenage boys.'

'That must've devastated every young man in your school,' Kenan jibed.

'Maybe, but my mother encouraged it – much safer than worrying who I was losing my virginity to after the prom. Of course, I did that too,' she tossed in and noticed him wince.

'I'm sure, but I can do without the details.'

'Since then I've lived and breathed cooking but recently I've sensed some burnout.' Lily spoke her thoughts out loud. 'Patrick O'Brian spotted me on a local Nashville TV programme and became my mentor and business manager. He's a big name on the Cooking Network and he really created *Luscious Lily*.' She saw no need to share with Kenan their disastrous personal relationship because it wasn't relevant anymore. 'I never have time to cook these days, unless it's in front of a camera, so I'm debating what direction to take after this project. If we take Mandy with us when we go off we can split the time between work and play and it might help me get things straight in my mind.'

'I hope you're not suggesting this for my sake. Mum and Dad could manage her.'

'She doesn't need to be *managed*, Kenan.' A rush of hot embarrassment raced up his neck. 'You're her father and, from what I can tell, you haven't taken the job very seriously. She's a confused little girl who needs you to be there for her.'

'I know, although there's more to it than you realise.'

'I'm sure, but sometimes we don't see what's in front of us.' For Mandy's sake Lily couldn't let this go.

The muscles in his neck corded with tension and he jerked the wheel to one side, steering the car over to a stop by the side of the road. Kenan turned to face her and seized a hold of her shoulders. 'I see what's in front of me right now. A beautiful fearless woman fired up by injustice and so full of life she almost bursts with it.'

Suddenly Lily didn't want to talk about Mandy, her own plans or anything. She met his searing gaze straight on and held her breath. But just when she thought that she was finally going to feel his lips on hers, he pulled back and let her go.

'We'd better go home now,' he said, sadness etched in every word.

He put the car into gear and drove into the dark night. Lily's heart was racing but she deliberately didn't say another word. She made herself rest back in the seat and let her mind wander. She'd left Nashville to search for something she'd lost along the way, but was now more confused than ever. *Go figure.*

CHAPTER 11

Lily diced, chopped, tasted and seasoned – disappearing into her cooking zone. She closed down her mind to everything but the task in hand or the food would suffer. She'd already made fresh fettuccine noodles, which had been a real challenge without her trusty pasta machine. Rolling it out multiple times in an effort to get it thin enough she'd smiled to herself, knowing she was making it in the exact same way as generations of Italian women. Lily broke off a bite of chicken breast to taste and sprinkled in a few grains of salt before declaring herself satisfied.

'Miss Lily, we're here!'

She turned around and smiled at the sight of Mandy in the doorway, jumping with excitement and pulling at Kenan's hand.

'Miss Lily has sharp knives over there. Be careful, sweetheart.'

Lily laid her knife down on the counter. 'Would you like to help?' she asked the little girl, rewarded by the brightest smile this side of the sun.

'Yes, please.' Mandy bounced across the room.

'How about you break the woody tips off the asparagus?' Lily laid the bright green spears on a paper towel.

'What's 'sparagus?' Mandy peered at them suspiciously.

'It's a vegetable and tastes really good,' Lily explained, struggling not to laugh at her helper's furrowed up brow.

Mandy poked at the hard spears. 'I like baked beans. Peas are nasty and cabbage is yucky.'

Lily suppressed a smile. 'Trust me, I'll cook them real good and you'll have a buttery sauce to dip them in.' She bent down to whisper in the little girl's ear. 'You can eat them with your fingers.' Kids could be persuaded to try most things if it involved breaking the normal rules. She'd have to wait and see if the same theory applied to the man who hadn't taken his dark, searching eyes off her since walking into the room.

Mandy's long sigh said she wasn't convinced. 'We'll see.' The contained set of her face was so like her father's Lily nearly choked, but managed to turn it into a cough at the last moment.

'Anything I can do?' Kenan's deep rumbling voice sent a curl of desire racing through her bloodstream.

'Sit down and stay out of the way while we make magic,' she jested and winked at Mandy. 'We'll tell you everything we're doin' so you can have a go one day.' Lily tossed him the challenge and he made a derogatory snorting noise in response.

'Very unlikely.' Kenan slid out one of the old wooden kitchen chairs and sat down.

Lily turned away and forced herself to get back to concentrating on lunch. Her hands flew over the chopping board, making efficient piles of onion, peppers and mushrooms. 'I'm goin' to fry these in a minute, Mandy. It'll keep them fresh and crisp because we don't want them over-cooked. Later we'll add them to our chicken, pasta and sauce.' Although she loved most traditional Southern food she'd grown away from the cooked-for-hours green beans of her childhood. 'Stand away, Mandy. These will sizzle when they hit the hot oil.' She dropped a handful of onions into the frying pan and the room filled with the sudden pungent aroma. 'Aren't the peppers pretty?' she asked Mandy, throwing the minced vegetables into the mix.

'I don't like pepper. Pepper's hot and burns my mouth,' Mandy asserted.

'Not this kind. They're sweet, I promise.' She caught Kenan's smile at his daughter's sceptical look. 'Now the mushrooms. The pan must be hot or they'll steam and get soggy. We don't want soggy mushrooms, do we?'

'I don't want them at all. They're nasty and rubbery.' Mandy screwed up her face.

'These won't be. No rubber mushrooms allowed in my cooking.' Lily focused on stirring the mixture, tossing in a sprinkle of salt and a generous one of pepper when Mandy wasn't looking. 'Kenan, pass me the bottle of Chardonnay over by the kettle please. It's already been opened.'

He stood up and grabbed the wine from the countertop. Kenan placed the bottle in her outstretched hand and she was startled at the brush of his warm skin. 'Thanks.'

'Oh, you're welcome.' Kenan held her gaze and a deep flush of heat crept up her throat.

'We're goin' to make a sauce in this other pan while the vegetables cook.' She turned to the small sauté pan she'd dug out from the back of one of Betty's cupboards and added a generous slug of wine to the warm chicken stock. It wasn't easy to juggle everything on the top of Betty's small electric stove after being used to her own oversized gas-range. Two pots of water were coming to a boil on the back burners ready for her pasta. She needed both because few people outside of Italy or professional cooks had the required massive pots for cooking pasta. Lily stirred the bubbling sauce and picked up a clean spoon to taste the fragrant mixture. 'It needs more flavour, Mandy. I'm going to add herbs. Fresh ones are best from the garden but these dried ones will do. Smell this.' She tipped out some basil in her palm and it held it under the little girl's nose.

'It's funny. Sort of sweet.'

Lily beamed. 'You're a smart girl. It's called basil.'

'Excuse me interrupting,' Kenan jumped in. 'In England we pronounce it basil, Mandy.' He put a different inflection on the word and flashed her a quick grin.

'I suppose the oregano and parsley I'm going to add also get some weird pronunciation?'

He folded his arms and fixed her with his dark-eyed gaze. 'Parsley is still parsley, but without being pompous you've got oregano wrong as well.'

'And we all know pompous is the last word to describe you.' Lily's cheeky assertion silenced him. She pointedly turned her attention back to Mandy. 'Right, there's all the herbs goin' in.' After a quick stir she picked up a clean spoon. 'A good cook tastes all the time they're cooking to get the seasoning right.'

Betty bustled into the kitchen with a huge bouquet of red roses cradled in her arms. 'You'm a lucky lady, my dear. Someone's spoiling you today. The florist just brought these to the door.' She gave Kenan an approving smile, but his unrevealing expression didn't change.

Lily reached for the flowers and studied them for a moment. Laying them down on the countertop she removed the gift card and read the short message. A knot formed in the base of her stomach.

'Is something wrong? Who're they from?' The hard-edge to Kenan's voice brought her back to where she was. Lily slipped the card into the pocket of her jeans.

'No one special. Now let's get on with finishing up lunch or it'll be spoiled. Mandy, we'll leave this sauce on a low heat to stay warm. I'm going to blanch the asparagus next.' She slipped back into professional mode. 'That means I'll cook it briefly and shock it in an ice water bath so it'll stay crisp. We'll eat it before our chicken.'

Lily's mind raced in ever-decreasing circles as she shared the spears out between their four plates, aware of everyone's eyes on her as she placed the food in front of them. 'Squeeze the lemon over your asparagus this way, Mandy.' Lily demonstrated and got a wary smile in return. 'Now, pick up one and dip it in the melted butter.' She took a bite of hers and the glorious fresh taste of the asparagus, the hint of acid in the lemon, and the rich buttery sauce made her forget everything else. She watched Mandy take a cautious nibble. 'What do you think?'

'It's funny. But okay funny,' Mandy declared and Lily declared that a big success.

'Pretty good,' Kenan commented.

Lily couldn't help smiling. His succinct praise meant more than anything and as his admiring gaze focused on her she wanted to turn the clock back before the flowers arrived. Patrick always spoiled things.

She got up to finish off the main course. She slipped the perfectly cooked slices of chicken into the sauce to warm through. 'Fresh pasta only takes a couple of minutes to cook. The Italians say it should be al dente, which means to the tooth. It should still have a slight bite.' She dropped handfuls of pasta into the boiling water.

'I've always heard the water should be as salty as the Mediterranean Sea.'

All the time she chattered on Lily sensed Kenan's gaze on her face. Although he wanted to find out more about her love of cooking, she guessed he was wondering about the flowers she'd received and her strange reaction to them. He wasn't a fool. 'I'll dish up over here seeing there's not much room on the table.'

For the next few minutes she gave thanks for Betty who never met a hole in the conversation she couldn't fill. Lily picked at her lunch while the older woman told them fascinating tales of growing up in the village.

'Mandy, how about you go out in the back garden to have a run around while I get cleared up, and then we'll have dessert?' Lily suggested. 'I've made my first attempt at a sticky toffee pudding so you'll need plenty of space in your tummy for it.'

'Okay. Miss Betty told me she has pixies living in the bottom of her garden.' The little girl fixed her bright, sunny smile on Betty. 'Will you come and show me?'

'What do you say, Mandy?' Kenan asked, his face severe and uncompromising.

'Please,' Mandy muttered.

'Of course, my sweet.' Betty gave her an encouraging smile

The two of them left and Lily found herself alone with Kenan who instantly fixed her with the same uncompromising stare he'd just used with such a sobering effect on his daughter.

'The dishes can wait,' he said firmly. 'We'll do them after you've told me what's wrong and don't bother saying it's nothing to do with me.' He reached over and picked up her hands, needing the reassurance of touching her again. 'Maybe I flatter myself, but I think my opinion matters to you. I know yours does to me,' he added quietly, his voice gruff with emotion.

Lily lowered her gaze to the table, but he used one finger to tip her chin up to meet his gaze.

'Are you going to make me ask questions, or be your normal forthright self and come out with it?' He tried for a smile, rewarded by a softening in her pretty blue eyes.

'The flowers are from Patrick O'Brian.'

'Why does your ex-manager sending you flowers bother you so much?' Kenan asked.

'He's my ex-fiancé too,' Lily blurted out.

Kenan fought to suppress his disappointment at the unexpected answer.

'I guess I should've told you but—'

'It might've been nice but you don't owe me any explanations.' He fought to keep his voice steady and unemotional, while being churned up inside.

'It's a long story.'

'I've all the time in the world,' he stated.

'About four years ago Patrick was scouting the country looking for new talent for the Cooking Network. He spotted me doing a short segment on a Nashville TV programme and wooed me – professionally and personally. There weren't too many good-looking, charming, Yale-educated Irishmen around Tennessee when I was growing up and I fell for him big-time. I was flattered when he showed an interest in me and my fledgling career.'

Kenan hated hearing Lily sell herself short and it took all his self-control to hold his tongue.

'He became my business manager and when we needed a hook to get the network on board Patrick basically created *Luscious Lily.* I went along with it because he obviously knew what he was doing.'

'Wasn't it unprofessional of him to date you as well?' That was the most polite way he could phrase the question. In the army it would've been completely out of order and he thought the same rules applied to most large corporations.

Lily blushed. 'Yeah. But it goes on, and everyone turns a blind eye. Unfortunately a lot of young women feel they've no choice. Patrick's never said so but I always wonder if I'd have got my show if I hadn't slept with him.'

He hated to see her doubt herself. 'You wouldn't have kept the show if you weren't good, sweetheart. The top bosses at the network aren't stupid.'

'I guess.' She shrugged. 'The day we hit the number one spot in the ratings he took me to the top of the Empire State Building and proposed, complete with champagne, red roses and an obscenely large diamond, of course.'

Kenan clenched his jaw and forced himself to ask. 'Did you love him?'

Lily's eyes shimmered. 'I thought so, but even before he betrayed me I was having second thoughts. We were always going out to parties and the right places to be seen. I guess it was fun at first but I got tired of it. The few nights we did stay in all we did was talk about work.'

It sounded a lousy sort of relationship to him, but what did he know? His own worst arguments with Olivia started when he complained about them never spending any time on their own. She hadn't wanted to hear about his work and so he'd stopped talking about it in the end. There was none of the companionship his parents had always shared, to him one of the lynchpins of a good marriage. This wasn't something he'd expected to find in common with Lily.

'I get what you mean. Olivia was the original party girl. I should've seen we weren't suited from the beginning.'

She gave him a curious look. 'How did you two get together in the first place?'

'Her father was a general and we met at a regimental dinner. Olivia was beautiful and classy. Out of my league.' Kenan stared off into space.

'We're a pair of misfits, aren't we?'

Lily's half-hearted attempt to laugh rescued him from maudlin thoughts. He leaned close enough to smell today's spicy orange scent on her warm skin, overlaid with hints of the wine they'd drunk.

Kenan knew he had only to touch her lips and they wouldn't need to talk any more for a while. 'How did Patrick betray you?'

'You're relentless, aren't you?' Lily sighed. 'I discovered him enjoying himself with a young, blonde intern on my top grade Italian marble kitchen countertop. He didn't see it as a deal breaker and said it needn't have any effect on us. I found out later that she wasn't the first by a long chalk. I shoved his expensive ring in the garbage disposal and turned it on. Then I fired him as my manager and now Patrick wants me back because it hurts his ego to be humiliated and rejected, plus he needs the money I brought him. His last couple of projects haven't done well and his career's on the line.'

'I almost think the worst offence he committed was choosing your favourite marble for his indiscretion.' Kenan tried to make a joke, but as all the colour drained from her face he knew he'd screwed up. He grabbed her hands again and squeezed hard. 'Honey, I'm sorry. I'm a thoughtless bastard sometimes.'

'Yeah, you are,' she said sadly, but struggled to smile. 'For some reason I still think you're a decent person underneath and I fancy you like the devil.'

'I fancy you too if it helps.'

'Sure does. Helps boost my ego a little.'

He smiled. 'Anyway, you're rid of Patrick now. He can send as many stupid flowers as he likes,' Kenan declared.

'You don't get it.' Lily shook her head. 'People don't get rid of Patrick unless he agrees and thanks to my soft-hearted mother he knows I'm here. I don't need this – or him. Getting this programme organised is my way of proving myself.'

'You'll do it. I've got faith in you,' Kenan proclaimed and foolishly met her shining, deep blue eyes head on. She might as well have grabbed him by the throat. 'Oh, Lily, you'd challenge a monk, and that's something I've never claimed to be.' He reached out and stroked her cheek, her soft skin heating under his fingers.

'Good. I've never been into the whole robes and shaved head thing.'

Her teasing laugh released something deep inside and he gave in, lowering his mouth to hers. Kenan trailed a slow path around her lips and with the quietest of sighs she opened to him, wrapping her arms up around his neck and winding her fingers in through his hair. Drawn in, he deepened the kiss, unable to resist sliding his hands down to rest on the curve of her hips and pulling her closer.

'Daddy! Guess what? Mummy's back.' Mandy's high, excited voice behind him startled Kenan into letting go of Lily. He jerked around to see his elegant ex-wife, her stunning face spoiled by an unpleasant sneer, walk into the kitchen.

CHAPTER 12

Every muscle in Kenan's body tensed and on impulse he reached for Lily's hand, clutching it like a lifeline. 'Olivia, I didn't expect to see you this soon.'

'I'm sure I don't know why. I told your parents it would only be for a couple of days.' Mandy wriggled in closer to her mother. 'You didn't think I'd leave my sweet girl for long, did you? I'm not her father.'

'Don't start, please.'

Olivia smoothed over her long blonde hair, cinched at the base of her neck with a black taffeta bow. 'You never were much for talking, were you?' Her gaze shifted to check out Lily.

'Mummy, that's Miss Lily. She helped choose my princess necklace.' Mandy pulled at the shiny pink strands around her neck.

'I'm sure she did, dear.'

Kenan itched to wipe the supercilious expression off his ex-wife's face as she fingered the elegant strand of pearls around her own neck. He'd been bowled over by her classic beauty when they first met, unable to believe his luck when she agreed to a dance. Later he had discovered that he'd been her brief rebellion against her father's efforts to steer her into a far more suitable marriage. Kenan was her bit of rough – a tough, working-class Army officer not given to flowery manners. Once the initial physical attraction dimmed on both sides, they discovered there was little left to keep them together. Only Mandy's unplanned arrival caused the marriage to last as long as it did.

He suddenly realised everyone was waiting for him to speak. 'Sorry. This is Lily Redman. She's a well-known American chef and I'm working for her at the moment.'

'Pleasure, I'm sure,' Lily drawled. 'You've done a bang up job with Mandy. She's precious.'

'Thank you.' Olivia managed a brief nod. 'Is anybody going to show some manners and invite me to sit down?' She stared around at them all and Betty glanced at Kenan.

'Of course. Feel free.' He pointed towards an empty chair.

'Here? In the kitchen?' Olivia's voice dripped with disdain.

Kenan fought to keep a lid on his temper. 'We'll go into the living room, if that is all right with you Betty?' She nodded.

He tugged at Lily's hand but she didn't move. 'I'll wait here for you.'

'Please,' he whispered.

'Are you sure?'

'Kenan, this is private between us.' Olivia's haughty manner put his back up.

'Lily comes, or we don't talk,' he asserted and a tinge of pink coloured his ex-wife's porcelain skin.

'Have it your way. Mandy, dear, you need to stay here with Mrs . . .' She gestured towards Betty and dropped her daughter's hand before gliding out of the room without a backward glance.

'Daddy?' Mandy's tear-filled eyes tore him up. 'Why is Mummy cross? Have I been a bad girl? I didn't mean to be naughty. She's not going again, is she?'

Kenan went over and lifted her up into his arms. 'Oh, my sweet. You're the best little girl in the world. Daddy's probably done something wrong. I'm sure Miss Betty will find you some yummy sticky toffee pudding to eat while we talk.' He pressed a kiss into her fair hair. 'Just remember to leave some for us.'

A tiny smile pulled at Mandy's lips. 'Of course we will, Daddy.'

Kenan set her back down and Mandy instantly ran over to Betty with a big smile.

He took hold of Lily's hand again. 'Come on. Let's get this over with.' She didn't say anything but followed him out of the kitchen. In the living room Kenan steered Lily towards the sofa so they could sit together.

'Before we discuss our daughter, I believe I've the right to know what your relationship is with Miss Redman,' Olivia stated coolly.

'I don't. You gave up that right the day we signed the divorce papers. Have I asked about your latest conquest?'

'Nasty, Kenan, nasty.' Olivia rested her pale, slim hands in her lap.

'All you need to know is that I'm working for Lily at the moment. Our personal relationship is none of your business.' He refused to drag Lily into all this.

'Let's forget her for now. We need to talk about Amanda. There needs to be a change.' She splayed her hands and scrutinised the immaculate pale pink manicure. Kenan remembered her telling him once that bright-coloured polish was common.

'You've had things your way for the last six years,' Kenan growled. 'I kept my promise not to contact Mandy because you thought it was best.' He seethed, hating the fact that she always made him sound uncaring. 'What's brought about this need for change?'

'I'm engaged to be married. The wedding will be in September.'

'Congratulations,' Lily burst out and Olivia's disdain couldn't have been more obvious if it was displayed on a flashing neon sign.

Kenan cleared his throat. 'Uh, yes, of course. Who's the . . . lucky man?' *Poor devil.*

'Lord Henry Cunningham,' Olivia said with a restrained half-smile, the most she ever allowed herself in order to avoid premature wrinkles. 'He's got a rather nice little estate in Surrey, a house in

Belgravia and a shooting lodge up in Scotland,' she preened.

'Of course, you love him madly?' Kenan's cynicism flowed right over Olivia and she gave in to another satisfied smirk.

'Naturally.'

Kenan leaned back slightly. 'Let me guess, Lord Henry would rather you weren't encumbered by an eight-year-old daughter. He wants an heir, and doesn't want to be reminded you're . . . damaged goods.'

An ugly flush rushed up Olivia's neck, flooding her face. 'If you want to put it so crudely then, yes.'

Kenan used every ounce of self-control he possessed not to snap. It had torn him apart every day of the last six years to be apart from Mandy, but he'd done it for his daughter's sake.

'I'd still see her for holidays and things, of course.' She waved her hand carelessly. 'You've always complained about her not knowing you, so what's the problem?'

'How about the fact that I don't have a home or a job at the moment. I only left the Army a few months ago.'

'Oh, Kenan, don't bother with the sob story.' Olivia blithely rejected his attempt to explain. 'We both know your family aren't wealthy but you made a bundle—'

'That's enough, Olivia.' He didn't dare look at Lily properly. Later she'd get a well-deserved explanation. He hadn't been able to find a way to tell her about the most difficult parts of his life yet because he was a coward. '*If* I agree, how're you going to explain this to Mandy? She might never forgive you . . . or me.'

Olivia rolled her eyes. 'Cut out the drama, Kenan. Amanda's a sensible little girl. I'll do the explaining if that's what's bothering you.'

'We'll do it together,' Kenan insisted. 'She's got to see it as a way to spend more time with me rather than losing you.' His mind raced, trying to work out how to put a good spin on this.

'Whatever you like. She won't be losing me anyway, I've told you that. You do twist things. I need this done today because I promised Harry I'd be back in London tonight.'

'My God, you can't wait to get rid of her, can you?' Kenan couldn't believe Olivia.

'You're making this more difficult than it needs to be, as usual. It's hard being a single parent. You'll discover it's not a bed of roses,' she sniped back.

An odd noise caught Kenan's attention and he turned around. Mandy stood in the open door, her white face streaked with tears and her little shoulders heaving with loud, gulping sobs.

'Now look what you've done.' He glared at Olivia, then got up and ran across to Mandy, swinging her up into his arms. Her hot hands grasped the back of his neck and she snuggled into the curve of his shoulder. 'Let's go in the garden, sweetheart.'

This was a test. If he could get through this maybe he'd be worthy of being called a real father at last. Kenan mentally crossed his fingers and hoped he wouldn't let down another important person in his life.

CHAPTER 13

Lily couldn't breathe the same air as Kenan's ex-wife a second longer. Whatever had possessed him to marry the cow? Sure, Olivia was beautiful but it must've resembled making love to a block of ice.

She jumped up from the sofa and headed towards the kitchen, not caring a whit about being rude. Baking would take too long, the situation demanded something quick and soothing.

Rifling thought Betty's pantry, Lily found a couple of cans of tuna – normally she'd use fresh, but today perfection wasn't the point. She grabbed a half-used jar of walnut halves and spied some Red Delicious apples in the fruit bowl. She flung open the fridge and pulled out a carton of eggs, lovely fresh brown ones from a local farm. Selecting two she popped them in a saucepan and added water and a touch of salt before turning them on to boil. While they cooked she'd make the mayonnaise.

She took two more of the eggs and separated them. Usually she'd keep the whites for making meringues but today she didn't bother. Lily slid the yolks into a glass bowl and added a touch of salt and dry mustard to begin the process. The stress began to seep from her tense body and she allowed herself a tiny smile.

'Very charming, I'm sure.' Olivia sauntered into the room. 'It's interesting to see Kenan turn to a domestic sort of woman for a change. The fact that I couldn't cook didn't bother him, but of course I had other attributes he admired like class and breeding.'

Lily didn't even look up and concentrated on squeezing a fresh lemon into a clean bowl and added a touch of white wine vinegar. Adding half of her lemon and vinegar mix to the egg, Lily whisked briskly.

'I can't imagine that it's part of your plan to end up as a stepmother?' Olivia needled.

This was the tricky part of making mayonnaise but Lily routinely did it in a busy kitchen full of people so refused to allow herself to freak out. She slowed down her breathing and steadily added the first few drops of oil, taxing her patience to the utmost. If she got this wrong it would curdle and be hard to retrieve. She smiled happily as the mixture began to thicken the right way.

'I can't imagine what's amusing you. Motherhood's no joke and I'm sure Amanda will be difficult until she gets used to the . . . situation here,' Olivia persisted.

With half the oil incorporated, Lily added the rest of the lemon and vinegar mix and then

121

streamed in the remainder of the oil. It was a pleasure to imagine beating Olivia's pea-sized brain as she whisked away. She reached for a spoon to check the seasoning. *Perfect.*

'It does come out of a jar you know,' Olivia sniped.

With the mayonnaise made she'd now pour her energy into stuffing the stuck-up Brit back in her box. Lily could chop and bitch at the same time – no problem.

'Not this good it doesn't,' she said with an upbeat grin plastered all over her face. 'I suppose it depends how sophisticated your palate is. Some people aren't fussy.' *Take that, you stupid creature.* Lily selected an apple and washed it off. She sliced it neatly in half, removed the core and began to turn it into a fine dice. Some chefs preferred to peel their apples but she loved the added texture and vibrant flecks of colour it gave to the dish. Her timer went off and she turned away to run her boiled eggs under cold water.

'Very sure of yourself, aren't you?' Olivia prodded.

'I am when it comes to my cooking,' she replied in a steady voice, while peeling the hot eggs.

'You're wasting your time as far as Kenan's concerned.' Olivia pulled out a chair and lowered herself elegantly onto the seat, crossing her legs in one sleek movement.

Lily almost reminded her of the earlier conversation when the other woman considered sitting in the kitchen beneath her, but saved her breath and diced eggs instead. Far more productive.

'He's not good husband material,' Olivia stated bluntly.

'Who says I'm looking for one?' Lily started chopping up the walnuts, then went back to the cupboard. Betty didn't have any celery so she needed something else for crunch. She discovered a small can of water chestnuts, which would work just fine. Also she spotted a packet of tart dried cherries and knew they'd add the perfect finishing touch. Tuna fish salad was her mother's favourite go-to dish in the summer – the warm weather version of chilli, their winter comfort food.

'It's a lonely life without a man's support,' Olivia stated decisively. 'I've done it and don't intend to go *there* again.'

'I'm able to take care of myself perfectly well, thank you for your concern,' Lily retorted, heading back to the cupboard where she found some paprika for a slight kick of heat and touch of colour. Sprinkling some into the dish she tossed it gently together and then tasted before adding a tad more of the smoky spice. Finally satisfied, she covered the bowl with plastic wrap and set it in the fridge. Now it was time to make Olivia wish she'd never started this discussion.

'Do you want to go back in and see Mummy?' Kenan asked, dreading the idea of setting off another flood of tears. He'd calmed Mandy down enough to staunch the first round, leaving him worn out. Women and tears always did him in.

Mandy nodded and plugged her thumb back in her mouth.

'All right, come on then.' He slid her off his lap and Mandy grabbed his hand and clutched on so tightly there was a distinct possibility he'd lose all feeling in his fingers.

They walked back indoors and Kenan came to an abrupt halt in the kitchen doorway. Lily and Olivia stood inches apart in the centre of the room with his fiery employer brandishing a large knife in her right hand.

'Uh, Lily, is everything okay?' His mind spun in circles, wondering how he could get the knife away without frightening Mandy or anyone getting hurt.

'Fine. Why wouldn't it be?' Lily met his gaze and calmly laid the knife back down on the counter.

Maybe because you looked about to murder my ex-wife. Not that he'd blame Lily – Olivia was enough to tempt the most committed pacifist.

'Mandy, would you like to make some special princess cookies?' Lily grinned and Kenan felt a little hand creep around his leg. Mandy peaked over at Lily.

'What's a princess cookie?' she whispered and the deep hurt in her soft, unsure voice cut right through him.

'Send your Mom and Dad away and I'll share the secret with you.'

Kenan wanted to kiss her right on her luscious pink lips. 'Good plan, kiddo. What do you think?'

He wanted to give Mandy the choice. She nodded and a tiny smile brightened her face. Kenan braced himself. 'Olivia, how about we go back in the other room.'

'But Lily and I hadn't finished our . . . discussion,' she protested.

Kenan walked across and planted a hand on his ex-wife's shoulder. 'Oh, I think you have.' He wouldn't allow Lily to be abused any longer. 'Come on.'

She shook off his hand and threw Lily a venomous glare. 'Don't think this is over,' she said and swept from the room.

Kenan shrugged an apology to Lily and she mouthed okay right back at him. He crouched down in front of Mandy. 'Is it all right if I go and talk to Mummy while you make something fun with Miss Lily?'

'Yes, and don't come back until they're done. Isn't that right?' Mandy asked Lily.

'Sure is, honey. Come over here and wash your hands and we'll get started.' Lily waved a hand behind her back to shoo Kenan out of the kitchen.

He left while the going was good but before he walked into the living room he hung back in the doorway and watched Olivia, unnoticed. Nothing in her expression or the quiet way she sat indicated any turmoil. He remembered visiting her an hour after Mandy was born after being banned from the delivery room. She'd greeted him with a quiet kiss on the cheek, her make-up redone and not a single silky blonde hair out of place. At first he'd thought there had to be more hidden underneath the public facade but had soon come to the conclusion that there really wasn't. He hoped Lord Henry Cunningham knew what he was getting into.

'So, are we ready to sort this out?' He stepped over to where Olivia sat, ramrod-straight on the sofa. Kenan remained standing with his feet spread and arms crossed not wanting to be comfortable in any way.

'Oh, do sit down, and stop acting as if this is another of your macho missions.'

Her languid drawl got to him, as it always did. From day one Olivia's upper-class manner intrigued and revolted him in equal measure and made him feel loutish and ignorant.

Kenan picked the chair furthest from her and dropped down into it, resting his hands on his thighs. 'I want this done properly through a lawyer.'

She scoffed. 'What an unnecessary expense.'

'No, it's not,' he insisted. 'We did it your way last time and see where it got me – six years of never seeing my daughter. That's not happening again.'

Olivia picked up her grey leather handbag and retrieved a silver case from one of the pockets. She opened it and passed over a business card. 'Contact Peregrine Worseley. He's Henry's solicitor and will be representing me from now on. I want mandated visiting three times a year and expect you to be agreeable if I request extra visits.

I won't argue about anything else unless you become unreasonable.' Her green cat-like eyes narrowed. 'I will insist her education be completed here in England until she turns eighteen, so don't think you're going to whisk her off abroad to live in America or anywhere else.'

He bit back the urge to protest. 'Fair enough.'

'By the way, you might think twice about getting tangled up with the tart in the kitchen.'

Kenan could have happily wiped off her smirk with a sharp, hard smack. Lily was worth a hundred of her.

'I have our daughter's morals to consider and won't have her exposed to . . . unsuitable influences.'

Kenan's hands clenched, the fingers pressing deep into his flesh. 'Be careful what you're saying. We both know there are things you wouldn't care to have revealed about your behaviour when I was deployed.' A slight flush tinged her delicate skin as his barb hit home.

'I believe we've said all that's necessary.' Olivia picked up her handbag from the sofa and stood. 'I'm going to say goodbye to Amanda.' She checked her watch. 'Ring for a taxi to collect me as soon as possible. I want to catch the four o'clock London train.'

Kenan instantly flipped open his mobile and made the call. 'He'll be about twenty minutes.' Olivia frowned but didn't say anymore. He'd offer to drive her to the station himself, but he knew his limits and he had about reached them. He worried about how he would cope with Mandy. He'd tried to explain the situation out in the garden, but wasn't sure it had sunk in.

Olivia left the room without a backward glance and for a few minutes he was rooted where he sat. One thing at a time. Firstly he would focus on getting Mandy through today. Kenan dragged back up to standing and strolled back into the hall. He lingered outside the half-closed kitchen door, hearing Olivia's slow firm voice and Mandy's quiet high-pitched questions.

He leaned against the wall and waited, ready to pick up the pieces.

CHAPTER 14

Kenan lay stretched out on the sofa with an exhausted Mandy plastered to him, sound asleep, her bare feet tucked in between his legs.

'You awake?'

Lily's low whisper startled him. Kenan glanced up to see her standing in the doorway and her vibrant beauty made the room glow, making what he needed to do next even harder.

She kicked off her high-heels and crept across the carpet, kneeling down and resting her head against his thigh. He couldn't resist stretching out one hand to play with a handful of her soft curls and the sharp scent of her lemon shampoo teased his senses. Kenan pulled his hand away and rested it on Mandy's back, rubbing his fingers around in small circles to soothe her in her sleep.

'She'll be all right. I'll make sure of it. I'm not letting her down again,' he said, as much to himself as to the woman now staring at him.

'You can only do your best. No one's perfect. Not even you, Superman.'

'Don't get away with much where you're concerned, do I?'

'Nah. My staff could've told you that, soldier boy.' Lily gave his leg a gentle squeeze.

The breath hitched in Kenan's throat and suddenly her smile faded. Written in her shimmering eyes lay the knowledge of what he was about to say. The realisation of how well she understood him shook him to the core.

'Lily, I have to put Mandy first for the foreseeable future. It's not fair of me to continue whatever we've started when I can't make you any promises.'

'Did I ask for any?' Her unwavering voice touched him more than anything, but he refused to weaken.

'No, but you'd be a strange woman if you didn't want to know where you stand – especially after Patrick.' He gave in to a wry smile. 'Hate it, don't you?'

'What?'

'Me, being right.' Lily attempted a disdainful glare.

'It's not working, love,' Kenan declared.

'What isn't?'

'Your attempt to be haughty. That's Olivia's province, not yours.' His voice roughened. 'I hate letting you down, in so many ways. You realise I won't be able to go with you tomorrow.'

'But I can't manage on my own,' Lily complained.

'I've got a suggestion you might or might not

like. My younger sister, Jane, is coming home tonight. She's been travelling for the last month since she finished university for the summer. She hates waitressing and chambermaid work, so I'm pretty sure she'll jump at the chance to take over. She's a competent driver. I taught her myself.' He couldn't help sounding proud. 'I'm sure you two will hit it off.'

'Got it all planned, haven't you?'

Kenan didn't blame her for being resentful. 'Don't make it any harder for me, please.' He caressed her cheek and she sighed, arching into the stroke of his fingers.

'This'll only be a pause, if I get my way,' Lily said, a glaze of tears filming her pretty eyes.

'And we know you always do that.' His attempt to be flippant failed miserably. Lily eased away and he did not try to pull her back, for both their sakes.

'Why don't you ask your sister to come over and see me in the morning and we'll go from there?' Her brave attempt at normalcy cut through him, but he kept his mouth shut.

'Okay.'

Lily unravelled her legs and stood up, tugging at her pink miniskirt. She leaned over him, purposely giving him a far too tempting view right down the front of her low-cut shirt. A mischievous tug of humour pulled at her lush mouth. 'You won't be able to stay away long. I've put a spell on you.'

'Witch,' he growled as she played with his hair.

'I'm off to do some work.' At the door Lily glanced back over her shoulder. 'I'll see you in the morning.'

Her smile was artificially bright but he wasn't stupid enough to comment. Kenan slumped back against the cushions and closed his eyes.

Mandy wriggled and stretched before rising up slightly and staring blankly down at him. Kenan watched the memory slam into her and her little face screwed up all set to cry again.

'Hey, sweetie, it's all right. Daddy's here.' He used his best soothing voice – the one that usually worked on young soldiers after a harrowing mission. 'I hear there are fresh cookies ready to be eaten.'

'Can we eat them before our proper tea?' she asked with wide eyes.

'Tonight a very special princess is allowed to have cookies instead of a proper tea, for being brave and beautiful.'

'Thank you, Daddy.' Mandy smacked a large, loud kiss right on his nose. 'You're the best.'

Kenan hoped she still thought so when she knew him better.

Lily toyed with her morning cup of coffee, unable to eat anything as she kept listening for Kenan's car outside.

'Is everything all right, dear. You'm a bit quiet this morning?'

She struggled to respond to Betty's question without bursting into tears and it took all her acting skills, honed by years in front of TV cameras. 'Yeah, I just didn't sleep well.'

'I hate that. Fair sets you up wrong for the day,' Betty commented, with a shake of her head.

'It sure does.' *The fact the man I'm pretty sure I've fallen in love with has gone all noble on me doesn't help.* Lily didn't resent Mandy – heck, she loved the kid to death – but she didn't see why caring about her and his daughter needed to be mutually exclusive.

The doorbell rang and Lily about jumped out of her skin. Betty gave her a knowing smile and patted her hand.

'It'll be all right, you wait and see.' She smiled and bustled away out into the hall. Lily's view of life was a lot less optimistic but she kept her scepticism to herself.

'Miss Lily! Miss Lily!' Mandy raced into the kitchen and right into Lily's arms.

'Were you a good girl for Daddy last night?'

Mandy glared in disgust. 'Of course. I beat Grandpa Bill at Snakes and Ladders and ate all my sausages and baked beans. Daddy told me I only had to eat biscuits, but Granny told him off and said that wasn't enough to keep a fly alive.' She jumped on Lily's lap with a heavy sigh. 'Why do we want to keep flies alive? They're yucky.'

Glancing across the room Lily met Kenan's dark, brooding gaze and swallowed hard. She quickly turned her attention back to Mandy. 'I can't imagine, kiddo.'

'Did you know I've got an aunt?'

'I did. Is she here?'

Mandy jerked around and pointed to the young woman standing over by Kenan. 'That's my Aunt Jane. She's fun. She did my nails for me, look.' She spread out her hands for Lily's scrutiny.

Lily caught Kenan's eye and shook her head, before he said something stupid. Dark purple nails might not be suitable for an eight-year-old but Mandy didn't need to be slammed down any more.

'Lily, this is my sister, Jane, who clearly got dressed in the dark this morning.' Kenan's laconic tone made clear his bewilderment at her striking combination of an old pink taffeta dress, black leather jacket and combat boots.

'Your daddy hasn't a clue about fashion,' Jane said to Mandy, with a laugh. 'This was all the rage at London Fashion Week.'

'Really,' Kenan said, with more than a touch of sarcasm. 'You look—'

'Kenan.' Lily gave him one of her sternest glares and he stopped grousing.

'Sorry, kid,' he apologised to Jane, who seemed totally uncaring. 'This is Lily Redman who I've been working with.'

'I'll bet you have,' Jane said with a smirk.

Lily had taken it for granted that Jane Rowse would be like the rest of her family, conventional and slightly old-fashioned. This was her kind of girl. She eased Mandy off her lap and held out her hand. 'Great to meet you.'

'You want to tell me what this job's about and we'll see if we suit each other?' Jane stated in the same plain-spoken way as her older brother.

'Sure. How about we go in the other room, if it's all right with you, Betty?'

'Of course, dear. I'll find this little love a few sweeties in my special box.'

Lily glanced at Kenan again. 'Do you want to join us and put Jane straight about what an evil boss I am?'

'No. You go ahead.' The throbbing pulse in his neck betrayed his struggle for control around her. 'I'll stay here with Mandy until you're through. Jane's smart enough to size you up all by herself,' he said sharply.

Lily guessed his nerves were as taut as her own. Hopefully she'd be on her way to Keswick soon and they wouldn't be tormented by constantly being around each other. Before they could make a move the doorbell rang again.

'Goodness. It's like Paddington station here today.' Betty laughed and scuttled off. A minute later she returned and frowned at Lily, holding out another bouquet of red roses. 'These just came for you.'

'Toss them in the garbage.'

The lines on Betty's face deepened. 'It's a bit difficult like.'

'What do you mean?'

135

'Your American man brought them himself.'

Lily wavered unsteadily on her feet and Kenan's firm hand cradled her elbow. 'Patrick's here?' she whispered.

'I sure am, sweetheart, and come to claim back my bride-to-be.' His smooth Irish lilt rolled over her and she wished a chasm would open up under her feet.

The back of Lily's neck burned from everyone's curious stares.

CHAPTER 15

'You goin' to find us somewhere we can talk, honey, without an audience?' Patrick's charming smile took her by surprise, although goodness knows why because he deployed it more than any other man she'd come across.

'I suppose we could go into the living room,' she said grudgingly.

'Don't sound too enthusiastic.'

The amusement in his voice riled her. 'And you don't need to push your luck,' Lily snapped. She tugged on her hand until Kenan loosened his grip, not daring to look up at his face. 'Follow me.' Out in the hall she pointed towards the door. 'Get in there and stop being a smart ass.'

'I've missed your Southern lady manners, Lily Elizabeth.'

She trailed in after him but he stopped abruptly inside the door and turned to face her. Patrick lifted his right hand and touched her cheek while treating her to the sexy smile he always used on gullible women.

'Get your hands off of me,' she hissed. 'Why are you here anyway?'

Patrick slowly dropped his arm away and strolled over to the window. He appeared to study the scenery outside but she'd no doubt his devious brain was working overtime. He swung back around and for a few long seconds Lily quailed under the mesmerising power of his deep green eyes.

'I'm here for you, of course.' He spread his arms out in supplication. 'I screwed up, Lily.'

'Finally something we agree on,' she jibed right back.

'I made a stupid mistake. It won't happen again.' He managed to sound so sincere Lily expected to hear violins wailing in the background. 'Give me another chance, please.'

'You've got to be kidding me.' A curl of anger unravelled inside her and Lily mentally thanked Kenan for helping to bring back her innate confidence. Once she'd been overawed to attract this man and they'd shared good times before it all turned sour. He was intelligent, incredibly knowledgeable about food and the business and had brought her into his world. It had taken a long time to see below the charming surface to the calculating man underneath.

'We're a pair, Lily. We go together. That girl meant nothing.' He took a step closer and Lily backed up towards the door.

'Do you seriously think I'd marry a man who'll have *meaningless sex* with any woman who'll bat her eyelashes at him? I'm worth more than that, Patrick. Leave now, and don't come back. Don't send any more flowers either or I'll set the police on you. There are laws against stalking.'

His eyes narrowed. 'You're forgetting something, sweetheart.'

Lily's heart thumped in her chest but she was determined not to show any fear. 'What might that be?'

'Who's the reason you have a career beyond frying chicken in Tennessee for has-been country music stars? We both know you won't last long without me steering your career. *Luscious Lily's* a hollow facade, sweetheart. They'll soon find you out,' he sneered.

A rush of heat flamed her cheeks. He mustn't guess how accurately he'd nailed the fears she'd hauled around ever since they had parted. 'I appreciate all you've done, but I intend on making a success of *Celebrity Chef Swap*. It will be all the proof anyone will need of my abilities.'

He gave a small shrug. 'You win. For now.'

'You don't get it, do you? I mean every word.'

'Sure you do. I get the fact I need to be punished. But we aren't done, Lily.'

Lily jabbed her middle finger in the centre of his chest. 'Quit patronising me. You're pissing me off. Now go.'

He didn't move.

'Didn't you hear the lady, mate?' Kenan shoved the door open and strode in, glaring at Patrick.

'Who might you be?'

Kenan's features turned to stone at Patrick's

supercilious tone and Lily waited for the trouble to really start.

'This is Kenan Rowse,' Lily interrupted. 'He's working for me and we're . . . good friends.'

'It's okay, love, no need to cover anything up for my sake.' Kenan sidled over to Lily and seized hold of her hand. She tried to pull away but he clung to her like superglue. 'We're a couple. Lily's off the market where you're concerned.'

God, she felt like a piece of meat being fought over by two warring lions.

'Good grief, Lily. Going down in the world, aren't you? I guess this thug makes you look classier.' Patrick laughed at them both and Lily grimaced, counting the seconds in her head. She made it to three.

Kenan sprung forward and sank his fist into Patrick's face. He scored a direct hit on his adversary's nose and jets of bright red blood sprayed everywhere. Patrick howled in pain and crumpled to the floor. For a second all Lily thought was that at least the blood wouldn't show up too much against the patterned carpet. Then anger roiled through her. 'Are you mad?' Lily yelled at Kenan.

'Did you expect me to do nothing? I sure as hell wasn't going to stand there and let him—'

'Insult me?' Lily thrust herself right in his face. 'Grow up, Kenan. I don't need you or anyone to fight my battles.'

'Sorry.' He lowered his eyes to the ground and

sucked in a hissing breath, clutching his hand. Pain pulled at the edges of his stoic expression.

'So you should be.' Lily turned away and bent down over Patrick. 'Are you all right?'

'No, I'm damn well not. I think he's broken my nose. I'll set the police on him.' Patrick scowled at Kenan.

'Sorry, mate, but no one talks about Lily that way in front of me,' Kenan declared with a steely voice.

Lily suppressed a smile, the whole caveman thing didn't *really* impress her but . . .

'You're a barbarian.' Patrick spat out the words, wiped at his nose, and struggled to his feet. 'Think carefully, Lily. If you choose him I'll make sure your career is dead in the water. You might have got your own back by firing me as your business manager, but I've got a ton of influence at the network and you'd be wise not to forget it.'

Kenan stepped forward but Lily grabbed his arm to hold him back. They didn't need this getting any more out of hand.

'Go, Patrick, now,' she ordered. He glared at them both but complied and headed for the door. 'As for you . . .' Lily flung Kenan's arm away and he winced in pain. 'I hope you've broken every bone in your hand. I'm going to talk to Jane now and hopefully by tomorrow morning I'll be out of here. God, you two men are both throwbacks to the Dark Ages.'

Kenan stepped out of the way as she stormed out of the room.

Lily ran through the house and flung the back door open, desperate for air. On the patio Jane Rowse lay sprawled out in a deckchair soaking up the day's warm sunshine.

'Three guesses. Kenan annoyed you?' Jane laughed and tipped her head back, peering out over the top of her oversized Jackie O sunglasses.

'You could say that,' Lily conceded.

'Don't tell me. He thumped your pretty boy ex, didn't he?' Jane's eyes, the exact match of her brother's, shone with glee.

'Well, yeah.'

'I'm pretty sure the Irish charmer deserved it. I only saw him for those few minutes but he struck me as a jerk. He must be a stud in bed because I can't see any other reason you'd have stayed with him.'

'Not really.' A small grin sneaked past Lily's defences. 'To tell you the truth – pretty dull and talk about quick.' Lily chuckled.

'Figures. Probably afraid it'd mess up his hair. I can't see him getting sweaty and out of control,' Jane teased.

'Kenan would throw a fit to hear you talk this way.'

'Oh, don't come over all pompous on me. My precious brother still thinks I'm a little girl. He prefers to imagine me as a virginal, teetotal, hard-working student tucked up alone in my own bed by ten o'clock every night.' Jane's loud raunchy laugh broke apart the last of Lily's anger and she

142

joined in, falling into the other deckchair and laughing so hard her ribs hurt.

'You mean that's not true?' Lily jested, setting them off on another round of helpless giggles.

'Hasn't been for a long time,' Jane drawled out the words and threw up her hands in abject surrender. 'Still want me to work for you?'

Lily stuck out her hand. 'Shake on it. We're going to have fun.' Jane pumped her hand several times and grinned.

'Great.' Jane's face turned serious. 'I'll work hard you know.'

'I'm banking on it. I don't waste time where my career's concerned.'

Betty came out of the kitchen door holding Mandy by the hand. 'Can this little dear stay with you a while? If not I'll take her back to her Granny's house? I've got to go see my sister over in Portmellon for a couple of hours because she can't get out much and I need to pick up some shopping for her. I'll be back before lunch.'

'Of course.' Lily helped Mandy clamber up onto her lap. 'Where's your Daddy?'

'He's gone to the doctor to have his hand made better.'

Lily frowned across at Betty. 'How did he get there?'

'Drove himself, the silly man.'

Guilt swamped Lily and her throat tightened. He'd been misguided but still got hurt defending her. 'Jane, why don't you go on home and pack.

When Betty comes back we'll go ahead and leave.'

'Okay.' Jane's eyes widened in surprise. 'I thought you wanted to make more plans first?'

'Not necessary. Kenan got everything lined up so we can wing it from there. I'm keen to get going.'

'Fine by me. You're the boss.' Jane's silvery eyes scrutinised Lily in typical Rowse fashion. She stood up, stretched out her long, skinny arms and slipped her feet back into the combat boots she'd kicked off to sunbathe. 'I won't be long. I travel light.'

Lily steadied Mandy as the girl wriggled out of her grasp and plopped down into Jane's chair.

'Tell me a story.'

Children didn't let you wallow, that was for sure. Lily plastered on a smile and dragged through her memory. If nothing else this would pass the time until she could escape from Kenan. He'd burrowed so deep inside her in such a short time that Lily couldn't imagine being without him. The trouble was she had to, for a myriad of reasons, not least of which was the little girl grinning over at her in happy anticipation.

It would have to be a princess tale. *Here goes.* 'Once upon a time there was a princess called Snow White . . .'

Patrick lay back in the driver's seat of his rental car and pressed a handkerchief against his nose in an effort to stop the bleeding. He picked up his

144

phone and called up his favourite researcher back in New York. 'Kayley. Listen good to what I'm saying, sweetheart, and I'll be expecting a call back within thirty minutes and no excuses.' He rattled off the details and hung up. Patrick pulled the lever and tipped his seat back and closed his eyes.

The jangling sound of his annoying Adele ringtone, chosen because everyone else thought her cool, startled him back from a nap. 'Yeah?' Patrick listened closely, and despite the pain, he grinned. A certain lady would be his next target. Miss Olivia Bellingham, lately Mrs Kenan Rowse. Divorced because of her adultery but with sole custody of her daughter for the last six years. 'Where's she living now, Kayley?'

'In London with her fiancé, Lord Henry Cunningham. Do you want her contact details?'

'Sure.' Patrick noted everything on his iPhone and ended the conversation.

His future depended on getting Lily back. He didn't care if she rejected his bed, there were plenty of others willing to fill that position, but losing her work-wise would be a disaster. She was the golden goose who'd save him from bankruptcy. He hadn't put all this work into her career to lose it all now.

Patrick checked his nose and decided it was dried up enough to head back to his hotel.

Lily Redman would regret her rash actions and a certain Englishman would wish he'd kept his fists to himself. No one got the better of Patrick O'Brian.

CHAPTER 16

The doctor's words resounded in Kenan's ears. 'You're lucky it's only badly bruised.' Right now it hurt like hell and he didn't feel particularly fortunate. He'd pissed Lily off big-time, given his little sister enough ammunition to use against him for a lifetime and risked his custody agreement with Olivia. Pretty standard for him.

Kenan pulled up in front of Cliff House but didn't see any sign of Jane's bright purple Volkswagen Beetle. He eased out of the car and slowly walked up the path.

'There you are, my 'andsome.' Betty opened the door before he even knocked. 'You've 'ad to wait some time at the 'ospital.'

'Yeah well, A&E's always overrun.'

'Come in and I'll make us a nice cup of tea. I've got a fresh saffron cake too. You can tell me what they 'ad to say about your poor 'and.'

'Thanks, but I ought to help Jane and Lily get sorted out before they leave.' Betty's smile faded. *What now.*

'I'm sorry, my love, but they've gone.' She rifled

146

in her apron pocket and pulled out an envelope. 'Lily said to give you this. She and your monkey of a sister were 'aving a right old giggle together.' Disapproval ran through Betty's voice and Kenan wanted to hug her. No one else cared if he'd injured himself or not. *Stop pitying yourself, you sad moron. It's your own fault as usual.*

'Thanks.' He hesitated, torn between wanting to rip the letter open right away or tear it up, unread. It sure as hell wouldn't be a get-well card.

'Come into the kitchen when you're done and don't worry about Mandy, she's 'appy watching the telly a bit longer. Your Jane tried to persuade her to go back to your place with 'er when she went to pack, but Mandy wouldn't shift until you got 'ere.' Betty smiled. 'Dear little soul's worried about you.'

She left him alone and Kenan sat down on the stairs and eased open the envelope to pull out the single sheet of paper stuffed inside. Despite everything he smiled as he raised the paper to his nose and smelled Lily's spicy citrus scent, today's particular teaser. Kenan stopped the wayward thoughts and unfolded the paper.

Kenan.

Jane and I have left for Keswick. It's best this way. We'll be in touch if we need anything.

Lily.

He shoved the paper in his pocket and heaved himself up to standing. Kenan headed inside and found Betty in the kitchen. He slumped into the nearest chair and Betty pushed a cup of tea in front of him without saying a word. He managed to nod his thanks and stared out of the window, going over and over in his mind what an idiot he'd been.

'Daddy, Daddy, Daddy.' Mandy bounced into the kitchen and jumped into Kenan's lap. A vicious pain shot up through his hand and he bit back a curse. 'Do you like *Angelina Ballerina*, Daddy? She's a mouse and she dances. Can I have ballet lessons, Daddy? Please?' She patted his hand and he jerked away. 'Does it hurt, Daddy?'

'Yes it does, poppet, but it'll be better in a few days. Do you think you could help Miss Betty find me some ice? The doctor told Daddy to put ice on it so it won't blow up like a balloon.'

'I don't want your hand to go pop like a balloon, Daddy.' Mandy's big blue eyes filled with tears and her worry pushed away everything else. Kenan pulled her into him for a big hug, ignoring the fierce pain.

'Daddy was joking, Princess. It's just hurt inside which makes it all puffy but it'll soon be back to normal.' She didn't look convinced and snuggled into his neck, digging her nails into his back and clinging like a limpet. 'I promise, Mandy. Now how about that ice?' Kenan tried to distract her and her fingers eased their death grip.

'Okay, Daddy.' She slid off him and fixed her attention on Betty. 'We've got to nurse Daddy.' He caught the older woman's smile and relaxed a little.

'All right, my love. Come 'ere and we'll get 'im fixed up.'

Kenan lay back in the chair and stretched out his legs while Betty found a plastic bag and helped Mandy fill it with ice from the small freezer compartment in the top of her fridge. They wrapped it in a clean towel and his daughter advanced on him, her whole attitude stiff with determination. He prepared to be frozen alive.

'You ready to take a break?' Lily rubbed the back of her neck and glanced over at Jane. They'd delayed lunch at her request and pressed on their way.

'I'm easy. There's a motorway services place in about another ten minutes, or we can get off and go somewhere local instead,' Jane offered. 'The services have a terrible reputation and live up to it in my opinion. Lousy overpriced food, screaming kids and dirty toilets.'

'Wow, that's a great review. They should employ you to do their PR,' Lily joked. 'Okay, I'm convinced. Get off at the next exit and see if we can find something interesting. How much longer 'til we reach Keswick?'

Jane's loud guffaw filled the car. 'Get it right, Lily, or they'll mark you down as an ignorant Yank.

149

You don't say Kes-wick, it's pronounced Kezzick as though the *w* wasn't there.'

'I won't even ask why they put it there because I'm sure there's some logical reason.'

'It's to catch out American tourists. Do you need any better reason?' Jane asked with a distinct smirk. 'To answer your original question, after we've eaten and get back on the road it'll soon change into the M6. After that it's just under two hundred miles, so should take us about three hours.' She slowed down for the exit. 'Don't worry we've enough miles behind us now. Kenan's not going to catch up.'

Lily flushed and glanced out of the window. A picture of Kenan's handsome face wracked with pain caught her unawares and she waited for the wave of guilt to pass.

'He'll get over it.' Jane's careless words were belied by the tight line of her jaw. Lily didn't intend to put the girl in an awkward position between them.

'Yeah, well, we won't worry about him now.' Lily closed the delicate subject of Kenan Rowse. 'I need you to find somewhere with Wi-Fi so I can check emails and look at Mike Braithwaite's site again to refresh my memory.'

'He's hot.' Jane flashed a wicked smile.

'How do *you* know?'

'He's been on the telly lots. Hordes of women watch just to drool over him. My friends will be sick when they hear I've met him. He's your dark, brooding Heathcliff type. All northern bluntness and no social graces. You get the impression he'd toss a woman over his shoulder and whisk her off to his ruined house on the moors to have his wicked way with her. I tell you one thing, he wouldn't have to ask me twice.'

Lily grimaced. Just what she didn't need – another dour, sexist man.

'Hmm. Let's eat and go through our game plan.' She didn't respond to Jane's shrewd glance. Her new assistant was rather too close to the old one for her sanity.

'This looks decent enough.' Jane pointed to a pretty old pub set back off the road. 'Several cars there even though it's late afternoon so hopefully that means it's popular.'

'Give it a try,' Lily agreed. They turned into the car park and Jane found them a space near the front door. 'Come on. Time to try some more food off my wish list.'

An hour later they were back on the road and Lily made notes as Jane drove. Her intention to choose a light sandwich failed when she spotted a man at the next table indulging in a plate of Cumberland sausage, mashed potatoes and the English version of baked beans. When the spicy, browned up sausages arrived she was glad she hadn't resisted. She finished her report and shut down her iPad. 'Will it bother you if I take a nap?'

'Help yourself. I'm good,' Jane insisted and Lily

decided to take her assistant at her word, leaning back in the seat and closing her eyes.

'We're nearly there, Lily.'

She stirred as Jane's voice penetrated her consciousness. Lily gazed out of the window, not recognising where the heck they were.

'Longarth Hall's at the end of this driveway according to my trusty companion.' Jane patted the GPS mounted on the dashboard.

'Oh, right. Would you mind pulling over a minute. I'd like to freshen up my hair and lipstick.'

Jane smirked. 'Mike Braithwaite *will* be impressed.'

Lily didn't bother to contradict her assistant. This was done for her own confidence – a shield between her and the world. A fluff through her curls and adding a layer of *Sizzling Pink* topped with a slick of lip gloss and *Luscious Lily* was back in business. 'All right, kiddo. Let's brave the lion in his den.'

As they swept around the next corner Lily's heart rose in her mouth. Longarth Hall was as grand, imposing and well-kept as the website photos claimed. She couldn't help wondering if the chef would live up to his publicity photos too.

'Yes, he's as hot as his pictures.' Jane giggled and shoved a hand up through her spiky dark hair, shaking it back into its carefully disarranged style.

'Are you and your brother both psychics?' Kenan had guessed her thoughts too many times already. 'No, don't answer that, just park and we'll go in.' Lily needed to put the man out of her mind.

Jane stopped near the front door and before they could unload a uniformed hotel employee came out to help.

'I'll get this lot up to your room while you check in at reception,' the man said, as he unloaded the trunk. *Boot, Lily, it's a boot here.* Kenan's joking reprimand filled her head and she wished he'd go away.

Lily thanked the porter. She'd maybe guessed half of what he said, his harsh, clipped accent completely different from the Cornish she'd begun to get used to.

They followed him into a spacious entrance hall and before she had a chance to look around a smiling young woman popped out from behind the desk.

'Come this way please, Miss Redman. If you'd care to come into the bar chef will join you briefly for a drink. He's getting ready for dinner service but insisted we let him know when you arrived.'

'That's very kind of him,' Lily responded, as she followed the woman into a large, sunny, rectangular room. Guests would immediately be at ease amidst the very traditional wood-panelling, antique furniture and gently faded Oriental rugs.

'Oh, my sainted aunt.' She stumbled to a halt. The amazing view spread out in front of her rendered Lily speechless.

The huge glittering blue lake framed by dramatic mountains reminded Lily of the gorgeous New

153

Zealand scenery in the *Lord of the Rings* movies. She hadn't expected this.

'Bloody beautiful, isn't it?'

Lily jerked around and realised Jane hadn't exaggerated. Mike Braithwaite spelled trouble in huge black letters and flashing lights. The ratings for *Celebrity Chef Swap* would skyrocket if she could win this man over. Time for *Luscious Lily* to go to work.

CHAPTER 17

'Welcome to Longarth Hall, luv.' Mike Braithwaite gestured for Lily to sit, pointing to a trio of comfortable chairs set around a low table over by the window.

'Thanks. This is Jane Rowse, my temporary assistant while I'm over here.'

The chef's smoky, long-lashed eyes swept down over her in one long drag and a rush of heat coloured Jane's cheeks.

'Coffee?' he asked, gesturing to a waitress before Lily got a chance to do more than nod her agreement. 'I've only got about a quarter of an hour to spare so tell me the details of this programme quick as you can.'

Lily launched into her standard public relations spiel, keeping things short and to the point. This blunt speaking man couldn't be more different from Luc Pascal and his flirtatious French ways. The more contrasting personalities she reeled in the better the show would be.

Mike only interrupted with a couple of brief questions and stayed silent the rest of the time, watching her intently with his dark, shrewd gaze.

'I think we can do a deal.' He nodded and his stony face cracked into a cynical smile. 'I can only imagine what kind of airy-fairy chef you'll swap me with.'

Lily didn't comment. She'd love to put him with one of her more esoteric chefs. The more the fish came out of the water the better for interesting viewing.

'Tomorrow, after breakfast, I'll give you a tour of my kitchen and we should be able to get things fixed.'

'Wonderful. I'm excited about having you on board. It'll be a great opportunity for us both,' Lily declared.

'Let's hope so.'

Over enthusiasm obviously wasn't his thing but Lily held her tongue.

'I've got to get back to work now,' Mike declared. 'I've selected your dinner menu for tonight. Seared breast of wood pigeon followed by Cumbrian beef fillet and rounded off with my renowned apple and sultana bread and butter pudding.'

His abrasive manner irked her slightly but she excused him on the grounds of justifiable culinary pride. Braithwaite had won national and international prizes for his bread and butter pudding so he'd every right to want her to taste the best he could produce. The one thing she always got important guests to try was her famed coconut cake.

'Enjoy your dinner.' Mike jumped up and turned

to fix his dark, fierce gaze on Jane. 'I'll see *you* later.' He stalked out of the room without another word.

Lily didn't want to imagine Kenan's reaction if he was here. He'd rip the chef apart for making a move on his sister considering Braithwaite was well into his thirties and had a well-earned reputation as a notorious womaniser.

'I'm going up to ring Kenan before dinner and find out how he got on at the hospital,' Jane said.

Lily didn't reply for a moment. 'I think I'll stay here a while longer. I might have a wander out around the garden. Our table's booked at half-seven for dinner so I'll be up to change before then,' Lily said. She'd give them free rein to talk about her if they liked. Lily didn't care. Not much.

The man's cooking was divine. Combined with his devilish good looks, Lily knew she had another winner on her hands. Women would swoon over him as his food melted their resistance. His food could be summed up as classic English with a modern twist. Everything was locally sourced, perfectly cooked and well-seasoned. The presentation was simple but elegant, nothing fancy but perfectly put together. Her new companion would describe the chef himself that way too. Lily must bite her tongue on doling out any advice.

'Don't. Okay?' Jane threw her a warning glance.

'Don't what?'

'Interfere. I may be only twenty-one but I'm not

a dumb kid. I'm aware he's trouble.' Jane's face split into a wide grin. 'I might choose to indulge anyway, but it's not your problem. I won't get in trouble or have my heart broken because it's not my style.' She finished off her coffee and gave Lily a sly smile. 'Oh, and by the way, I'm sure you'll be pleased to hear Kenan's hand's only badly bruised, no bones broken.'

Lily took several steadying breaths. 'Good.' *Very eloquent*. 'It's been a long day so I'm goin' to head on up to bed. Are you coming?' Jane snorted and shook her head. 'He won't finish in the kitchen for ages,' Lily warned.

'Mind your own business, boss, and don't wait up for me.' Jane gathered up her oversized leopard print bag and left the dining room heading in the direction of the bar.

Lily sighed and straightened out the hastily jotted notes she'd made during the meal. While the tastes, textures and aromas were still vivid she must get busy and type up her impressions on her iPad. With a sigh she dragged to her feet and headed for the stairs.

Up in the suite she and Jane were sharing, Lily flung open the French doors leading onto the small balcony and stepped outside. The mild summer air was tinged with a hint of cooler night sneaking in around the edges of the day. She slumped down into one of the white wood chairs and without thinking pulled her cellphone from the depths of her bag. Surely it would be the simple act of a friend to call and ask after Kenan's injury?

Lily startled as the phone came to life and vibrated loudly in her hand.

'Where's Jane? I need to talk to her and she's not answering her damn phone,' Kenan's deep, gruff voice boomed into her ear.

'Hi to you too, and thanks for askin' how our day's gone. We had a good drive and Mike Braithwaite's perfect for—'

'Lily, I don't mean to be rude, but I really need to get hold of Jane.'

'She's downstairs somewhere. I'm guessing her phone's turned off because she's waiting to pounce on Mike Braithwaite when he finishes up in the kitchen.' She couldn't be bothered to prevaricate. Jane didn't care so why should she?

'What are you talking about? She just met the guy,' he snapped.

'She's a grown woman, Kenan. I'm not her keeper any more than you are. She's interested, he's interested so what'd you want me to do – slap a chastity belt on them both?'

'Of course not. I'm sorry. You surprised me that's all.'

His more conciliatory tone took away some of her irritation. 'Fine. Forget all that and tell me what's wrong?'

'My Mum's gone missing.' He raced on, talking so fast she only caught about one word in three.

'Relax and take a deep breath,' she insisted. 'Start

at the beginning and give me the details. Remember I can't always get your cute accent when you gabble away.'

'Sorry again.'

Lily could picture his wry smile from here.

'Mum and her friend Annie went for a walk around Heligan Gardens, over on the other side of Mevagissey, this afternoon. They had a cup of tea and Annie needed to get on home but Mum stayed to see the Melon Yard. She was supposed to ring Dad when she was ready to be picked up and he got worried when he didn't hear anything. He decided to go on over and arrived right at six o'clock when they were closing. There was no sign of her. They've got the police out now and dogs,' Kenan's voice roughened. 'As far as we know she doesn't have her heart medicine with her and we're worried she's been taken ill.'

'Is it a big place?' Lily was almost afraid to ask.

'Over three hundred acres.'

'Heck. You gotta stay strong, Kenan. I'll run Jane to ground and I promise she'll be on the phone to you in less than ten minutes.'

'Thanks.' His single, choked out word pulled at Lily.

'I gotta go.' She hesitated but needed to say what was in her heart, wise on not. 'I wish I was there with you.'

'Not as much as I do.' His honesty shocked her and it was a struggle to hold herself together.

'I'm hanging up, Kenan, not because I want to, but because you need me to.'

'Yeah, I know.' He sighed.

Pressing the button to end the call Lily refused to give into the urge to scream out her frustration. Kenan didn't have time for her to give in to emotional, womanly nonsense now.

She checked to make sure she had the room key card safely in her pocket before heading out and down the stairs towards the kitchen.

'Jane's on her way up to her own bed. You happy?' Mike Braithwaite's deep, booming voice from the kitchen doorway startled Lily half out of her skin.

'What the heck . . .' She jerked around and watched a tight smile pull at his dark features as he paced across the hall to place himself right in front of her.

'I assume you're checking to make sure she's not spread out on my kitchen counter with her knickers off.'

The linking of the words seduction and kitchen counter sent a rush of embarrassing heat to her face.

'Correct me if I'm wrong, but you aren't her mother, are you?'

She ignored his teasing question. 'Jane's brother was trying to get hold of her about an important family matter. I couldn't care less about anything else.'

'I believe I'll call you Lily Liar from now on.' He

treated her to a full-blown smirk. 'Jane's over the age of consent and, yes, I'm a lot further over it, but as you said earlier it's none of your business.'

Lily bit the tip of her tongue. Kenan needed to hear from Jane now, not next week. Plus she didn't intend screwing up her business deal with Mike Braithwaite because she couldn't hold her temper. 'I've gotta go and give her the message. I'll see you in the morning.'

'I can hardly wait, luv.' He took another step closer and gripped her shoulder with hands large and strong enough to stop an elephant in its tracks. 'By the way, if you and the delectable Jane care to stay an extra night I might be able to finish what I started.' He gave a mischievous grin.

Lily caught a glimpse of a younger, more carefree man and wondered if being with Jane made him different.

His large white teeth gleamed in the near darkness. 'You can try to warn Jane off, but I'm pretty sure she'll tell you where to go. She's a feisty woman and that appeals to me.'

Lily knew he was right and she didn't have time for any more of this now. 'Goodnight.' She walked away with Mike Braithwaite's laughter ringing in her ears and ran back upstairs. The second she slipped the key card into the lock the door flew open and Jane pounced on her.

'What the hell are you playing at?' She shoved her cellphone in Lily's face. 'Mikey texted.'

'Mikey?' Lily almost laughed but the waves of

anger rolling off Jane stopped her. 'I wasn't checking on you. Kenan called and needed to talk to you. You weren't answering your phone and I offered to track you down. Braithwaite didn't believe me either but that's not my problem.'

'Kenan better not be checking up on me too,' Jane groused.

'Oh, grow up. Do you want to know what's wrong or are you goin' to pick at me all night?' Lily snapped.

'You didn't say there was anything wrong,' Jane protested.

'Maybe 'cause you didn't give me a chance. It's your Mom. She's gone missing in Heligan Gardens.'

'Oh my God, how—'

'Be quiet and listen. If you don't call Kenan in the next couple of minutes he'll have nibbled every nail off.' Lily shushed her until she got out the whole story. 'Now get on the phone and save your apologies for later.' Lily sneaked in the slight dig and received a faint smile in return. 'After that we've got plans to make.'

CHAPTER 18

Patrick maintained a steady speed on the treadmill and watched the door. He'd achieved a faint sheen of sweat on his spray-tanned skin already, hopefully enough to be masculine but not repulsive. Kayley was due a large raise for finding out where Olivia Bellingham came to work out every weekday morning at eight. With the help of a large sum of money under the table he achieved a temporary membership of the exclusive Energia gym, and here he was.

The main news headlines started on the wall-mounted television near him as a stunning woman strode into the room, her blonde ponytail swinging with every step. Patrick wasn't the only man staring at her lithe body encased in black Lycra. What the devil did Kenan Rowse see in Lily when he'd had this elegant beauty? Patrick turned the speed up on his controls and began a fast run. Now he had to leave it to the luck of the Irish and hope she'd pick the empty machine next to him. *Bingo*. He purposely didn't look over as she got set up and started.

Today the body of an eight-year-old . . . Patrick

came close to smiling. He couldn't have arranged a more perfect way to strike up a conversation.

He glanced at her and grimaced. 'Makes you wonder about the state of the world, doesn't it? How can anyone do that to a child?'

She fixed her big, blue eyes on him. 'It's monstrous. They should hang him when they find the person responsible.'

'Yeah.' Patrick made himself turn away so as not to appear too interested just yet. From the corner of his vision he saw her increase her speed. Ten minutes later he finished his own workout, threw a towel around his neck and headed off to the changing rooms. He'd been told that Olivia's routine was a thirty-minute run, followed by a shower and then a carrot smoothie at the juice bar.

He'd be waiting.

After his shower, Patrick finished dressing and combed his damp hair the right amount to look groomed without being overly fussed over. He shouldered his bag and headed out to position himself ready to make his move.

'My usual carrot smoothie, please, Crispin.' Olivia's cut-glass tones made the server jump to attention.

'Good choice, sweetheart.' Patrick laid on the Irish with a trowel and a smile tugged at her neat, pink lips. 'Cheers.' He raised his glass and took another sip of his own carrot smoothie. The vile mixture was sweet and gloppy but he'd do whatever it took to win her over. She returned the gesture and as their eyes met he caught a flash of interest.

'We don't get many Americans here. Are you in town for business or pleasure?'

'Mainly business. I'm wrapping up research for a TV programme I'm producing.' He leaned a little closer and her delicate floral scent sent a curl of desire surging through his body. He hadn't expected the bonus of actually fancying the woman. 'It's a cookery programme.'

Olivia's eyes narrowed and she fiddled with her juice glass. 'That's interesting. I came across an American chef called Lily Redman recently. I don't suppose you know her?'

His feigned shock would've earned him an Oscar. 'Yeah, I sure do. In fact she's over here working for me at the moment. How do you know her?'

Her jaw tightened and Patrick knew he'd scored a bull's eye.

'The common creature has got her claws into my ex-husband,' Olivia stated with a sneer.

'Not Kenan Rowse?' he asked artlessly.

'How do you . . .'

Patrick pointed to his bruised nose and an unpleasant smirk crept across her face.

'Really.' She only hesitated a moment before carrying on. 'I believe I'd like to hear more.'

'Would I be a typical, crass American if I asked you to have lunch with me?'

'Yes, but I'll accept anyway.' Olivia's smile cheered Patrick no end.

He'd work his magic over a few lettuce leaves and a bottle of Perrier. By this afternoon he'd have talked her into being his conspirator in their exes' downfall. And perhaps into his bed.

Kenan paced around the Heligan car park wearing deep ruts in the loose gravel. Jane's last text half an hour ago said they'd just driven through St Austell.

'She won't get here any faster with you glowering at the road.' Pete punched his shoulder.

'Yeah, I know. I suppose there's no news?'

Pete briefly shook his head. He'd led a party down through the Jungle part of the gardens earlier, even though no one really thought she'd have walked that far.

A car horn beeped and Jane's bright purple car screeched to a halt right next to Kenan's feet. Jane leapt out and threw herself into his arms, dissolving into loud wet sobs.

'Hey, kid, it'll be okay.' Kenan switched into big brother mode. 'You got here fast.'

'We left at midnight.'

'We?' Kenan glanced back over Jane's shoulder and the breath caught in his throat. 'Lily?' His vision filled with her vivid mass of red hair. 'What're *you* doing here?' Kenan whispered in disbelief.

'Charming, I'm sure. I'm pleased to see you

haven't turned all smooth and polite while I've been gone.' She grinned over at Jane whose sobs had slowed to an occasional hiccup. 'Boy, I'm glad I came. This was worth giving up an audience with the super-arrogant Mike Braithwaite for, wasn't it?' Jane started to protest but Lily ploughed right on. 'Is there any news?' Her worried frown touched Kenan's heart.

'No.' He returned to reality with a mental thump. 'The search groups had to stop for the night and are gathering again now. More people have arrived to help. The police will be sending everyone back out with new instructions in another fifteen minutes or so.' He pointed to the cafe behind them. 'They're serving hot drinks and bacon butties over there. Go and get yourselves some breakfast.'

'I'm starved,' Jane declared then slapped her hand over her mouth. 'God, I'm a heartless cow when Mum could be—'

'Stop it,' Kenan cut her off. 'Mum's always on at you to eat more, so do it for her, okay.'

'Okay, big brother. I'll obey orders.' Jane threw him a fake salute and ran off to leave him staring at Lily.

'When did *you* last eat?' Lily demanded, her fierce glare belied by the gentle hand she rested against his cheek. 'Don't bother answering as I've a pretty good idea. I know food's never a priority with you.' He didn't say a word but leaned into her touch out of sheer relief not to have to pretend for a few minutes. 'You need to eat and don't argue. We'll go together.' She slid her arm through his and led him across to join the rest of the group hanging around the cafe. Inside, Lily let go of his arm and dropped the overloaded pink bag she hauled around everywhere onto the nearest vacant table. She dragged a couple of chairs over and pointed to one. 'Sit. I'll be back.'

Kenan slumped down and allowed his tired eyes to close for a minute, the first rest he'd had since the nightmare began.

'Drink this.'

A mug of steaming hot black coffee appeared in his hand and Kenan inhaled the best perfume going – straight-up caffeine. He took a long swallow and was grateful for the instant satisfying burn all the way to the base of his stomach. Lily steered a sandwich towards his mouth.

'Open wide.'

Helpless against her encouraging smile he took a large bite and chewed slowly before forcing himself to swallow.

'Good boy,' she teased.

Kenan managed about half of the sandwich before his stomach rebelled and he gently pushed her hand away. 'Can't manage any more. Sorry.' He set down the mug and slid his good hand up to stroke her cheek. Very tenderly he traced his fingers over her glossy pink lips.

'Listen up,' a brawny uniformed police officer yelled, getting everyone's attention. 'The new search plan's been put together and the helicopter's ready to do the first sweep. Five minutes and I'm handing out fresh assignments.'

'Go on,' Lily encouraged. 'You need to be over there. I'll get some food then find out where I can help.'

'Come on, Kenan. The police need your input.' Pete grabbed his shoulder and noticed Lily. 'Hello, didn't realise you were here. Evelyn's in the kitchen of course. Go on back and she'll fix you up with some food.'

'Will do, thanks.'

Kenan hated to leave her, still unable to get his head around the fact that she'd come back for his sake. He stood up and touched her arm to make her look at him. 'Thanks. I'll see you later.'

Lily remained glued to the ground until Kenan disappeared from sight. It hadn't been a hard decision to come. Later she'd find out whether or not it was wise. For now, she'd allow a deliciously greasy bacon sandwich to set her straight. She sniffed the air and followed the mouth-watering smell and found Evelyn bustling around a kitchen as usual.

'Lily!' She exclaimed, her face breaking into a wide smile.

Any fears Lily harboured about whether she'd be welcome were instantly put to rest. 'A little bird told me you're doin' some great food here. You got any goin' spare?'

'Of course we do. Sit down and I'll bring us some over. I could do with a break.'

She disappeared back in the kitchen and soon re-emerged with a loaded plate. Evelyn placed the stack of sandwiches on the table between them and pulled a chair out to sit down. Lily immediately seized one and took a large bite, unable to stop herself sighing with pleasure.

'Before you ask, here's the rundown,' Evelyn's voice was full of her usual good humour. 'The bacon comes from a pig farm about twenty miles away. I made the bread fresh this morning and the butter was churned at an organic dairy down the road.'

'It's all wonderful. Fresh, simple ingredients treated with respect. I'm finding more and more these days that I want to simplify recipes and get back to a more basic treatment of food,' Lily stated, before taking another massive bite.

'Sounds reasonable. Of course it's the way we've always eaten really. I grew up on a farm and we grew or raised most of our own food. Pete's family were the same way. That's why the business is a natural direction for us.'

A pang of envy shot through Lily. She'd thought she had something of that closeness with Patrick until she realised for him she was nothing more than a meal ticket.

'Eat up, there's plenty more where that came from.'

Lily shamelessly seized another sandwich off the plate.

'I didn't think you'd come back with Jane,' Evelyn said.

Lily took another large bite partly because it'd be a shame not to, but more to give herself extra thinking time. She felt Evelyn's scrutiny from behind the tortoiseshell half-glasses she needed when cooking. 'I couldn't stay away. I had to be here for . . .' Kenan's name caught in her throat.

'We saw it, you know. The day you stopped by the farm. Kenan's a stubborn man but he'll be worth it,' Evelyn stated in a firm no-room-for-argument way.

'I'm not sure. It's complicated.' Evelyn's rumbling laugh took her by surprise and Lily met her new friend's smiling green eyes.

'Life always is, dear. No one's straightforward.'

Lily shrugged. 'But you and Pete seem so . . . steady together. As though you were meant to be.'

'I could tell you some stories but we haven't time now. Come up for tea one day when things are quieter and we'll talk.' Evelyn straightened and stared over Lily's shoulder.

Lily turned around to see Kenan, white-faced and with his right hand gripping the wooden door-post. He stared silently at them both. 'Have you heard something?'

Kenan opened his mouth and tried to speak.

CHAPTER 19

'Great news isn't it?' Pete boomed out.

'What is?' Lily asked cautiously, with her gaze fixed on Kenan's ghostly face.

'Didn't he tell you?' Pete's ruddy skin flushed deep crimson and he shifted awkwardly from one foot to the other.

'Oh, for goodness sake, get on with it,' Evelyn barked. 'Kenan's turned into a mute and Lily's going to explode in a minute.'

Her exasperation with her husband's shilly-shallying around made Lily smile.

'Mrs Rowse is fine,' Pete said with a big smile. 'She'd left the Melon Yard after her friend went and wandered around a couple of the walled gardens. She got distracted by a particularly beautiful rhododendron – her words not mine – then tripped over and turned her ankle on the rough grass.'

Lily snapped out of her trance and walked across to Kenan and straight into his open arms. He rested his injured hand on the curve of her back and wrapped the other around her waist. She wasn't sure who was comforting who.

'And?' Evelyn urged Pete to continue.

'She couldn't walk more than a couple of steps and she tried shouting but there was no one around. Sensible woman had a bottle of water and, despite what Kenan's dad believed, always carries spare heart pills. Said she got disorientated and wasn't sure of the way back so waited it out until daylight for someone to come. The poor woman was mortified when she saw the huge crowd of people out searching for her.'

'I'll bet.' Lily sighed with relief. 'So she's really all right?'

Pete nodded. 'The paramedics tried to insist on taking her to the hospital but she refused, so they checked her over and strapped up her ankle. She promised to call the doc to see her up at the house. All she wants is to go home and sleep. I don't blame her.'

Kenan's muscles relaxed and he eased his vice-like grip on Lily. The hint of a smile tugged at his stern mouth. 'Dad couldn't decide whether to shout at her for scaring us all or kiss her silly.'

'Which did he choose, as if I couldn't guess?' Lily joked, as Kenan seized hold of her shoulders and captured her mouth with his own. His hard, searching kiss sizzled through her blood and when he finally let go it was with a triumphant grin.

'Right first time,' he said.

His smug expression would have garnered him a smack if she hadn't been as dizzy as a schoolgirl after her first kiss.

'I always am.' Lily tried for light and casual, despite her racing heart threatening to burst through her chest.

'Get a room you two, for heaven's sake,' Pete jested.

His suggestive laugh doused a bucket of metaphorical cold water over Lily and she eased away from Kenan's warm embrace. '*You* need to go home,' she told him firmly.

'*We* need to.' He slid his arms back around her waist and squeezed. 'I'm not letting you out of my sight for the rest of the day. Don't argue.'

Lily got an unexpected kick out of him turning macho and possessive. *What was up with her?*

'Jane's taking Mum and Dad home. I told them I'd bring you and we'd stop by Betty's to pick up Mandy before coming to join them.'

'Go on the pair of you.' Pete shooed his hands at them.

'Thanks, I mean that.' Kenan turned back to Lily. 'Are you ready?'

She gave a brief nod and was reassured by his softening smile.

They walked back outside and ran straight into the gauntlet of people still hanging around and rehashing the morning's excitement. Lily held Kenan's hand, hoping it would help as he fought to hold onto his manners long enough to thank everyone.

Finally they reached his car and Kenan pushed

her back against the door. He spread his hands on the roof and his steel-grey eyes pierced her with their intensity.

'One more kiss and then I'll behave myself.'

Before she could protest he claimed her mouth again and she softened into his hot, reckless taste. 'Oh, Kenan, stop.'

'I know we ought to go. I know all the sensible things, but I lose every atom of sense around you. You're a witch, Lily Redman.'

'Abracadabra,' she replied and laughed. 'If I'm a witch, you're the very devil, Kenan Rowse.'

'Once I'm sure Mum's really all right, maybe we can go out on our own later.'

'I thought you'd decided this – us – was a bad idea?' Lily pushed him gently away, determined not to be a pushover. 'You've got too much to sort out in your life, remember?' Her body might have responded to him in an instant, but it didn't mean the rest of her had to follow suit.

'I've been rethinking things.'

'Yeah, I bet you have,' she retorted. 'You'll turn noble again later and remember all the reasons we can't make this work and dump me again.' She should have stayed in Keswick and continued the job she'd travelled four thousand miles to do.

The emotion drained from his face, leaving behind an unrevealing blank slate. 'You've got a real high opinion of me, haven't you?'

His ice-cold words trickled down her spine and Lily felt terrible. 'I'm sorry. I shouldn't have said that.'

'It's what you were thinking and I don't blame you, Lily. I haven't treated you right from the beginning.'

She didn't have a clue what to say and neither of them were good at apologising. Lily stretched up to drape her hands loosely around his neck. 'This isn't the time or place. Drive me back to Betty's. You need to take Mandy home with you and look after your mother. We'll talk when you can get away, whether it's tonight or not until tomorrow. And I mean talk properly.'

His sheepish grin made her smile too.

'Whatever happens I've got to get back on track with my work,' Lily declared firmly. 'I'm determined to make a success of this show and prove I don't need Patrick to succeed. After that . . . I'm not sure.'

'Fair enough.' Kenan nodded. 'Hop in.' He opened the car door and stood back to let her get in before walking around to get in the driver's seat.

'Can you manage to drive okay?' She touched his swollen right hand, now pretty much one Technicolor bruise. Kenan gave a terse nod, but didn't speak. Something else to add to the list for later.

Lily rested back in her seat as he started up the car and pulled out onto the main road. Usually the narrow roads bothered her but today she was too exhausted to care and decided closing her eyes for a few minutes was the best use of her energy. She was vaguely aware of leaning into Kenan's warm shoulder each time they went around another curve, only barely awake enough to realise how secure he made her feel.

'Hey, sleepyhead, we're here. Get ready for the Mandy onslaught.'

'Thanks for letting me rest.' She yawned.

'It's never a hardship to spend time looking at you.' Kenan gave her an enigmatic smile as he pulled into an empty parking spot close to Cliff House and stopped the car. He rested his hands on the steering wheel and his jaw tightened. 'I've got things I have to tell you.'

Lily met his uncertain gaze as he glanced over at her, full of apprehension.

'Don't worry, it's not all bad.'

She searched for a suitable reply but her car door was suddenly wrenched open.

'Miss Lily, oh, Miss Lily, you came back.' Mandy flung her thin, hot arms around Lily's neck. 'I told Daddy you would and he got cross and said he didn't think so. He's silly.'

'You're right.' Lily caught Kenan's hint of amusement. With a recipe she followed the steps all the way through to achieve the complete dish so now she'd put her professional knowledge into play and deal with one thing at a time. 'Guess what, kiddo, I didn't go to bed last night and I'm really tired. Why don't you go with your dad while I take a nap. We'll play again tomorrow.'

Mandy pouted. 'But I want you to come with us now.'

Lily half-smiled, expecting the little girl to stamp her feet with temper.

'That's enough, sweetheart,' Kenan interrupted, his tone stern enough not to brook any argument. 'Hop in the back seat while I go and thank Miss Betty for having you. Granny Eileen can't wait to see you.'

'Yes, Daddy,' Mandy grouched, but had stopped whining.

'I'm here.' Betty appeared by the car. 'I'm some pleased Eileen's all right. Tell her I'll pop down and check on her tomorrow.'

Lily quickly jumped out and flashed a smile in Kenan's direction. 'I'll see you later.'

'Oh, yes, most certainly.' A touch of humour tugged at his mouth before he glanced back at Mandy. 'Seat belt on, young lady.'

Lily waved them off and watching them go she wondered just what her future held.

'So, Mum, have you done frightening us all to death?' Kenan asked, as he hurried into the living room with Mandy in his arms. His mother was propped up on the sofa with all manner of cushions around her and being fussed over by his grey-faced father.

'Don't you start. Your father's driving me half-mad. The daft man won't let me out of his sight from now on.' Eileen beamed at Mandy. 'You come here, sweetie, and give your old Gran a kiss. You're the best medicine going to make my silly old ankle better.'

Mandy wriggled out of Kenan's grasp and threw herself in Eileen's arms before he could say anything about being careful or quiet. He caught his Dad's eye and they exchanged a rueful smile. Women paid no attention to men, ever.

'Why don't you get a book and I'll read to you?' Eileen asked.

'You should be resting, Mum,' Kenan interrupted and received one of his mother's famous do-not-cross-me glares. He threw his arms up in a gesture of surrender. 'Okay, I'll shut up and leave you ladies alone. I'm off up for a shower.' He mustn't be selfish. He was needed here tonight so he'd have to wait until the morning to see Lily. Thank goodness he knew she'd understand.

'Of course, dear.' His mother gave him a knowing smile. 'Lily turned up trumps today, didn't she?'

He nodded, unable to say any more without making a fool of himself.

'Don't be long, Daddy. Miss Betty gave me a new Cinderella book today and I know you love princess stories too,' Mandy proclaimed with certainty.

'I certainly do, sweetheart.' Sometimes it was hard to reconcile this new version of his life with what had gone before, but as each day went by Kenan thought he was getting the hang of the idea.

Kenan made his way up to the bathroom and indulged in a long, hot shower instead of his usual two-minute military special. He towelled his hair dry and pulled on clean jeans and a dark green T-shirt. His stomach clenched as he wondered how he'd cope tomorrow if his confessions frightened Lily off.

He opened the wardrobe door and reached up to take down the metal box he'd stashed on the top shelf. He carried it over to the bed and sat down. Kenan unlocked the clasp and rifled through the contents to take out what he needed.

A loud knock on the door startled him. 'Who is it?'

'Me. Can I come in?' Jane answered and he made haste to shove the envelope he'd removed under the pillow out of sight.

'Sure.' Kenan stretched out on the bed, as if he'd been resting.

She flung open the door and stepped inside. 'Sorry, dear brother, I didn't know you were sleeping.'

'I wasn't, you're good.'

'Did Lily say anything to you about Mike Braithwaite?' An embarrassed flush crept up Jane's neck.

Kenan knew he shouldn't find it funny but . . . 'She did mention he'd be ideal for the programme.'

Jane wandered across the room to look out of the window meaning he couldn't see her face straight on. *Smart woman.* 'Yes, he'll be perfect.' She fiddled with the ends of her spiky hair, twisting them into knots. 'I got on pretty well with him.'

'And you're telling me this . . . why?' Kenan folded his arms behind his head.

'I'll do a deal with you.' Jane swung back around to face him. 'Lily thinks I'm going back with her to finish the interview with him but I don't intend to.'

Kenan wondered, not for the first time, what on earth made women tick? 'Feel free to smack me for being dumb but I don't get it? I thought you'd be speeding up the motorway as fast as your tiny car would permit?' He raised himself up on his elbows to judge her reaction better.

'I'll ignore the childish insult about my vehicle. I might only be twenty-one but I'm pretty shrewd where men are concerned you know.'

Kenan wasn't sure if he was supposed to indicate pleasure at this assertion so kept his mouth shut.

'Mike expects me to come running back and fawn over him because I'm sure it's what all his other women do. To make sure he understands I'm different, it's exactly what I'm *not* going to do,' Jane declared with complete assurance.

'Don't even try to explain. I'm a man so I won't get it.' Kenan's heavy sarcasm was ignored. 'So basically you're going to drop Lily in it?'

'What do you mean?' Jane frowned.

'Well, nothing's changed with me, has it? I still can't go off and leave Mandy with Mum and Dad, especially now, so what's Lily supposed to do?'

Jane smirked. 'It's not a problem. Mandy loves me – I'm the cool aunt who paints her toenails and dresses funny. I'm pretty sure the idea of spending a week with me fussing over her non-stop will top being with you.'

Kenan had to give her credit, she'd manoeuvred him into a corner and there was no logical reason for him to turn her down. Plus, he really didn't want to. 'Okay, you win, if Lily agrees.' He swung his legs off the bed and stood up. 'But don't mention any of this to Mandy yet.' Kenan shoved his hands in his pockets.

'Why not?'

'I'll be seeing Lily tomorrow and then she'll know all about my less than illustrious past and then spending time in my company might not be top of her list.'

'Are you going to tell her everything?' Jane's brow furrowed.

'Yes. Now scram.' Kenan shooed her from the room and retrieved the envelope from under the pillow before folding it neatly into his wallet. He couldn't continue to put it off, no matter how badly he wanted to bury his head in the sand. The idea of Lily thinking less of him ripped him apart, but she must know the truth before he asked her to make any sort of choice on the future of their relationship.

But tonight he'd lose himself in Cinderella's problems and make his little girl happy.

CHAPTER 20

Olivia toyed with her small, green salad and laid down her knife and fork. 'You planned all this didn't you?'

Patrick flinched under her sharp, green-eyed gaze. 'What do you mean, sweetheart?' He put on his best innocent American act.

'You didn't just happen to be at the gym this morning. I want the truth, now, or I'm leaving.' Her eyes flicked over the narrow, diamond watch hanging on her slim wrist. 'I'll give you five minutes.'

He'd have to tell her enough to satisfy her curiosity without revealing everything. 'You're right. I was there on purpose to meet you.'

'Why?'

Patrick flashed the famous smile that usually did the trick but the Englishwoman's expression stayed cool and unreadable. 'Because I think we can help each other out.'

'I can't possibly imagine how.'

Talk about icy. He'd never been attracted by the whole upper class Brit thing, but she needed to believe otherwise or he'd never get what he wanted. 'I want to know more about your ex-husband

and . . .' he slid his hand halfway across the table, stopping just short of her fingers, 'I kinda think you might care to hear more about Lily.' The pulse in her neck throbbed and he knew that he'd hit the jackpot. 'You want me to go first?'

'If you like.'

Patrick rolled out most of Lily's story, playing up her lowly origins, her lack of culinary training and blatantly lying about her lack of business skills.

'She certainly doesn't dress like a professional chef,' Olivia observed, her lips turning up in a sneer.

'It's part of her image. I created the *Luscious Lily* persona and it's been a huge hit. People are taken in by the sexy character and overlook the fact that she's a very ordinary cook.'

'She's lucky you came along.' Olivia rested her cool hand over his and gave him a sympathetic smile.

'You wanna believe it.' It was time to lay his cards on the table and see if she took the bait. 'She's trying to screw me over but two can play that game.'

'How about three?' Olivia murmured.

'Maybe.' Before they went any further he needed to be sure they were on the same page. 'What's in this for you?'

Her eyes narrowed in calculation. 'Kenan let me down and it would give me great pleasure to pay him back. He had the potential to go far in the Army and in return I'd have been the perfect military wife. I knew exactly what was involved because I'd grown up with a father who had a career in the Army. After we married he turned boring, hated the social side of military life and expected me to follow suit.'

'I can't imagine you as the little wife stuck at home, darning his socks and having dinner on the table at six every evening,' Patrick needled, pleased when she grimaced.

She took another sip of her water and gave him a sly half-smile. 'Hardly.'

Patrick decided to take a stab and see what reaction he got. 'I'm surprised you wanted to be tied down with a kid?'

'These things happen.' Olivia shrugged. 'Being a single mother wasn't part of my plan, but I love Amanda dearly, of course.'

'Of course,' he demurred, not convinced but also not stupid enough to say so.

A sliver of anger flashed across her smooth features. 'He turned very bourgeois because I sometimes went out with . . . good friends while he was away. We could have still had a perfectly decent marriage but he insisted on divorcing. It was a huge embarrassment.'

So he'd found out what they had in common finally. 'Lily's very moralistic too,' Patrick said, calculating that he'd asked enough questions for now. He dared to cover her hand with his own and she didn't move away.

'Tell me exactly what you've got in mind and

then maybe we can . . . get to know each other better.'

She swept her eyes down over him and Patrick couldn't help grinning. Olivia was definitely not faithful wife material and the thought made him a very happy man.

'Betty, how do you think a combination of dark chocolate, red wine and raspberries sounds?' Lily glanced up from checking her ingredients meticulously arranged over the kitchen counter.

'I thought you were going to make some buns?' Betty frowned.

'I'm going to experiment with a few different flavours.'

'Being 'onest, dear, I think red wine's a bit nasty, raspberry seeds get stuck under my dentures and I prefer a nice bit of Cadbury's milk chocolate to that there dark stuff,' Betty said with an apologetic smile.

Lily chuckled. 'You'll be a perfect challenge. If I can win you over it'll be a hit.' She found the corkscrew and opened the wine, pouring half the bottle into a saucepan. 'I'll bring this to a simmer then reduce it down to concentrate the flavour. The raspberries will be turned into a silky purée, which I'll sieve to get rid of the offending seeds. I'll use that in the centre of the buns as well as in the cream. The chocolate will be melted and piped into the shape of butterfly wings. It won't be easy but I'm pretty sure it'll work.'

'I expect you're right. I'll be off and leave you to it.'

Lily checked the kitchen clock. 'Oh, I didn't realise the time. I'll be in the way of you fixing your lunch.'

'Don't worry about me.' Betty shook her head. 'I'm off to see my sister and she's making us a pasty. I'll try one of your buns when I get back this afternoon.' She smiled at Lily. 'If you haven't burnt the house down by then, of course.'

'I'll try not to. I didn't thank you properly yesterday for having me back and now for letting me mess around in here.'

'That's all right, my dear. You'm a bit of an odd one sometimes, but I'll miss you when you go back to America.' Betty sighed.

Lily's throat tightened and she stared back down at the table to hide the tears pressing at her eyes.

'Just make us something good to have with our tea later,' Betty said and bustled out of the room.

Lily stood completely still, frozen in place. She hadn't bargained on getting involved in life here. This was supposed to be a base for planning out her show – nothing more. Falling in love with everything from Kenan, to Mandy and Cornwall itself hadn't been on the cards.

All she could do was cook to push everything to the back of her mind for now.

Before she went any further, Lily took a new pink spiral-bound notebook from her bag and selected one of her fine-tipped purple pens. Over the years she'd accumulated a whole stack of books with details of every recipe she'd ever made, complete with meticulous comments and pictures. She laid her camera on the counter ready to take photos of every step.

For the next hour she disappeared back into her cooking zone. She always found baking one of the most satisfying things going. Few people could resist a fresh, homemade cake. Maybe it would prove to be Kenan's weakness. She was determined to try cooking as many different things for him as possible until she hit on the one that excited his taste buds. Lily opened the oven and checked on the last batch of buns. She'd had to bake six batches to get the quantity she needed to practise on and longed for her industrial sized oven more than once during the whole process. Pressing gently on one of the tops it sprang back perfectly and brought a smile to her face.

'Perfect,' she said, laughing to herself in the empty kitchen. 'Now, my beauties, you need to cool down before I can make you all pretty.' She set them out to cool, missing the blast chiller she normally used to speed things up. Today Mother Nature would have to do the job.

Lily washed her hands and wandered out into Betty's back garden. She flopped down on the old wooden bench, put her feet up and turned her face up to the sun. Her delicate skin didn't allow for too much of this so she must keep a close eye on the time.

She waved away a bee buzzing near her face and fought against drifting off to sleep.

'My God, woman, are you mad?' Kenan yelled across the garden. He reached Lily in two long strides and shook her awake.

She stared up at him, obviously bewildered and dazed with sleep.

Kenan hauled her to her feet and ignored her piercing shriek.

'What the hell are you doing?'

'You're going inside, right now.'

She dug her feet into the ground, placed her hands on her hips and glared hard enough to frighten any other man. Kenan didn't hesitate and swung her up into his arms in a tight grip. She beat her hands on his back, but he didn't stop walking until he had her back in the kitchen. Unceremoniously he dumped her down on a chair.

'You're a maniac, Kenan Rowse,' she yelled.

Lily tried to stand up and he instantly shoved her back to sitting. 'Do what you're told for once. Stay there,' he ordered. Kenan snatched a kitchen towel and soaked it under the cold tap before wringing out some of the water and crossing back over to her. 'This will sting.' Very gently he pressed it against her face, hating that she flinched under his hands, and then draped it around her neck. 'I'm getting you something cold to drink.' He raided the freezer and tossed a handful of ice into a large glass before filling it up with water. 'Get that down you.'

For the first time she didn't argue with him and gulped the drink down, finishing it in a couple of large swallows. 'Thanks,' she murmured.

'You're welcome. Look, I know you're into the whole pink thing, but isn't this taking it a bit far?' He pointed at her hot, tender skin.

'Yeah. What time is it?'

'Nearly two o'clock, why?'

Lily's eyes widened in shock.

'How long were you out there?'

She stared down at her lap and murmured something he couldn't catch.

'What did you say?'

'About forty minutes,' she said, her voice filled with shame.

Kenan shook his head in disbelief. 'At a wild guess I'd say that's about thirty more than your delicate skin can take.'

'Do you get a kick out of being right all the time?' A touch of her normal spunkiness had returned.

He guessed she couldn't be suffering from sunstroke if she was answering him back again. 'Far from it, sweetheart. In fact, that's partly why I came but we'll wait until you've . . . cooled down some. Why don't you go have a cool shower?'

'Shit.' Lily smacked the table. 'I forgot.'

'What?'

She gestured towards the kitchen counters and

he glanced around, seeing buns spread out to cool on every available inch of surface.

'I'm in the middle of baking. These have to be decorated.'

'Not now they don't,' he protested. 'You need to—'

'I'll be fine. Stop being an old woman. I'm not wasting a morning's work for a slight touch of sunburn,' she declared in her usual, no-nonsense way.

'Slight touch? You're the same colour as a tomato dropped into a bowl of boiling water. You're insane.'

A sly smile crept across her face and she rested her hand on his right arm, stroking the dark hairs and sending shivers all the way down to his toes.

'If you help it'll be done sooner. After they're finished I promise I'll follow orders,' Lily wheedled.

'What do you think *I'm* going to do?' He splayed his large, ungainly hands out in front of her.

'You'd be surprised what they can do.' She giggled.

'Cut it out, woman,' he growled, unable to think straight when she used *Luscious Lily* on him.

Lily removed the damp towel from her neck and draped it over the back of the chair. 'Come on.' She tugged at his hand.

'All right,' he groused, determined to at least make a gesture at not being a complete pushover. 'What do you need?'

Lily picked up a small, sharp knife. 'Watch me.' Very precisely she removed the centres of the bun and set the discarded cake to one side.

There were enough to feed a whole battalion, but Kenan didn't comment. It would only get him into more trouble.

'Normally you'd use the cake you remove to make the butterfly wings, but I've got these instead.' She pointed over to a large tray of fancy chocolate shapes. 'You can eat any of the leftover cake if you want.'

'No, thanks. I'm not much for sweet things,' he insisted.

'Try some, please. I want to know what you think.'

Her deep blue eyes widened and he was sucked in again. Kenan crammed a handful of cake into his mouth and chewed. 'Not bad.' He ate some more.

'Don't overdo it. I might get a swollen head,' she teased.

Kenan rested a hand on her shoulder. 'Look, I'm not a foodie, you know that. It's nice and light. Is that better?'

'It'll do.' Lily nodded and reached up to press a kiss on his mouth. 'Mm, you taste yummy.'

It took all his restraint not to grab hold of her and kiss her senseless, but Kenan swallowed hard and tried to smile. 'Let's get on with this.'

'Yes, sir.' She snapped off a salute, picked up another knife and a bun and they got started.

Kenan sneaked a couple of looks her way as she worked. With her gaze fixed firmly on the job in front of her, she handled the knife as competently as any surgeon. He found her intensity a real turn on and memories flooded back of the satisfaction of working a successful army mission. In the aftermath of his last stint in Afghanistan, he'd pushed the good things away with the bad. Maybe he could retrieve them again one day.

'Right. We're done with that part. Now I'll pipe the cream in one and show you how to place on the chocolate wings because that's going to be your task,' she said.

He watched with a sinking heart as she pinched one of the chocolate wings between her fingers and pressed it gently in the middle of the cake.

'Your turn,' she declared.

Kenan picked up one but it broke in his large fingers before he even got it as far as the designated spot. 'It's no good, I—'

'Be patient and try again,' she said soothingly. 'I'm pretty sure the first time y'all tried to march you weren't all in step. This is no different. These are only practise for an idea I've got. It's no big deal.'

He groused but she ignored him. Finally he got one right and held it up for her approval.

'Brilliant. We'll soon be done at this rate.' Lily beamed as if he'd handed her a priceless diamond necklace. 'As you do that, I'll finish them off with a sprinkle of the special raspberry sugar I made.'

Kenan nodded and carried on, more affected by her obvious pleasure than he'd any right to be.

'All finished.' She sprinkled on the last handful of sugar and headed to the sink to wash her hands. 'Get yourself cleaned up while I make us some coffee and then we'll have a tasting session.'

He couldn't help smiling and Lily grinned right back at him. 'Behave yourself, soldier boy, and wash your hands.' She fake-glared at him and wagged her finger in his face.

'Yes, ma'am.'

Kenan did as he was told, then sat down out of the way. He watched as she got the kitchen in perfect order again, cleaning every surface until they all shone.

Lily carried over two mugs and set them on the table along with a plate of the finished buns.

'There you go. Drink that and eat one of those. Tell me what you think and then start talking about what you really came here to say,' she stated bluntly.

He shifted in his seat, trying to put off the evil moment. 'What about your sunburn? Didn't you ought to see to that first?'

'Don't try to wriggle out of it, Kenan. Trust me, I've had a lot worse than this before. If it'll shut you up, I'll run upstairs and slap on some lotion. By the time I come back down you'd better be ready,' Lily warned. 'I mean it.'

'Right,' he muttered, unable to meet her eyes. He wouldn't be ready if she took ten hours.

CHAPTER 21

Lily watched Kenan unobserved from out in the hall. He sat slumped forward in the chair with his eyes closed. Gathering up her courage she went back into the kitchen.

Kenan opened his eyes and tried to smile. 'Feeling better?'

Lily nodded and her breath caught in her throat. 'How about we go and sit in the other room,' she suggested.

He shook his head. 'No point in moving. Now are you going to stand there all day or come join me?' Kenan pulled out a chair and patted the seat. 'Where do you want me to start?'

'First, I want you to give me a critique of the butterfly bun.' She chose that partly because she really wanted his opinion, but mainly to ease him into talking freely. Lily wasn't a smart Southern woman for nothing.

'Uh, well, it was good.' He admitted with a shrug. 'I finished it.' Kenan pointed at the few crumbs left on his plate.

'Be more specific.'

Kenan made an effort to smile. 'You're relentless.

I suppose I liked it better than most cakes I've eaten. It wasn't too sweet. The raspberry and dark chocolate were good flavours together.' He let out a heavy sigh. 'Will that do?'

'Sure.' Lily guessed she had better not press him too hard.

'What do you want next?' he asked.

'How do I know? You're the one with the story to tell.' Lily sat down and wished he'd just get on with it, all the while dreading this was something she'd rather not hear.

'Lily, I'm shit at doing this and I'm not even sure why I need to.' He shoved a hand through his hair, mussing up the crisp, dark waves.

'Maybe because it's eating at you and you care what I think?'

'I do care.'

He sounded downright angry about the fact and Lily guessed he'd rather be anywhere else on the face of the planet than sat here opening his heart to her.

'You're under the impression I'm an honourable, straight up and down sort of man, but I can't let you go on believing that any longer.' Kenan slammed his hand on the table.

'What on earth are you saying?' Her heart thumped in her chest and she wondered what the hell he was about to confess.

'Just listen, honey.' His voice quieted. 'I didn't join the Army straight from school. I went to university first and my parents were so proud.' A heavy thread of sadness ran through his words. 'I studied economics and after I graduated I worked as a city trader in the London financial district. I rarely came home because I thought Cornwall was dull and boring. I was so damn full of myself.'

Lily reached over to squeeze his hand. 'Hey, you're not the first young man to think that.'

'Maybe not. I made a ton of money before I turned twenty-five. I was flying so high I thought nothing could touch me.' He swallowed hard. 'I got engaged to a girl who worked for one of the other large banks. She was bright, beautiful and all set to go right to the top.'

'What was she called?' Lily asked.

'Victoria. Victoria Elizabeth Worthington.' Kenan pushed her hand away. 'I cheated on her more than once. You know my parents – it's not how they brought me up, but I thought I was above old-fashioned, working class morals. Victoria found out of course and dumped me.'

His taut face creased into deeper lines and a grey pallor shadowed his tanned skin.

'I don't blame her for leaving you, but you learned your lesson – right?' Lily asked. 'Everyone makes mistakes. Believe it or not I've made a few too.' She tried to smile, but the searing pain in his eyes only worsened.

'I'm sure you have, but I'm guessing yours didn't kill anyone.' He spat out the words.

'Kill? Don't be ridiculous. I can't believe—'

'Victoria took a transfer to her New York office

to get away from me,' he said, his voice cracking. 'It was in September, 2001. She'd only been there a week and went to an early morning meeting in the World Trade Centre.'

Kenan pushed his chair back and clutched his head with his hands. Lily got up and knelt down on the floor in front of him. She reached up and wrapped her arms around his shoulders. All she could do was hold on and absorb his silent, dry tears.

Suddenly he jerked upright and gently pushed her away, as though he didn't deserve her comfort.

'She was her parents' only child, Lily, and I killed her because I was an ass.' He reached into his trouser pocket and pulled out a small, brown envelope, laying it on the table. 'Read those.'

Cautiously she opened the flap and shook out a pile of newspaper cuttings. An attractive dark-haired woman stared up at her and Lily swallowed hard. The headlines cut through her heart. *High-flying trader killed in New York bombing. Destroyed – a young woman's bright future gone in an instant.*

Lily forced herself to meet Kenan's anguished eyes. 'Did you consider talking to anyone at the time?'

He scoffed. 'No, I joined the Army instead as a sort of penance. They took me in with no questions. I'd just been commissioned when I met Olivia, and you know how well that turned out.'

Lily wanted to ask more about his marriage but held back. It would have to wait.

'I didn't always stay the right side of the line in Afghanistan the first time I went,' Kenan confessed. 'If I didn't break the rules I skimmed pretty close in a warped effort to make up for Victoria's death.'

'Did no one realise you needed help?' Lily asked, but he couldn't meet her eyes.

'When I came back I met Olivia and fell hard for her. Within a couple of months I talked her into getting married and next thing she was pregnant with Mandy. We never had a chance to get to know each other and before too long I was sent back to Afghanistan, although it probably wouldn't have made any difference in the end.'

'What happened?'

'Gossip is a way of life on most military bases and not long before our tour was up I started hearing rumours that Olivia was enjoying herself rather too much while I was away. Back home again I tackled her about it but she laughed and said it didn't mean anything. Didn't mean anything? How could it not, Lily?'

'I don't know,' she murmured, wanting to wrap him in her arms again and never let go, but didn't make a move to touch him.

'I couldn't get it out my head. Mandy was close to two by then and all I wanted was for us to be a family. Olivia and I wanted very different things from life and I think if she hadn't got pregnant our relationship would've run its course much earlier. She resented me for not giving her the life she'd expected. She's not a bad person and I still hoped we could . . .' His deep, rough voice throbbed with frustration. 'We struggled along but our marriage descended into one long argument. My temper was on a short fuse and when Olivia came home late again one night I lost it big time. If Mandy hadn't come downstairs crying because she couldn't sleep, I'm pretty sure I'd have hurt Olivia. I frightened her, and myself, and she ordered me to leave.'

Lily chose her words carefully. 'Sometimes it's the only way.' Her thoughts went to Patrick and how she'd come to the point where she couldn't ignore his behaviour any more. 'You stayed in the Army after your divorce?'

'I didn't know what else to do.' Kenan shrugged. 'Olivia didn't want me around Mandy and I couldn't blame her for that. After a spell as a training instructor I went back to Afghanistan about fifteen months ago.'

'Is that when your colleague died?'

He nodded. 'One thing you can't afford out there is to lose your concentration.'

'You're human, Kenan, mistakes happen.' Lily longed to find a way to get him to ease up on himself, but by his fierce glare knew that she'd failed.

'One second of not paying complete attention can condemn you and your mates to death,' he stated baldly. 'Do you know what gets to me more than anything since I left the Army?'

She didn't answer, pretty sure he wasn't really asking.

'People bandy around stupid comments about their jobs and how stressed they are. They say some project or other is a matter of life and death. They haven't a bloody clue.'

Lily flushed. 'I guess I'm guilty there, I'm afraid. I take my work too seriously at times. I'd never looked at it that way before.'

Kenan leaned forward and snatched up her hands. 'I didn't mean you . . . oh, hell, this is coming out all wrong.' He let go of her hands and jerked up to standing, shoving the chair back away from him so hard it crashed to the floor.

'You're not going anywhere until you're finished, so you might as well sit back down.' Lily met his anger straight on and a slight curl of humour pulled at the corners of his mouth.

'Bossy woman,' he complained half-heartedly.

'Yeah, and what're you goin' to do about it?' Lily challenged.

Kenan sighed and lifted the chair back upright. 'Sit down, I guess.' He slumped back on the chair with a ghost of a grin softening his hard, taut face. 'One morning last spring I led a foot patrol in the centre of town. A group of kids were kicking a ball around and I spotted one little girl about Mandy's age. I couldn't keep my eyes off her. I kept thinking about the fact I was a father in name only and how much I missed Mandy. I should've been watching for snipers, but I slipped up.'

It took all Lily's courage to meet his smouldering eyes.

'My mate, Chris, pushed me down as the first bullet hit, and the guy behind us bought it. Eighteen he was, only been there a week.'

The steely remoteness of his words chilled Lily through to her bones.

'The kids began to scarper when the shots started, but when I looked up from the ground I saw the little girl trip over a rock. Next thing the sniper picked her off too.'

'But she was one of his own people?' Lily couldn't comprehend such a thing.

'War's not pretty, sweetheart. Not everyone follows the so-called rules.' He leaned back and stared blankly at the wall behind Lily's left shoulder. 'I crawled over to see if I could help her as her father came out from their house. The agony on his face as he picked her up in his arms was the worst moment of my life.'

'What was her name?'

'Kalinah,' Kenan said softly. 'I see her pretty face most nights. Hear her laughter and then her screams.'

Lily only hesitated for a second. 'Betty wondered the other day if you suffered from PTSD?'

'Most do at some level.' Kenan shrugged. 'I function okay, most of the time.'

'Would you ever consider talking to someone?'

He reached over and stroked her loose hair, teasing the wild curls. 'What do you think I'm doing right now?'

Lily blushed. 'I mean a professional?'

'You're a professional chef. You'll do for now. One step at a time, sweetheart.'

Kenan leaned in to kiss her and didn't stop until she'd lost the ability to think, let alone speak. He wrapped his arms around her and pulled her so close that she felt his heart beat against hers.

'Until you, I've not let myself be close to another woman since the divorce five years ago. I know that's unusual, but I'd screwed up so badly and had to sort myself out first. I couldn't risk messing up another person's life. Regaining my integrity was a priority.' He hesitated. 'Lily, right now I'm struggling to learn how to be a good father.'

'You're doing a great job.' She knew Kenan needed her to understand the underlying message he was giving her. 'We both need time. How do you feel about being friends?'

'With benefits?' His quirky smile shot through her and pooled somewhere deep in her gut.

'That's negotiable. I've not exactly been racing to leap into bed with another man after the mess with Patrick. He shook my judgement, badly.' Lily gave in to a smile. 'Of course, that was before I met you.'

He got the satisfied look of men the world over when they realised a woman wanted them *that* way.

'Before I came here today I decided that if you were still speaking to me after our talk, I was going to ask you something.'

'What are you getting at?' Her heart raced.

'How do you feel about having your old driver back?'

'How come?' she asked.

'Jane's proposing to send me off with you while she plays at being the World's Best Aunt with Mandy.'

Lily didn't understand. 'But what about—'

'Mr Mike Braithwaite? She's got a warped plan to force him to come running after her instead of the other way around,' Kenan explained with obvious confusion.

'She's a devious little madam.' Lily laughed, despite everything.

'Jane's my sister, what would you expect?' he said with a satisfied grin.

'Mm. Well, I guess we can give it a try.'

'Good.' He cupped her face, stroking his large thumbs slowly down her neck and setting her on fire. 'Can we learn to be friends and maybe more?' Kenan took her mouth in another hot, searching kiss. 'I'm willing to give it a try.'

His sexy smile melted her resolve. 'I bet you are,' she exhaled and succumbed as he kissed her again. Kenan teased her lips and she opened to him, tasting the lingering hint of sweet raspberries and essence of red wine. 'I'll probably give you more talking therapy along the way,' Lily warned.

'I bet you will.' He pulled her up to standing and wrapped his arms around her waist, pulling her up against him.

'Go home now and do what you need to get

sorted out. We'll leave in the morning and head back to Keswick.'

His dark eyes studied her so intently she squirmed. 'You're an amazing woman. I'm not sure I deserve the chance—'

'You may not, but I guess we'll find out,' Lily stated bluntly.

One day at a time. Anything more was tempting fate.

CHAPTER 22

Kenan cleared his throat. 'Give me your bags and I'll load the car.'

They had decided to make an early start and the sun had not yet risen over the sea. Lily yawned and stretched her arms above her head, making the shocking pink T-shirt cling like plastic wrap.

'For God's sake, do you have to do that?' he protested with a groan.

'What are you talking about, soldier boy?' Her drawl thickened.

'If I'm going to be stuck in a car with you for seven hours, you'd better put a cardigan on or something. Cover up some of that . . .' He waved his hand vaguely in her direction and a rush of heat lit up his face.

Lily smirked and opened up the enormous pink bag she dragged everywhere and pulled out something pink and scrunched up. 'Will this do?' She held up a bit of skimpy lace and pulled it on. It covered her arms, but even if she pulled the edges together it didn't reach all the way over her lush, full breasts.

'It'll have to.' Kenan shook his head. 'How any grown man confronted with *that* would drool over my sister with her whacked-off hair and ragbag assortment of clothes is beyond me.'

He grabbed her bags and headed outside leaving Lily to stare at him with her mouth open. Today she could manage to get herself into the car without his help. He soon had their luggage organised in the best way to optimise the available space. Kenan eased into the driver's seat and glanced over at his passenger. 'All set?'

'I sure am,' she declared with a bright smile. 'I take it I'm not supposed to repeat what you said about Jane? It wasn't kind.'

Kenan shrugged. 'Best not to. I think I'm just obsessed by you and don't know how to handle it.' He shut up before dropping himself in it any more.

'Whoa. Careful there. You're on dangerous ground.' She chuckled. 'You'll turn into a metro-sexual if you're not careful. Sharing your feelings is first. You know what comes next, don't you?'

He grated the car into gear and jerked away from the kerb.

'Don't answer – I'll tell you.'

Had a feeling you would.

'You'll start using moisturiser and we'll get matching mani-pedis,' Lily pronounced with a decided smirk.

'What the hell's that when it's about?' he grouched.

'Don't tell me you've never had a manicure and pedicure?' Lily's fake shock lit up her face.

'Not bloody likely.' Kenan scowled and turned on the indicator ready to get on the A30. 'Stop being daft, woman. Why don't you do something useful like get some more sleep?'

'Okay, I get the hint.' She tossed her hair around and pouted. 'Can I lean against your shoulder?'

Lily snuggled up against him and today's scent, a lethal choice reminiscent of full-blown roses open to the sun, teased his senses.

'No. Not unless you want to crash at seventy miles per hour. Stick to your own side of the car,' he ordered and she gave him a sly nod.

A few minutes later he heard her steady breathing and let himself relax a little. Kenan tuned in the radio to his favourite Classic FM station and Handel's *Water Music* came on. He eased back into the seat and slipped into his driving mode. Alert but relaxed it didn't tire him – in this place he could keep going forever. He merged onto the M5 for the long uninterrupted stretch before it changed into the M6 and headed north. Kenan turned the air conditioning on low, enough to keep them cool without being chilled. After basic army transport it was a luxury he didn't mind indulging in.

'Are we there yet?' Lily's laughter took him by surprise. 'Isn't that what kids always say?'

'Yes, and the poor parents trot out the same answer – not long now – even when it's a complete lie.' He remembered family holidays to their cousins in Scotland when he and Jane nearly drove their parents up the wall. 'We've about another hundred miles to go on the M5 and after we turn onto the M6, it'll still be nearly another three hours. Let me know when you need a break.'

'Don't tell me, you're a typical man with a huge bladder and no desire to eat. You just want to get there,' Lily said, screwing up her face.

'Pretty much, but you're the boss.'

She checked her watch. 'I'd say in about thirty minutes we'll stop for brunch. Jane found some little town and a cute café with Wi-Fi, so I'll leave it to you to see if you can best her.' Lily gave a heavy sigh. 'What's that awful noise on the radio? Don't you have any decent music over here?'

Kenan clenched his teeth. He should've guessed their taste in music would be as diverse as everything else. 'That *awful noise* as you call it is Handel. Hasn't he reached Nashville yet?'

'Nasty, nasty. As I'm paying your salary I get to pick what we listen to.' Lily fiddled with the controls, grimacing at several stations before stopping at one belting out *Ring of Fire*. 'You need an education in good country music. Even you must have heard of Johnny Cash?'

'Yes,' he said curtly.

'Old school country songs should be right up your alley. They're great stories, full of unhappy people, alcoholism, unfaithful husbands and other fun stuff,' Lily declared with enthusiasm.

'Wonderful. Just what I need.' He gave her a wry smile and was rewarded by one of her sterling grins in return.

'Hey, it'll make you feel better about your life. When I was really pissed with Patrick it worked wonders to listen to Loretta Lynn complaining and whining about her men.' Lily turned the volume up and leaned back, humming along with the music.

Kenan watched out for his exit and pulled off the motorway. The gold-award winning pub they were headed for was number one on the list of possible stopping places he'd mapped out last night.

'Where are we going?' Lily turned down the radio.

'Brewer's Arms at Riley.'

Her face lit up. 'Awesome. You planned this, didn't you?'

'All part of the job, sweetheart,' he said casually, covering up his pleasure. The map he'd memorised in his head had them turning left off the motorway and going a couple of miles into the nearest village.

An hour later he had a contented woman in the car. She totally ignored him while he started to drive again, immersed in making notes.

'That was something else,' Lily declared and stopped typing. 'Light but perfect.'

'The mushroom soup was pretty decent,' Kenan conceded.

'Decent? I guess from you that's high praise. How about the roasted vegetable panini?'

'It'll tide me over until dinner.'

A frown creased the space between her eyes and, not for the first time, he wanted to do better for her.

'Good crusty bread, and the veg almost tasted meaty.' Kenan made an effort and got another wide smile.

'You nailed it in one. I'll turn you into a food critic yet.'

He held his tongue on how doubtful that was and let her carry on with her extravagant descriptions of the food.

'Okay, I'll shut up now. I've seen your eyes glaze over which can't be good when you're driving. We'll listen to some more good music and I'll be quiet until we get to our next culinary extravaganza,' Lily pronounced and immediately followed through.

The car filled with the sound of wailing fiddles and some woman's strident singing, bemoaning the fact her husband loved his pick-up truck more than her. Kenan went back into driving mode and tuned it out.

He sighed with relief when he pulled off the motorway at last for the last few miles to Longarth Hall.

'Is that a tired worn out sigh or tired of me sigh?'

Her bright eyes sparkled and set his body on edge. 'I've driven over four hundred miles, and I've already admitted to being obsessed with you, so which do you think?'

Lily flushed underneath her pretty freckles. 'Okay, we'll go with just tired. You can have a rest and a long, hot shower when we arrive and then an amazing dinner. I'm sure you'll love Mike's food.' She pulled a lipstick from her bag. 'I'll shut up for now. Let's prepare to beard the lion in his den.'

Kenan watched in admiration as she managed to slick on a perfect, fresh, glossy layer of pink while he steered around the last sharp corner and came to a stop. *Luscious Lily* was back on.

'Brought a bodyguard with you this time, luv?' Mike said as he swaggered into the dining room that evening, stopping at their table. 'Is he here to keep you on the straight and narrow?'

Lily had no clue what he was talking about. 'This is Kenan Rowse, Jane's brother.'

'Pleasure, I'm sure.' Mike ignored Kenan's outstretched hand.

Lily watched Kenan drop his hand back down, with a dismissive sneer and hoped she wasn't in for trouble.

Mike dug around in the pocket of his chef's trousers and pulled out a folded piece of printer paper. 'This was sent to me from some place called the Phoenix Clinic. They asked me to pass the message on to you because they hadn't been able to contact you direct.' As he passed it over to Lily an angry, red flush crept up his neck.

Lily scanned through the message and glanced

up to meet Mike Braithwaite's blatant curiosity. She reread it, unable to believe what it said and then passed it over to Kenan, her hand trembling. 'Mike, I don't have an assistant called Kayley. I'm a very light drinker and I've never taken drugs. I sure as heck don't need to follow up with a rehab centre I've never heard of. I hope you believe me?'

'Whatever you say, luv.' Mike shrugged. 'We all have our demons. Doesn't matter to me as long as you don't screw up the programme.'

Kenan squeezed her arm, his signal for her to think before she spoke again. He was being wise, but she hated anything to undermine her professionalism.

'I'm too busy to have you under my feet tonight, so be in my kitchen tomorrow morning at seven. You'll see how I work and hopefully we'll get the details hammered out this time before you get on your way.' He gave a curt nod. 'Enjoy your meal.'

Braithwaite strode away towards his kitchen and Lily glanced over at Kenan.

'What do you make of this?' She waved the email at him in disgust.

'Do you want me to check into it?'

Lily tried to smile. 'Don't tell me you're a computer genius too?'

'No,' he answered with a brief smile. 'But I've a friend who is.'

'Why am I not surprised?' Lily took hold of his hand. 'Thanks. I—'

'You might not like the answer,' he stated frankly.

'It doesn't matter. I need to know.' Lily hesitated,

but then ploughed on. 'You believe what I told Mike, don't you?'

'Of course I do. You're an honest, straightforward woman. If it was true, you'd say so.'

God, the man knew her so well it was scary.

A smiling, fresh-faced waitress appeared and slid a plate in front of each of them. 'Enjoy. If there's anything else I can do, please let me know.' She left and Kenan shook his head at Lily.

'Is this the kind of stuff you cook?' He prodded suspiciously at their appetiser.

'Mine's far simpler. I call it down-home Southern cooking with a modern twist.' Lily grinned. 'This isn't overly fancy, Kenan. They're calling it "Chicken Liver Parfait on a Warm Rosemary Brioche with Cinnamon Apple Chutney", but really it's pâté on a roll with fruit chutney.'

'You really get a kick out of all this, don't you?' Kenan laid down his fork and leaned his elbows on the table, curiosity darkening his eyes. 'I know I'm a philistine where food's concerned. I grew up eating the regular stuff my mum cooked, and when I worked in the City it was fast food grabbed on the run or expensive showing-off type dinners with the other traders. The Army was plain English food or ration packs out in the field.'

Lily couldn't resist rubbing her fingers over his forearm, teasing the dark hairs. 'Just be open to trying different things – that's all I ask.'

'I'll do my best for you always, sweetheart.' Kenan's raspy voice startled her into letting go.

'In a minute I'll forget I'm supposed to be working.' Lily couldn't wonder too much about the promise he'd just made.

Lily took out her iPad and started to make notes on the entrée, a succulent fricassee of venison. Next came a tangy raspberry sorbet followed by a delectable fresh fig and almond tart. She took her time with each course and managed to largely ignore Kenan. He solidly worked his way through the meal without saying a word.

'Chef says for you to join him for coffee in the lounge,' the waitress announced, clearing away their dessert plates.

'Mm. We don't get asked?' Kenan observed dryly.

'Don't start,' Lily warned him and smiled at the girl. 'Tell him we'd be honoured.'

'Oh, yeah, course we are.' Kenan's raised eyebrow made it clear what he thought of Braithwaite.

'Come on, put on your best charming manner.' Lily jumped up and beckoned to him. With a resigned sigh Kenan stood and trailed after her out of the dining room.

'The view's incredible,' Lily chivvied him along as they crossed the hall. 'Might be better than Cornwall,' she teased, rewarded by a snort of disbelief. She spotted their host at his favourite low table over by the window.

'Coffee's coming.' Mike signalled to a nearby waitress.

'With some of your awesome homemade fudge?' Lily asked hopefully, and he managed a dour nod.

With the coffee poured, Lily chattered away about the meal and he responded and loosened up, sharing his recipes and where he sourced his food.

'Tell me something, why didn't Jane return with you?' he asked out of the blue. 'I thought she was your assistant.'

Lily almost choked on a mouthful of chocolate nut fudge. She watched Kenan place his cup carefully back on the saucer, but the bland expression on his face didn't fool her for a minute.

'She was only standing in for me last week,' Kenan replied. 'I'm free again now so there was no reason for her to come back.'

'So she's staying in Cornwall?' Mike persisted.

'Until classes start again. Yes.' Kenan didn't elaborate.

'Fair enough.' Mike pushed away his cup and jerked his chair back from the table. 'We'll see about that.' He stood, gave a curt nod to them both, and stalked off.

'Whew, what do you make of that little exhibition?' Lily asked.

'Maybe my sister's smarter than I thought, although goodness knows why she's interested.' Kenan shook his head.

'Jane said he looked the type to toss a woman over his shoulder and haul her off to his house on the moors,' Lily tried to explain, although the man's appeal bewildered her too.

'And that's supposed to be a good thing?' he questioned.

'Don't ask me.'

'How about a walk?' Kenan suggested. 'We've been stuck in the car all day and I could do with walking off some of this food.'

'Works for me. Let's declare it a no-food, no relationship conversation zone,' Lily declared and he gave her a wary look. 'I want to find out what you like to read and your favourite movies – all the sort of stuff people talk about on first dates.'

Kenan gave her a dark, dangerous stare. 'Is that what this is?'

'I don't know. Want to find out?' Lily held out her hand and he took hold of it with a smile.

CHAPTER 23

Just when Kenan thought he was inching closer to understanding Lily she threw him for a loop. '*Texas Chainsaw Massacre*? Seriously?'

'Let me guess. You expected *An Officer and a Gentleman* or *The Princess Diaries*?' She burst into loud, unrestrained laughter and threw her arms around his neck, pulling him to her for a swift, hard kiss. 'You are so easy to tease. It's like taking candy from a baby.'

He'd been had again. Kenan had no choice but to throw up his hands in disgust at himself. 'You got me.'

They'd spent the last half hour walking around the well-tended gardens surrounding Longarth Hall while Lily started what she'd called her first date interrogation. So far they'd established he was a Beethoven nut to her Dolly Parton and her favourite actress was the feisty Angelina Jolie compared to his weakness for the lush-mouthed Julia Roberts.

'If you took me to a horror film I'd spend the whole time wearing earplugs and covering my eyes with my hands,' Lily confessed.

Kenan slipped his hands around her narrow waist. It bewildered him how she stayed so slim when she ate constantly and greedily and declared herself allergic to exercise. He suspected she had a high metabolism and burned it off by being so energetic about everything in life. 'Might be worth it. I could keep you safe,' he murmured against her ear and a rush of heat warmed her skin.

'We're supposed to be talking about our likes and dislikes,' she protested in a weak voice. 'What's your favourite book?'

He nibbled at her soft neck, working his way down to the place where her T-shirt dipped dangerously low. '*History of the English Speaking Peoples* by Winston Churchill.' Kenan slipped his right hand down to stroke over the curve of her hip and Lily's quiet moan made him smile.

'Very heavy. Exactly what I'd have suspected,' she teased. 'I collect *Southern Living* cookbooks.'

The way she wriggled against him drove Kenan just the right side of crazy. 'Are you ready to negotiate?'

Lily gave him a puzzled look and her expression turned suddenly serious as she plainly recalled their conversation in Betty's kitchen. 'I'm not sure.'

He eased away, not wanting her to think he was trying to put pressure on her. 'Fair enough.' Keeping his voice steady wasn't easy.

'Don't get me wrong,' Lily whispered. 'I really, really want to make love with you—'

'But it's hard to get past Patrick screwing you

over? Believe me I understand, sweetheart. It's not the right time,' Kenan spoke the words he guessed she didn't want to voice for fear of hurting his feelings. 'Yet.'

She nodded, and as she glanced back up her eyes glistened with tears. Kenan brushed them gently away and pressed a light kiss against her forehead.

'Don't worry. It's all good. We've had a long day. Let's go back in and I'll escort you to your room like a gentleman.'

Lily stroked her fingers over the roughening shadow on his jaw and Kenan steeled himself not to overreact to her touch.

'There are things which need to be right for both of us before we take that step together.' The curve of a smile lit up her beautiful face. 'Makes a change for me to be the right one, doesn't it?'

Kenan held onto his smile although it strained his acting abilities to the limit. He couldn't see how he'd ever let this woman go out of his life, but she wasn't ready to hear it yet. 'It certainly does.'

'What time do you want to have breakfast?' she asked.

He gave a wry smile. 'Is that a genuine question, or do you need me at breakfast to run interference with Braithwaite?'

'Don't you dare do a Patrick on me and imply I'm helpless.' Lily poked him in the chest and glared. 'Do you want breakfast, or not?'

'Not,' Kenan replied, daring to pop a kiss on

her cheek. 'Another first date confession. I hate solid food before noon. Just reading the description on the menu made me nauseous. I'll get coffee sent to my room while you wallow in greasy bacon and eggs.' He shuddered.

'Thanks,' she murmured.

Lily snuggled back into his arms, surrounding him with her unique scent and luring his fingers to tangle with her soft curls.

'What for?' he asked.

'Being honest. I'll give you a break on this one and won't try to convince you of the healing powers of breakfast,' Lily said, with a gentle laugh up against his chest. 'Now let's go to our own lonely beds before we lose the will to resist.'

Kenan held his tongue. He'd lost all his willpower the night he first set eyes on Lily. It had taken him a while to realise that and she hadn't got there yet. He kept his arm wrapped around her as they walked back to the hotel in silence, caught up in their own thoughts.

After a couple of hours observing Mike Braithwaite at work during breakfast service, Lily had a new respect for him. His knowledge of food was encyclopaedic and he managed his kitchen with the sort of calm, firm hand Lily envied. He treated his staff with respect and there was no sign of the macho sexism he flaunted in public. Maybe the brash, rough persona was his equivalent of *Luscious Lily*, in which case Jane wasn't an idiot after all.

'Right, luv, they can finish up without me,' Mike declared. 'Let's go to my office and hammer out a few more details so you can get on your way.'

Lily smiled as he escorted her to his so-called office, which consisted of two chairs and a rickety table shoved into one corner of the large kitchen. She set up her iPad and launched into the details that she went through with all her potential chefs.

'Sounds reasonable. Do I want to know who you're going to pair me with?' Mike's dark scowl didn't intimidate her any more.

'Oh, yeah, you'll love it,' Lily teased.

'I doubt it very much,' he scoffed. 'Spill the beans.'

'It has to be Jonathan Cabot in Boston.'

'Why?' he persisted.

The two men were such opposites in style and manner it would be great viewing, especially on the couple of crossover days that she had planned, when each chef got to settle the other in their kitchen before leaving them to work.

'Cabot's a soft-spoken man with impeccable manners.' Lily smiled, recalling her first visit with him when she'd been regaled with the story of his Boston Brahmin heritage, going all the way back to the first Massachusetts Bay settlers.

'Let me guess. Harvard educated. Preppy dresser. Would cut his tongue out rather than swear in front of a lady?' Mike's pithy summing up was so accurate Lily could only nod.

'Good TV. Doesn't bother me. If it helps put this place on the map I'll be as rude and obnoxious as you like,' he tossed out carelessly. 'Oh, by the way, your bulldog's out there pacing around the hall. You'd better go before he forces his way in here and tears me limb from limb.' The crack of a smile softened Mike's granite features.

'My staff will be in touch about contracts etc soon.' She shut down her iPad and put away all her gear. 'We've got to get going anyway. I need to be in Edinburgh by lunchtime.'

'I didn't feed you enough breakfast?' The dark slash of his eyebrows rose in question and Lily grinned back.

'It was incredible and you know it.' She'd packed away one of his famous breakfasts designed to fortify guests who intended to spend the day tramping for miles around the beautiful countryside. Lily had happily waded her way through a large platter of locally sourced bacon, eggs, sausage, potatoes, wild mushrooms, granary toast and creamy butter.

'I suppose you're going to see Lachlan McDonnell next.'

'How did you guess?'

Mike shrugged his massive shoulders, sending ripples down his tight white T-shirt and Lily couldn't help thinking the sight would've made Jane melt. 'He's the only chef up there on a par with me.'

'Why, you arrogant—'

'There's nothing wrong with being sure of your

224

abilities. You understand that.' Mike untied his apron and screwed it up, tossing it into the dirty laundry basket beside them. 'You'll see me again soon.'

She shook her head, getting up to leave. 'It'll be a while. I'm guessing it'll be spring next year before we're ready to start shooting.'

'Not what I meant, luv. I'm thinking a few days in Cornwall will be a pleasant change from this.' He gave a sly grin and walked with her towards the swinging doors leading out into the hall. 'Don't say a word.'

'You sure it's wise?'

'Maybe not. We'll see, won't we? Bye, luv.' He winked and left her to get back to his work.

Lily stepped out into the hall and waved over to Kenan. Her heart beat faster at the sight of him, immaculate as ever in what she thought of as his work uniform – white shirt, dark trousers and highly polished black shoes.

'Good morning, are you ready?' she asked.

She took it for granted that the car was neatly packed and all set for them to go. He'd have the route planned and know their arrival time down to the last five minutes with alternate plans in place for unexpected traffic conditions.

Kenan motioned to the mobile phone he held, and carried on talking. Lily's stomach tightened when she heard Olivia's name mentioned. Kenan grunted and swore, shoved his hands through his close-cropped hair and paced around the small lobby.

'Call me back tonight and I'll make a decision.' He slammed the phone shut and shoved it into his pocket.

'Something wrong?'

'Maybe, I'm not sure yet but I need you to trust me. I'll tell you later when I know more.' He lowered his voice to a murmur. 'Can you do that, Lily?'

She reached up and wrapped her arms around his neck as she pulled him close enough to feel his heart beat. 'Did you need to ask?'

'Yes, Lily, I did.' He frowned and played with her hair, nuzzling into the unrestrained curls. 'Do you expect me to trust easily after the mistakes I've made?'

'No, but I hoped you realised that I'm different. Was I wrong?'

'I want to. I really do,' he pleaded.

'I know and you will,' Lily replied, while crossing her fingers behind his back. 'How about we get going and concentrate on our next victim – I mean chef.' She plastered on a bright smile.

'I'm damn sure I don't deserve you, Lily, but I'll go along with it until you come to your senses.' He eased her hands away before cradling them gently with his own. 'Come on.' Kenan let her go and checked his watch. 'We're seven minutes late already.'

Lily threw up her hands in mock disgust. 'Well, kiss my grits, as we say in the South.' She laughed at his obvious confusion. 'Come on. I want to meet this hunky Scot and find out if it's true what they always say.'

Kenan mock-frowned. 'God, you're like every other woman. If you think I'm going to stand by and watch you gawk up under his kilt you've got another thing coming.'

Lily pulled her powder compact out of her bag and flipped it open. 'What do you think mirrors are for?' She grinned, slung her bag back over her shoulder, pulled her sparkling pink T-shirt back into place, and with an extra twist of the hips, walked out towards the car.

Kenan hadn't realised it yet but he'd met his match.

CHAPTER 24

'Can you find the Farmer's Market on Lodge Street?' Lily asked, closing up her phone. 'That was one of Lachlan's staff. If I understood her right, he wants to meet us at the Simpson's Butcher stall instead of at the restaurant.'

'No problem,' Kenan said with a nod.

'Do you need the map?' She reached into the door pocket where he stored his neatly folded maps.

'Not necessary. I've been to Edinburgh before a few times. I can get you close and drop you off while I find somewhere to park.'

'I should've guessed.' Lily smirked but he didn't react.

Kenan deftly negotiated a maze of side streets while Lily made the most of seeing something of the city. The down side to this trip was catching glimpses of exciting new places without having the time to look around properly. She'd have to come back another time and play tourist. The old buildings were austere and elegant in the light misty rain and she could imagine them as a setting for a dark, atmospheric movie.

'This should work. The market's through there.' He pointed towards a narrow street. 'Walk straight down and it'll be on your right. I'll join you soon.' Kenan pulled into the kerb and let her out, before immediately driving off.

Lily made her way through the crowds of locals out doing their shopping. She noticed the abundance of sensible raincoats and headscarves among the mostly older women and the fact they all carried their own shopping bags. Her own flashy pink outfit stood out like a wedding dress at a funeral and she hoped it wouldn't put her Scottish chef off before they had even started. The misty rain was wreaking havoc on her hair, turning it into the same frizzy halo as it did in humid Tennessee. Lily dug out a scrunchy and tied it back where it should annoy her less.

Ten minutes later she wasn't at all happy, as there was no sign of Lachlan or Kenan.

'Enjoying the glorious Scottish summer?' Kenan's deep voice close to her ear startled her.

'Wonderful,' Lily remarked and quickly got out her phone to send a text. 'I'm asking where he's got to. I don't have time to waste.' She got an instant reply. 'Charming. No wonder the Scots are renowned for being grouchy. He's asking where the devil we've got to and says if we're not at the Clan House in fifteen minutes our meeting's cancelled.' Before she could send a curt response Kenan snatched her phone.

'Hold on, sweetheart. Think a minute. Doesn't

229

matter right now whose fault this is. Remember you're the one who wants this meeting the most. It goes against your grain, I know, but my advice is to grovel.'

Lily sighed and took the phone back. She obediently texted a conciliatory message. 'Okay, soldier boy, get us back there fast or you're fired.'

'Yes, ma'am.' He grabbed her hand and basically dragged her behind him as he strode off back towards the main street. Of course he wasn't the one wearing killer heels on the rough cobblestones but Lily didn't dare to complain.

Fourteen minutes and twenty-nine seconds later Kenan brought the car to a screeching halt outside the Clan House. The colourful flags flying on poles all over the front broke up the severe effect of the imposing, weathered granite building. Lily noticed a large white wooden easel outside the door that proclaimed today's lunch special to be Scottish lamb. She didn't suppose he'd chosen it on purpose for her visit, but it was the dish he was renowned for.

'About bloody time too.' A massive man with broad shoulders and a barrel-shaped chest yelled at them from the doorway.

The chef's white coat, swirling dark plaid kilt and his bushy ponytail rivalling Lily's in colour and wildness, all created an awe-inspiring effect. Her first thought was how magnificent he'd look on TV. The second was that if they were going to work together she must stand up for herself right now.

'We'd have been here much earlier if your employee hadn't called and changed the plans.'

'Who rang?' McDonnell frowned.

'I think she said Martha. Her accent was kinda hard for me to understand, but I repeated where we were supposed to meet and she confirmed it.'

'Och, there's no one called Martha working here. Someone's playing games with you, lassie.' He shook his head.

Lily glanced over at Kenan, but he didn't react.

'I need to be back in the kitchen. I'll get you set up with some coffee for now and then you'll eat with me. You can poke around my kitchen when lunch is over.' He nodded and turned his back on them to disappear into the building.

'Well, go on, you're not going to get an engraved invitation.' Kenan gave her a slight push.

'You and our charmer would make a good pair,' Lily joked. 'Plus you'd look pretty damn sexy in a kilt.'

'Get in, woman,' he groused, but marred it with a sly smile.

Lily skipped up the steps and the elderly woman behind the reception desk peered at them over her half-glasses.

'You're to go in the morning room.' She gestured to an open door on the other side of the hall. 'Himself will send for you when he's ready.'

Lily thanked the woman and followed her instructions to discover a small, comfortable room waiting for them. The large bay windows overlooked the busy street outside and people scurried along trying to avoid the large puddles dotting the pavement.

'There ye be.' Another unsmiling woman tramped in and thumped a tray down on the low table in front of them before walking right back out.

'Do you think they win many awards for customer service?' Lily muttered behind her hand to Kenan, as they were left alone.

'Who cares?' He poured out two cups and pushed one over to her. He took a long sip and sighed happily, leaning back against the chair and closing his eyes. 'God, that's good. I needed that.'

Lily picked up her own cup. 'Did you find out anything on the email? Do you think something odd is going on?'

'I'm ready for ye now. Jump to it or the food will be ruined. I'll no be eating with you after all. I'm too busy.' Lachlan McDonnell's booming voice startled Lily and she jumped to her feet.

As Kenan picked up her bag and indicated she should go first, Lily noticed that a shadow of relief crossed his face. She would find out the reason why later, when she got him on his own again.

'Now, that's what I call real food.' Kenan scraped out the last spoonful of blackberry pie, swallowed it with relish and laid his dessert spoon back in the empty bowl. 'A decent piece of meat, vegetables I can recognise and a pudding to fill up any empty corners.'

Lily raised an eyebrow and smiled. 'The Philosophy of Cooking according to Kenan Rowse?'

'Hey, most blokes I know would agree.' He got the fact he was being teased but wanted to be honest. He understood this was important to her, but wasn't sure he could ever be a discriminating foodie, no matter how much she pushed.

'Would you call fried chicken fancy?' Lily probed.

'No, but—'

'Every chef's different the same way as every person eating it is different,' she said, cutting him off. 'Does someone in India typically enjoy the same food as say – your father?'

'Well, no, but . . .'

Lily leaned across the table and pressed a hard, warm kiss right on his mouth 'Okay, I won that round.' She laughed. 'By the way, in case you're in doubt, I loved lunch too. I've never been a huge fan of lamb. It's not real popular in the States, but I'm a convert now. The touch of ginger in the mint sauce was pure genius.'

'I'm pleased to hear it, Miss Redman.' Lachlan appeared right by her shoulder. 'Come with me to the kitchen and I'll put you straight about my ways.' He fixed his stare on Kenan next. 'You can get yourself back into the morning room and they'll bring you coffee. I don't need extra bodies cluttering up my kitchen.'

Kenan agreed before Lily could bother protesting. 'I'll be waiting.' He followed orders and made himself scarce.

After a waitress brought his coffee, Kenan turned his phone back on. He was glad Lily's questions had been interrupted earlier so he didn't have to answer just yet. This morning he had received an email from Grant, his computer genius, with a decent amount of interesting information he could use. Now he'd follow Grant's detailed instructions and see what happened. With luck he would sort this out and Lily would never need to know the sordid details. Patrick O'Brian needed teaching a lesson. 'O'Brian? It's Kenan Rowse here.'

'What the hell are you up to? Why is the screen showing my secretary's number?' Patrick barked.

'Let's just say I know someone with the same talents that you used to screw with Lily. Hacking emails. Deceptive phone calls. Easy enough if you know what you're doing.'

'I've no idea what you're talking about,' Patrick blustered.

'You must be desperate, mate,' Kenan scoffed. 'I've been thinking—'

'Must be hard. I'm not admitting anything, but what do you actually know about Lily?'

'More than enough,' Kenan snapped.

'You sure? Do you know her mother's an alcoholic and substance abuser and we all know these things are in the genes.'

'Don't talk rubbish.' Kenan refused to overthink the fact that Lily never said much about her mother, apart from the fact she was a lousy cook.

'Given you something to think about, have I?'

234

Kenan heard the sneer and ached to give the man another satisfying punch. 'Not at all. Stop harassing Lily or you'll have me to deal with.'

'Oh, I'm scared.' Patrick laughed and hung up.

Lily would never forgive him if he doubted her, it must be nonsense but . . .

'Come on. I'm done.' Lily appeared in the doorway and Kenan plastered on a smile. 'You should have enough caffeine in your system to drive straight through to Oxford.'

'Like you're going to sit still for six plus hours unless I give you a knockout pill,' Kenan tossed right back at her. He'd trust her until she proved him wrong. 'Give me your bag and we'll get going.' He snatched her flashy pink bag and headed out of the door, leaving her to follow.

'Don't you want to hear how it went?' Lily asked, bursting with energy.

'Of course,' Kenan said with a smile, as he unlocked the car and loaded up. 'Give me all the details, except you can leave out the part about your kilt investigation.'

'Spoilsport.' Lily sighed dramatically and plopped down into the passenger seat. 'You wouldn't believe his kitchen. It's like something out of the Dark Ages. He cooks on a massive black range that has to be fed with logs of wood all day. Different parts have higher or lower temperatures so it takes a genius to juggle getting everything done right.'

'I take it you won't be buying one for your Nashville kitchen anytime soon?' he asked, checking in the rear-view mirror before pulling out into the traffic.

She scoffed. 'Not likely. It'll stick to my trusty gas stove. Apart from a couple of ancient electric hand mixers he won't have any gadgets, so no microwave, blender or food processor allowed. Bizarre.'

'Makes bloody good food though,' he interjected.

'Yeah, I know.'

'So, who are you going to pair our refugee from *Braveheart* with?' Kenan tossed out and sensed her smile.

'Absolutely it has to be Peregrine Gaines over in San Francisco,' Lily declared with a hearty giggle. 'He's a trendsetting chef whose kitchen is the poster child for everything new and innovative. His wardrobe contains as much pink as mine and I'll be tactful and call him flamboyant.'

Kenan rolled his eyes. This woman spelled trouble on a multitude of scales, but God was she ever fun. 'We'll be on the motorway in a few minutes. I'll keep driving until you order a stop. Okay?'

'Yep. That'll work.' She launched right back into her story, this time all about Lachlan McDonnell's refusal to have a freezer.

Thankfully about halfway there she fell asleep. With his classical music playing at low volume, Kenan's mind drifted back to his dad's earlier phone call. Apparently Olivia had turned up out of the blue again in Cornwall and thrown a fit when she discovered he wasn't there. She'd spun a story about regretting the new custody agreement and threatened to return and take Mandy away. He'd promised to ring his father again later and then he'd need to make a decision. Glancing over at Lily his throat tightened at the idea of letting her go again. He'd asked her to trust him, but would he have no choice but to let her down again?

'Can you make a stop before we get to this place please. I need to freshen up.' Lily yawned and stretched, making her generous breasts push against the clingy shirt.

Kenan caught the satisfied smile that told him she'd done it on purpose. 'You don't deserve it but there's a coffee shop down the road.'

'Surely you can't drink anymore?'

'I've a high tolerance for caffeine,' he explained. 'Long days on the trading floor followed by years of exhausting patrols and crappy living conditions inure you to a lot, sweetheart.'

'I bet they do, and in more ways than you'll ever tell me unless I pull your nails out one by one with tweezers.'

Kenan looked away, and she didn't say another word.

Half an hour later – after two cups of coffee for him and a full make-up reapply for her – they were ready. He drove the last few miles and turned into a curved driveway running in front of the hotel.

Lily surveyed the stark, long, white building. 'What kind of name's The Bite anyway?'

'I'm sure you checked on her before she went

on your list. According to the online info I tracked down she's an oddball. The daughter of an Earl who turned into a hardcore punk and becomes a serious chef isn't going to name her restaurant Mitzi's County Cooking, is she?'

Lily's glittering sapphire eyes fixed on him. 'What do you guess she'll think of me?'

He took hold of her hand. 'You're two unique women. Hopefully you'll respect each other for that.'

'You're a flanneller, Kenan. You know damn well she'll sum me up as a frivolous girly girl,' Lily declared, her drawl deepening along with her frustration.

He checked his watch. 'If you don't get on with it we'll be late. Stop fretting and get out of the car.'

'You've been ordering me around all day. Who's the boss here?'

Kenan reached over and swooped in for a kiss. He ignored her half-hearted protest and deepened the kiss satisfactorily before letting go.

'My lipstick!' Lily yelled.

'Put more on.' Kenan got out of the car and strolled around to open her door. She deliberately took her time, but he didn't react and rested against the car, whistling an old army march until she finally joined him.

Lily straightened her skirt and put on a killer smile. 'Okay. Mitzi Carlton-Baines. Do your worst. I'm ready.'

CHAPTER 25

'For heaven's sake, stop pestering me,' Olivia hissed down the phone.

Patrick grinned. He stretched out on the hotel bed and kicked off his shoes, letting them drop with a thump on the carpet. 'I want to know how it went.'

'I did what we agreed.' Olivia sighed. 'I turned up in Cornwall and threw a fit when I found my poor neglected daughter abandoned again by her father.'

'Where are you now?'

'I'm stuck in a dreary cafe drinking lukewarm coffee,' she complained. 'I hinted I had business to see to and told them I'd be back in a couple of hours to pick up Amanda. Are you satisfied?'

'You did good.'

'Well,' she snapped.

'Well, what?'

'The correct word to use is well – not good.' Olivia's cut-glass accent sliced down the phone line. 'It irritates me to hear the English language butchered.'

'Excuse me.' Patrick chuckled. 'I don't remember

my grammar making a difference when I took you to bed.'

'Must you remind me. I . . . got carried away by the moment and don't intend to repeat my mistake. I'm engaged to a wonderful man who—'

'Wouldn't be pleased to find out his classy fiancée was screwing around?' Patrick sniped. He'd only known Olivia for a few days, but already felt unwanted sympathy for Kenan Rowse and the poor sap she'd talked into marrying her this time. Talk about cold. 'Don't you dare back out on me now or Lord Cunningham will hear the truth about you.'

'I should never have agreed to this farce. Is all this really necessary?'

Patrick made her wait. Hopefully she'd start to sweat – if upper-class English women did such a crass thing. 'You know it is. Your daughter is the one thing your ex-husband wants. This pays him back for attacking me and keeps your tame Lord, who you told me didn't care for the fact that you dumped her in the first place, happy.'

'How dare you. I did not dump her. I merely gave her father the—'

'Save it for the jury, sweetheart,' he interrupted. 'I don't give a monkey's why you got tired of playing mother.' Patrick snorted. 'Shove the brat into a boarding school, isn't that what y'all do anyway?' Silence. He'd scored a massive bull's eye. 'I've stirred the pot some more and put a flea in Rowse's ear to hint that his precious Lily's just out of alcohol and drug rehab.'

'You make me sick. I'll ring when I've got Amanda back in London. I'll get Henry's solicitor to draw up a new custody agreement in my favour.'

'That works, sweetheart. Go back now and play the part of the distraught mother.' Patrick hung up before she could beat him to it. It never did to let a woman get the upper hand. He'd made that mistake with Lily and it wasn't happening again.

'You're Lily Redman?'

Lily's heart sank as Mitzi Carlton-Baines's piercing blue eyes swept down over her in an openly scathing stare. Talk about opposites. Lily's image was as frothy and girly as possible. Mitzi was ripped leather, spiked jewellery, multiple garish tattoos and enough piercings to send a metal detector crazy. Lily suppressed an inappropriate laugh imagining the two of them swapping on the show.

'I certainly am, honey.' Lily launched into her well-practised spiel about the programme before she could lose her nerve completely. Five minutes later she decided to shut up and see what happened next.

'I did try to tell you I thought you were wasting your time coming and now I'm sure of it,' Mitzi declared in the polite, cutting British way Lily would love to be able to master.

'How about you feed me dinner and we'll talk later?' Lily wasn't giving up yet. 'I sure am starving and I've heard your Chocolate Amaretto Cheesecake Balls are to die for so I'll be sure to save a space.'

A hint of pleasure pulled at Mitzi's narrow, black painted lips. 'Deal.' She strode off and left Lily gaping.

'Might be your toughest challenge,' Kenan commented, and she could only nod. 'Come on. Lead me to another gourmet feast.'

She sighed and they walked along together, following the waitress to their table. Lily slipped back into work mode and made notes all the way through the delicious meal. Finally she got her hands on the notorious dessert and knew she'd tasted heaven. Lily groaned as she forced down a third cheesecake ball even though she was already stuffed.

'Don't even try to tell me this isn't wonderful?' she nagged Kenan.

'I'm not much for fancy puddings, but the salmon was decent.'

Lily leapt on his comment. 'Why?'

'Hell, Lily, I don't know.'

'Try,' she pleaded and leaned in over the table, watching his eyes drift down her cleavage. She'd do whatever it took to get him to talk more – about everything.

'It wasn't dry the way fish is sometimes and I liked the lemon sauce.'

Lily patted his hand. 'See, didn't kill you, did it?'

Before he could answer the waitress reappeared.

'Chef says to come to the kitchen.' She didn't wait for them to reply so Lily scrambled to her feet and dragged Kenan by the hand.

'You're coming. Don't argue.' On the way Lily quickly tied her hair back and smoothed down her skirt, not for the first time recently wishing she could return to dressing more like a normal person.

'Stand out of the way and shut up. I'm too bloody busy to answer inane questions until later,' Mitzi ordered as they stepped into the kitchen. 'We're fully-booked and I'm short-staffed tonight.'

In a flash of brilliance Lily knew she could turn this to her advantage. 'Get me an apron and find me a pair of kitchen shoes. You can put me to work.'

'You?' Mitzi's scepticism poured out unabated and Lily struggled not to take it personally. Her kohl-rimmed eyes darkened. 'All right. Put your money where your mouth is. Uniforms are over there. Alice will fix you up.' She gestured at a petite blonde girl hovering nearby.

Two hours later when things finally slowed down Lily knew she had the quirky chef in the palm of her hand. She had fitted right into the line – chopping vegetables, boning chicken breasts and whipping up a ton of fresh pasta – whatever was needed. The woman knew her business and now Lily had her *Celebrity Chef Swap* partner chosen as well. Sam Evans, her traditional meat and three veg, conservative, Mississippi wonder boy would be the perfect foil for this edgy woman.

'Well done.' Mitzi slapped her on the back. 'I think we can do a deal. I'm too knackered to talk details tonight though. Make it after breakfast.'

Lily's head reeled with tiredness but she managed to nod and say goodnight. Turning around she saw Kenan watching from over in the corner, his dark eyes full of admiration. She didn't intend trying to resist him any longer.

He dangled her pink shoes in his hand and waited. Kenan really hoped he wasn't reading her wrong, and as a sexy smile crept across Lily's weary face he knew that he'd hit the jackpot.

'Ready?' she asked, her voice husky with tiredness.

'Whenever you are, boss.' Kenan held out the shoes.

'You've got to be kidding.' Lily chuckled. 'My feet feel like plates of raw meat.'

He instantly thrust the shoes in her hands and swept her up into his arms.

'Put me down, you idiot,' she protested, ineffectively beating on his back.

Kenan ignored her and strode briskly across the room, catching more than a few admiring glances from the other kitchen staff who had stopped cleaning to watch.

'Are you trying to re-enact the final scene from *An Officer and a Gentleman*?' Lily giggled and tightened her grip around his neck.

'Haven't got a clue what you're talking about, sweetheart.'

She sighed and told him he was hopeless. Apparently his education was sorely lacking where romantic films to win over women were concerned. Lily rattled off every detail of the scene that most of her female friends could recite by heart and longed to experience for themselves.

'Your feet were hurting,' he stated plainly, and she gave a sad shake of her head implying he was a hopeless case. 'Enough nonsense. Let's get you to bed.' Kenan headed for the lift.

'Exactly what I had in mind,' she whispered.

A curl of desire snaked through him and he struggled to remain coherent while this armful of warm, perfumed woman whispered in his ear and made it abundantly clear what she wanted. Kenan cleared his throat, but still couldn't speak. He pressed the button and bit back a curse as the lift took its time arriving.

'Where's your key card?' he asked as they reached her bedroom door.

'In my bag. You'll have to put me down.'

Kenan wasn't about to attempt a search of the oversized pink creation she hauled around everywhere and reluctantly slid her down from his arms, waiting impatiently as she got the room unlocked. Lily grabbed his hand and pulled him in with her before kicking the door shut behind them.

'Strewth!' Lily exhaled. 'I wasn't sure I'd survive that.'

'Not sure Mitzi did either.' Kenan's laconic comment brought out another smile.

'Won her over though, didn't I?' she boasted.

'She didn't stand a chance once you grabbed a knife and started chopping veg like a madwoman,' Kenan teased,

'Any chef would do the same,' Lily protested. 'But before you say anything, I admit there was a less noble side to my offering to help out. She needed to see I wasn't a fluffy airhead just because of this.' She waved down over herself.

Kenan scoffed. 'I can't imagine anyone being stupid enough to believe that. You're an extremely competent chef and a damned fine businesswoman and don't you ever forget it.'

She stood gaping at him.

'Have I finally discovered how to silence you?'

'You keep surprising me,' Lily murmured.

'It's part of my innate charm.'

Her deep blue eyes burned through him and Kenan was afraid he wouldn't be able to take this as slow as he knew he should.

'Yeah. It is.' She sounded thoughtful. 'We've waited long enough, don't you think? Why don't you kiss me?'

'I don't know. Why don't I?' He caressed her face, making long sweeping strokes down over her warm, flushed skin. Kenan lightly traced around her mouth until she sighed and then dragged her into a deep, possessive kiss. 'You always taste wonderful. Perfect balance of sweet and hot.' He grinned. 'See, I can describe things when I want.'

'You sure can.'

Her sly smile and the way she wriggled her soft, luscious body up against his nearly sent Kenan over the edge and he fought for control. Easing back slightly he took hold of her hands, hoping she didn't notice how badly his own were trembling. 'Let's go and check out the view.'

Over by the large window he yanked back the heavy green velvet curtains and they stared out over the rooftops of Oxford, illuminated only by the streetlights and myriad of stars.

'I wish we had time to check it out properly,' Lily said.

There was so much he wished they had time for, and was very afraid this might be all they would ever have but he refused to spoil things yet. Not until he'd loved her in the way she deserved. Kenan didn't speak only turned her around in his arms and kissed her again. Tenderly he slid his hands down to the curve of her hips and shifted to align his body with hers.

'Are you sure about this?' He'd give her one last chance to reconsider.

The brilliant smile lighting up her eyes was Lily's response and Kenan didn't ask again. Quietly he led her over to the bed, laid her on the fluffy white duvet and began to undress her, taking his time as he had always done with presents as a child.

'You're so beautiful.' He traced a path down over her delicate freckled skin and wondered how he had got so lucky.

Lily reached up and pulled him to her, taking

charge of the kiss this time. When she let him go it was with a gentle, magical laugh. 'Love me, Kenan.'

Tears pressed at his eyes. Did she know? He'd hardly admitted it to himself before this second so she couldn't, right?

He slid off the bed and quickly undressed, tossing his clothes on the carpet, before joining her again. Kenan pushed everything else out of his mind and concentrated on the beautiful, trusting woman opening herself to him, and asking only to be loved.

'I won't break,' Lily teased, shifting herself under him so every inch of their skin touched and set him on fire.

'Good. I've wanted this – you – for so long.' Kenan stumbled over his words and she instantly put a finger to his lips.

'Don't overthink everything,' Lily purred and encouraged him with a slight roll of her hips. He didn't need asking twice and slowly made her his, relishing the radiant expression lighting up her beautiful face. Without another word being said they fell into an easy rhythm, moving together as though they were meant to be.

Before he could consider holding back the intoxicating effect of Lily's scent surrounding him pushed Kenan close to the edge. He stroked his fingers between them to bring her along with him and a cry wrenched from his throat as they both tumbled into a long shattering release.

Lily tightened her hands around his neck. 'Don't leave me. Not yet.'

He wanted to say he never would but couldn't lie. Especially now. Instead he kissed her again.

Kenan glanced at Lily's bedside clock. Nearly ten o'clock. His father would be going ape waiting for him to ring. Carefully slipping from the bed so as not to wake her, he grabbed his phone and crept into the bathroom.

'It's me. What happened?'

His father sighed. 'Sorry, son, but Olivia's taken Mandy back to London with her. First she got mad about the fact you'd left, then said she made a mistake and a daughter needed to be with her mother. Poor little Mandy wasn't happy.' His voice cracked. 'She was crying and it tore us up, but what could we do?'

'Nothing, Dad. It's not your fault. I shouldn't have trusted her.' He cursed under his breath. 'I'll go to London in the morning and sort this out once and for all. Mandy deserves better.'

'Yes, she does. Let me know if there's anything we can do.'

'I will, Dad, and thanks. I'll call tomorrow.' He slammed the phone shut before his father could offer any consoling platitudes.

Easing open the bathroom door, he silently crept across the carpet and climbed back into bed. Kenan wrapped himself around Lily's soft, warm body as she shifted back into him in her sleep. He pressed his face into the mass of her wayward hair in a desperate attempt to drive away the tears pushing at the back of his eyes.

He ran through every possible scenario in his head, but as daylight seeped in to the room Kenan was forced to accept what he'd known from the day they met.

CHAPTER 26

'So that's it? Wham, bam, thank you ma'am.' Lily used anger to keep her tears at bay.

'God, Lily, it's not that simple.'

Kenan's frustration boiled over, but she did not cut him any slack. The cool, rational explanation of his intended plans had shaken her to the core.

'I totally get the fact that you must go to Mandy and I'd think less of you if you did anything else, but I still don't see the connection with us,' Lily persisted, hating the additional strain her words etched into his grey, taut face.

'Oh, sweetheart. We can't pretend any longer. This was never going to work long-term and we were fools to think it might.'

'Other people manage to have long-distance relationships. Some have even been known to move because they loved each other.' Lily went quiet. She'd asked him to love her last night, and he'd let his body do the talking for him. Maybe she'd assumed too much?

'Yes, but they didn't have children and high-profile careers complicating things.' Kenan's steady, calm voice made Lily itch to smack him.

'Have you forgotten last night?' she persisted. They'd turned to each other over and over again in the night, neither able to get enough of the other.

'Of course not.' His dark, smoky eyes rested on her. 'But we can't live our lives around great sex.'

Lily wasn't fooled. He saw no choice and was sending himself away. For now she'd have to let him go, but this couldn't be the end. She'd kissed too many frogs to let her prince go without a fight. Taking a step back away from him, she clasped her hands together to stop them from touching him. 'Go, if that's what you're determined to do.' He gave her a puzzled look. Obviously he'd expected a battle, but taking a man by surprise was always a smart move and he'd seen nothing yet.

Lily ploughed on. 'Good luck, and give Mandy my love.'

'How will you manage to get to Wales?'

'You told me last night what a capable woman I was, so why are you doubting me now?' she needled him, satisfied when he winced at her sharp words.

'You know I didn't mean that. I feel bad for letting you down.' He stared at his feet.

'Yeah, well, I seem to arouse that tendency in men. I'll survive, it's what I do.'

'Right.' Kenan slung his bag on his shoulder and reached for her.

Lily held out her hands in warning. 'No. Don't

touch me. Just leave.' Hurt flashed in his slate-grey eyes, but she had to protect herself. One brush of his skin against hers and she wouldn't be able to do this. 'Drive carefully.'

'I don't know what to say.' He sounded totally defeated.

'Nothing. There isn't anything.' She turned her back on him and refused to turn back around until she heard the door close behind him on the way out.

Lily stared at the empty space where he had been and wept.

Kenan straightened his tie, pulled his shoulders straight and sighed. He pushed the picture of Lily's distraught face to the back of his mind. So much for integrity and honesty.

Eighty-seven Lilac Gardens, he checked the address and glanced up at the imposing Georgian house. Before he could lose his nerve, Kenan rang the doorbell. A stern-faced butler opened the door and stared out at him.

'Captain Kenan Rowse to see Lord Cunningham.' His old army title slipped out and softened the man's stony face.

'Is his Lordship expecting you, sir?' The steely politeness didn't fool Kenan.

'Perhaps. I need to speak with him on a personal matter.' He stared the man down and waited.

'Come inside and wait in the hall while I check if his Lordship is free.'

Kenan stepped in and stood in the middle of the marble-floored hall. While he waited he glanced around, taking in the array of old family portraits on the elegant mahogany table next to him, and an abundance of extravagant flower arrangements. A sweeping staircase rose up from the centre and Kenan half-expected Olivia to appear at the top, poised to make a dramatic entrance. The house suited her to perfection.

'Captain Rowse.' A genial, ruddy-faced man strode across from one of the rooms off the hall, holding out his hand in greeting. 'Henry Cunningham. Let's go into my study.'

Five minutes later Kenan found himself seated in a well-worn leather wingback chair with a cup of steaming coffee in one hand. He took several long swallows and relished the much-needed caffeine shot. 'That's good. Thanks.'

'I've an excellent chef, thank goodness.' He gave a wry smile. 'It wouldn't be wise to rely on Olivia for anything on the domestic front, would it?'

Her name hung in the air between them, the first time she'd been mentioned and Kenan cleared his throat, unsure how to reply. 'Probably not.'

'Don't worry. I don't have many illusions where she's concerned, but I'm all right with that.'

Kenan felt a reluctant admiration for the man.

'I'm sure you're anxious to see your daughter again. She . . . wasn't too happy last night, but children are resilient.'

Kenan clutched the coffee cup so tightly he was

amazed the handle didn't break. 'She's the reason I came.'

'Good heavens, Kenan, what on earth are you doing here?' Olivia swept into the room, elegant as ever in a pale green sleeveless dress. With her golden hair swept back and a strand of pearls circling her slim throat she fitted the part of aristocratic fiancée to perfection.

'Take a wild guess.' He struggled to keep his temper in check. 'I've come to discuss Mandy. You broke our agreement.'

'For a supposedly contrite father desperate to get to know his daughter, you couldn't wait to leave her, could you? I found her dumped on your crazy sister and elderly parents while you'd run off again with your trashy Yank.'

Kenan called on every ounce of self-discipline that he possessed to stay in control. 'My loving family were happy to look after her while I worked for a few days. Mandy and Jane planned a lot of things to do together and she was perfectly happy and well cared for.' He avoided any mention of Lily, not wanting to go there. 'You had no right to take her away and upset her again.'

A hint of colour flushed Olivia's creamy skin as the barb hit home. 'Nothing legal was in place, Kenan.' Her sharp, dispassionate words sliced through him.

'Only because we hadn't got around to it yet. I thought you could be trusted for once. Stupid me,' Kenan chided.

'Excuse me interrupting for just a moment.' Lord Cunningham's cultured tones silenced them both and Kenan could have kicked himself for sinking to Olivia's level. 'I need you to understand my position, Rowse. I love Olivia very much and when I asked her to become my wife I made it abundantly clear Amanda would always have a home with us.'

Olivia's face tightened. Clearly she expected Kenan to challenge Cunningham's assertion after the story she'd spun him, but he held his tongue. For now.

Cunningham carried on. 'Olivia decided the little girl would be better off with you, with the exception of regular visits, of course, and naturally I deferred to her.' He turned to look at Olivia.

Kenan heard the unsaid. The other man thought it unnatural, but loved Olivia enough to go along with her decision.

He turned back to Kenan. 'Olivia's agreed to honour your recent custody agreement.'

Olivia threw her fiancé a mutinous look. She must have been railroaded into it, but Kenan didn't care.

'If you're agreeable, I'll get my solicitor here as soon as possible,' Cunningham carried smoothly on. 'We'll get something drawn up and you can run it by your own solicitor at your convenience.'

'That sounds ideal. I appreciate your . . . concern and help, your Lordship.'

'I'm happy to help, and please call me Henry. My father only passed recently and I'm not used to all this nonsense yet. Olivia, why don't you go upstairs and wake Amanda? Captain Rowse and I will head into the breakfast room and you can join us when you're both ready.'

Kenan suppressed a smile as Olivia instantly left the room. He had never seen her so passive but guessed that she had too much to lose this time around.

Lily stared at the plate of congealing food.

'I thought you'd enjoy my take on American style waffles.' Mitzi's gruff voice startled Lily.

Mitzi's in-your-face fierceness was a bit much first thing in the morning, but Lily managed a slight smile. 'I'm sure they're delicious, but I'm not very hungry today.'

Mitzi's hard stare pinned her to the seat. 'Where's your man this morning?'

The possessive word cut through Lily. Kenan had never really been hers. That was the root of the problem. 'Gone.'

'You let him leave?' Mitzi's loud expression of disbelief made the diners on the next table turn and stare. She pulled out a chair and dropped into it, surprising Lily as the chef must be busy with breakfast service. 'You're a fool.'

'Excuse me?' Had no one informed Mitzi that English people were supposed to be reticent and polite, never discussing anything personal until you'd known them for decades?

'A blind person could see you two love each

other, so what's the problem?' Mitzi stated bluntly, pouring herself a cup of tea from the pot and adding multiple spoons of sugar and a huge slug of milk. 'Go ahead and tell me it's not my business.'

'Even if I do, it won't stop you, will it?' Lily said with a huge blast of irony.

'No. Outside of my staff I don't care for most people. My family are a bunch of stiffs, and I don't have many friends,' Mitzi stated plainly. 'I took to you last night, after I got past the bubblegum look, of course.'

'I'm not surprised you have problems getting along with folks,' Lily retorted. 'What've I done to deserve your—'

'Interference? By being an interesting person. You've a strong sense of self and I relate to that big time. I don't have much time for men as a rule. In my experience they hold women back.'

Lily had thought the same thing herself until she met Kenan.

Before she realised what she was doing, Lily opened her mouth and out poured the whole, sorry tale. As soon as she finished, Mitzi kept her response to one choice epithet, earning them another disgusted look from their neighbouring diners.

'So, what're you going to do about him?' Mitzi probed.

There was no one else to confide in and if she didn't run her ideas by someone she'd go mad.

Lily sucked in a deep breath and told Mitzi everything she'd thought of.

'Not bad, but how about this.' Mitzi tossed in a few thoughts of her own and leaned back in her chair with a sly grin on her face, staring Lily down.

'You're a genius.' Lily leaned across the table and hugged the other chef.

That was too much for the offended customers who stalked out muttering about how they'd make sure other people heard about this.

'Oh hell, I'm sorry,' Lily apologised. 'I forget I'm not back in the South where you're allowed to initiate physical contact with strangers without being thought weird.'

'Don't worry.' Mitzi grinned. 'Outside of the kitchen my reputation is pretty much in the dirt anyway, thanks to my dear family. I'll live. I've plenty of other customers who'd kill for a reservation here.'

'You've been great. I'd better get going now. My train to Wales leaves in an hour and I've still got to pack.' Lily screwed up her face.

'I bet Mr Efficient usually does all that, right?' Mitzi teased and Lily could only nod. 'Another reason to get him back. Off you go and keep me updated. If there's anything I can do to speed things along let me know.'

'Thanks. When I return to Nashville I'll get the programme details sorted out.'

'Everything will fall into place if you're smart and get your priorities sorted.' Mitzi pushed the chair back and leapt up. 'Remember what I said.' She strode away in the direction of the kitchen and Lily could only stare at her retreating back.

You can do this, Lily Redman. Get your ass in gear and get busy. There's no time to waste. Kenan Rowse isn't the only one who can plan and execute a military campaign.

She was ready for battle and he'd better watch out.

CHAPTER 27

'Darn it, Mary-Beth, why the devil didn't you call me first?' Lily would cheerfully swat her assistant around the room if the woman wasn't four thousand miles away in Nashville. 'Since when do you take orders from my mother?'

'Don't get at me, hon. You're the one a gazillion time zones away and never available. How was I supposed to know it wasn't a genuine email?' she protested.

'Uh, maybe because we know my mother's a technical illiterate.' Tricia Redman wouldn't recognise a computer or smartphone if she fell over it.

'I guessed she'd got someone else to send it. I'll change your plane reservation back again, it's not a big deal,' Mary-Beth assured her.

'Yeah, but it'll cost me a fortune. You knew I planned to come back in a couple of weeks, not two days.' Lily wasn't about to let this go easily.

'I guessed you'd changed your mind and hadn't got around to telling me.'

'Maybe someone's hacked into my email?' Lily ventured.

Mary-Beth laughed. 'You're gettin' paranoid. Check with your mother before you jump to conclusions.'

'I will, but I know what her answer will be before I call.' Lily couldn't believe she'd forgotten the errant phone call in Edinburgh and the odd email in Keswick. A sudden chill ran through her. 'I don't suppose you've heard from Patrick O'Brian?'

'No, why'd you ask?' Mary-Beth replied a shade too fast for Lily's suspicious mind. She'd come upon the two of them laughing and gossiping more than once and he was an expert at covering his bases. The name Lucinda Trecastani popped into her brain. She was the gorgeous Italian chef who had preceded Lily in Patrick's fickle affections and fell from grace after he metaphorically stuck the knife in. He would have no qualms in destroying Lily too. From his point of view, he made her so she was his to tear down again.

'I'm just curious.' She'd keep her ideas to herself for now. 'Go ahead and change my ticket back to the original date.'

'Are you goin' to be done by then?'

'Yeah, one way or the other,' Lily murmured.

'What do you mean?'

No way was Lily answering that ticking bombshell of a question. 'Nothing much. See you soon and thanks for keeping things going.'

'You're welcome.'

Lily turned her phone off and stared out of the grimy train window. She barely registered the beautiful countryside they were going past because her mind was zipping in tortured circles between her various problems. This wasn't getting her anywhere. Lily pulled out her iPad and started to re-read her research on her potential Welsh addition to *Celebrity Chef Swap*.

Aled Gruffydd was apparently the young darling of the progressive food movement in Wales, with an ego to match. She studied his publicity picture and decided he'd be perfect for the cover of any glamorous men's fashion magazine. His designer black shirt and skinny jeans, long black ponytail draped over one shoulder, piercing amber eyes and chalk-pale skin all drew the camera's attention. Being the combination of a superb cook and an interesting personality were her criteria, so in less than two hours she'd size him up for herself.

Lily stopped reading and snuggled into the corner of the seat, forcing her eyes to close. A vivid picture of Kenan, staring adoringly down at her in bed filled her vision. Mitzi's last order thumped in her head. *Priorities*.

'Daddy.' Mandy flung herself at Kenan, wrapping her skinny arms around his neck. 'I was afraid you wouldn't find me.' She sobbed into his shirt.

'I'll always find you, sweetheart, I promise.' It had been an uphill battle to get her to trust him, but it was the only thing that mattered. 'Mummy and I will get everything sorted today and then we'll go back to Cornwall.' Not many fathers got a second chance so it was up to him not to blow it.

'Good.' Mandy snuggled into his chest. 'Yesterday Aunt Jane was going to paint my nails green and Granny was making pasties for tea, but Mummy made me come back here and I don't like it.' She glared at Olivia who paled under her make-up.

Kenan felt unexpectedly sorry for his ex-wife. She loved Mandy in her own way but wasn't naturally maternal. He was pleased to see Cunningham take hold of Olivia's hand.

'I want to swim in the sea like you promised,' Mandy insisted.

'We will, but it'll be cold and you'll scream,' he teased.

'I don't care. All the children who live there swim in the sea and I will too,' she stated with determination. 'I want Miss Lily to come with us too. She's fun and she knows girl things.'

The words cut through him and Kenan was at a loss how to reply. 'We'll see,' he prevaricated.

'Daddy, she has to.' Mandy's big blue eyes shone with tears.

This wasn't the time or place to attempt an explanation. 'Leave it for now, poppet.' He pointed to the table. 'How about some breakfast? I bet you're starving.'

'I will if you do.' Mandy pouted.

Kenan met Olivia's amused eyes and they shared a smile for the first time in years. She clearly remembered his dislike of solid food before lunchtime. It eased something inside him as he remembered that there had been something good between them once, but it had been forgotten among all the bitterness.

He met Mandy's challenging stare. 'That's a deal. How about you get me a plateful?' She jumped right up and Kenan's stomach roiled as she put two fried eggs, bacon, sausage and mushrooms on a large plate, sliding it in his direction.

'You have to have toast too, Daddy.' Mandy tossed two pieces on the plate. 'There's the butter and marmalade.' She pointed to the offending articles and he dredged up a nod.

'Coffee, sir?' Mowbray appeared at Kenan's shoulder with the only welcome item.

Kenan stuck his fork in one of the eggs and watched the runny liquid ooze out. He cut a piece, sandwiching it between two bites of sausage in the hope it would help it slide down. Kenan swallowed without chewing. 'Yum. Thanks, sweetheart.' He began to shovel the rest down as fast as possible.

'Mummy tells me to put my knife and fork down between bites and chew properly. If not you'll get sick, Daddy.'

'Your Mummy's right.' He plastered on a smile. 'Daddy was too hungry to remember his manners.' Kenan cut a piece of bacon and proceeded to chew it very slowly, the fat sticking to the roof of his mouth.

'I'm sure he won't make the same mistake again, Amanda.' Kenan met Cunningham's laughing eyes and knew he'd been well and truly outed to everyone except his oblivious daughter.

'I certainly won't,' Kenan asserted, meaning a lot more than his table manners.

The atmosphere relaxed and everyone else began to eat too. Olivia ignored the generous breakfast and nibbled at a dry slice of toast while she sipped on her standard hot water with lemon. Her obsessive dedication to maintaining the perfect figure had caused many of their arguments, but now he saw it more objectively. Olivia wasn't particularly smart or career-minded, but what she did have were her looks and poise and time marched on for everyone.

'Worseley, my solicitor, will be here at ten,' Cunningham said, interrupting Kenan's musings. 'When you're ready to leave afterwards just let me know. My chauffeur is on standby to drive you back to Cornwall.'

'We couldn't possibly—'

'Yes, you can, Captain Rowse. You'll allow me to do this. If nothing else it will reassure Olivia.' He fixed his fiancée with a hard stare.

Kenan suppressed a chuckle as she rushed to agree. She'd met her match too. *Too?* His relationship with Lily was over. Over. He watched Mandy laughing and eating up and knew he'd made the right choice. The empty place in his heart would close up eventually. Last week Pete asked him to consider taking a job as Burton's Financial Officer. It would be a good, steady position doing work he'd enjoy. He would accept the offer and concentrate on being a good father. It would be enough.

'Thank you. I won't be ungracious.' Kenan hoped he didn't sound grudging. This couldn't be easy for the other man.

'Mandy, can I borrow your Daddy for a while? We've got some work to do,' Cunningham asked kindly. Kenan glanced down at the remaining food on his plate and could have hugged the man for rescuing him. He pushed back his chair and followed his host out of the room.

'Sorry to deprive you of the last bites of cold, greasy food. I could get Mowbray to bring in your plate if you like,' Cunningham said in jest, as they entered his study.

'Very funny. You can stick that idea where the sun doesn't shine . . . your Lordship.' Kenan grinned.

'Only trying to be hospitable.'

'Oh, you're that all right,' Kenan responded, but fell silent, suddenly feeling awkward. He cleared his throat and stood, feet spread, bracing himself. 'I appreciate all you're doing. Not many men would be as generous.'

'I love Olivia. I see her faults, but I've plenty myself. I'm older, set in my ways and seen a damn sight too much – you know how it goes. I would've welcomed Amanda to be a bigger part of our life but . . .' He exhaled heavily. 'Olivia doesn't want any more children and I can live with that.'

His calm acceptance was surprising. 'Don't you

need an heir for all this?' Kenan waved around the room.

Cunningham shrugged. 'Oh, it'll go to my cousin. You've seen war, Rowse, you know family is all that really matters in the end. Olivia's good company and I'm tired of being lonely. Children grow up and leave, after all. That's life.'

His cool logic made Kenan wince. He couldn't think ten years down the road – couldn't imagine sending Mandy off to university or walking her down the aisle to another man. He would still only be in his mid-forties himself. It would be time enough for him then. Not with Lily of course – but as Cunningham said – life happens.

'Sit down and we'll hash this out before Worseley arrives.'

Kenan followed orders, pushing the rest away before it drove him mad.

By the time they'd finished with the solicitor and had an early lunch, it was time to leave.

'Daddy, will everyone still be awake when we get there?' Mandy bounced up and down in the car as Kenan fastened her seat belt.

'Yes, sweetheart. It's one o'clock now and if we don't stop too many times we'll be there by about six. Granny's making the pasty you missed and Aunt Jane promises to do your nails first thing in the morning.'

Her eyes sparkled and she smacked a big, wet kiss on his cheek. 'You're the best, Daddy.'

I'm trying. 'No, you are, the best little girl ever.'

Kenan slid into the seat next to her and wrapped his arm around her bony shoulders. 'Jenkins, we'll get going if you're ready.'

'Certainly, sir.' The chauffeur nodded. 'Time to get this princess home again.' He winked at Mandy in the rear-view mirror and she beamed right back.

Things would all seem different once they were in Cornwall again. It had been his refuge after Afghanistan and would be so again now. Kenan had to believe he was right.

CHAPTER 28

'I can't meet you,' Olivia declared and her curt dismissal made Patrick's temper run hot and furious.

'It wasn't a question, sweetheart. Be at the coffee shop in ten minutes or His Lordship will get a very revealing phone call.' He hung up. Patrick had taken a trip to Lilac Gardens earlier to check out what Olivia was up to and he didn't care for what he'd seen – Kenan Rowse and the child leaving by chauffeur-driven car.

He grabbed his keys and wallet and headed out of the hotel. He walked briskly along the road and dived into the cafe to select a table before she arrived.

Ten minutes later Olivia swept in, turning heads even in a room full of elegant women. He didn't stand or pull out a seat for her and caught a flicker of disapproval in her cool eyes. He ordered two coffees.

'What do you want now? I've nearly wrecked my future thanks to you.' Her snooty tone set his teeth on edge.

'I'd like an explanation for why you've allowed your thug of an ex-husband to get his kid back?'

A tinge of colour heightened her fair skin and her fingers toyed with the edges of the tablecloth. 'I had no choice. Last night I was in the bathroom and Henry picked up my phone when one of your texts came in. He asked some pertinent questions and I was forced to admit some things I'd rather have kept to myself.'

Patrick glared. 'Exactly what did you tell him?'

'Who you are and your connection to Kenan. He was very displeased and—'

Patrick seized her wrist and gave it a subtle twist. 'What else? I'll find out one way or another.'

She sighed but did not reply until after the waitress had set down two coffees. 'He guessed we had slept together, and it took all my . . . charm to persuade him not to break our engagement.' Olivia picked up her cup of coffee, the slight tremble in her hand betraying her nervousness. Her voice dropped to a whisper. 'He said Amanda deserved better and I was to go back to the recent agreement I made with Kenan or we were through.'

Patrick's brain raced. 'You blew it, but I guess I can make this work. Your heroic ex is bound to be noble and dump Lily in order to put his daughter first. She'll be desperate to throw herself back into her work and I'll be waiting to fill the gap in her life.'

'What on earth do you see in the dreadful woman?' Olivia asked with a sneer.

She didn't have a damn clue and he needed to keep it that way. He was up to his neck in debt and had to get *Luscious Lily* back under his control soon.

'It's money, isn't it?' Olivia's haughty drawl made his flesh creep. 'That's what all this is about – plus your ego. God, you men are all the same.' She stood and tossed some money on the table. 'That's for my coffee. Don't contact me again.'

Patrick glared. 'Don't you dare threaten me, sweetheart. Photos all over the internet might be more than your precious fiancé can stomach.' He scrolled through his phone and shoved it in her face. Olivia blanched and he couldn't help laughing. 'Not suitable behaviour for the would-be Lady Cunningham, is it? If I need any more help from you I'll expect instant agreement, got that, honey?'

Olivia gave a curt nod and walked away from him. The pretty, young waitress caught his eye and headed over with a coffeepot in her hands. The hotel room was his until tomorrow so he might as well make good use of it. Then he'd head back to dreary Cornwall to plot his next move.

Lily sipped an excellent glass of Chardonnay and watched the man she hoped would be her last acquisition. Aled Gruffydd couldn't be more perfect if she'd created him herself.

Sharp, young and hip he exuded confidence and cooked the kind of food she'd never get Kenan to appreciate in a million years. Her Southern roots would never quite get the flamboyantly staged plates and edge pushing recipes that had made Gruffydd and The Tiger Cage famous. The language barrier would be an interesting twist wherever she put him. Lily barely understood a word of his heavy Welsh accent but was too fascinated by him to care.

She'd hate to have her kitchen open to scrutiny while she was cooking but he worked the sprawling open plan space like an Oscar winning actor. Lily ran her hand over the long narrow stainless steel bar topped with dark Welsh slate and the only thing separating the kitchen from the restaurant. Aled continually interacted with customers and she knew without doubt he'd be a big hit on the show. Heck, she'd use subtitles if necessary.

While she waited for him to join her to settle a few last details of their agreement, Lily refused to think about returning alone to her hotel. It had been tough dealing with her luggage on the train but once she'd got a taxi to Cardiff Bay she'd settled down. Naturally Kenan had found her a perfect place to stay in the amazing waterfront area, a regeneration of the old Tiger Bay docklands. It was a small boutique hotel run by a friendly local couple who were excellent chefs in their own right. Lily was already looking forward to breakfast. They'd promised her it would include laverbread, a seaweed based dish that she'd never tried before, and Penclawdd cockles.

'Cardiff Bay Red Mullet with a touch of cumin,

orange and tarragon. Specialty of the house. For a beautiful lady.'

Lily smiled as Aled placed the octagonal black stone plate in front of her with a flourish. The only reason that she had guessed most of what he said this time was because he'd handed her a copy of the menu he intended serving earlier.

'Have you time to join me for a few moments?' she asked.

'Of course.' He shouted something back over his shoulder in the direction of the kitchen and a loud conversation batted back and forth before he turned back to her with a broad smile. 'Eat.'

She picked up her knife and fork and took a bite. Aled might go for show but the man damn well knew how to cook. Lily couldn't wipe the smile from her face as she carried on eating. Her notes could wait until later.

'You know it's exceptional, don't you?' she said, and he gave a sharp nod. Lily launched into a quick rundown of the last few details and held out her hand. 'Do we have a deal?'

He shook it and grinned. 'Who are you going to swap me with?'

'It's not carved in stone yet but I'm thinkin' Billy-Bob Crockett, my third generation Texas barbeque pitmaster. Billy-Bob considers adding paprika to his potato salad taking a risk and his kitchen is in a double-wide trailer with picnic benches outside for his customers.' Lily thought

Aled paled under his already chalk-white skin. 'It'll be a challenge for both of you.'

'You'd better join me in a glass of finest Penderyn whisky,' Aled declared.

Lily was happy to celebrate, but without Kenan here by her side her enthusiasm felt forced. Aled Gruffydd completed her slate of chefs from this side of the pond. She now had six interesting characters to match up and swap with their American counterparts, all of whom would make for entertaining television.

As soon as she could Lily left Aled to his work and returned to her hotel.

In her room Lily immediately got out her phone, her head reverberating with Mitzi's words. If she followed this project all the way through she'd have no time to cook and none to consider Kenan's place in her life. What she was about to say might well be reported right back to Patrick but she didn't care anymore.

'Mary-Beth, glad I caught you. I need a favour. Can you get me phone numbers for Gus, Marianna and Sean please and then call me back.' Her fellow Cooking Network stars would fight over this opportunity and she was ready to let them.

'Why do you need them? Is it anything I can deal with?' her assistant probed.

'I'm considering taking a step back on *Celebrity Chef Swap*. I'd still be a consultant to steer the direction of the project, but I'm thinking of getting someone else to actually headline the show. I thought I'd sound them all out.' The idea she'd been mulling around for days finally emerged.

'Are you mad? We've worked on this solidly for the last six months. I don't get it?'

'Mary-Beth, what do I love doing above anything else?' She'd love to convince her assistant, but didn't have high hopes.

'Cooking, but what's that got to do with it?' Mary-Beth snapped.

'If I do this it'll leave me no time to cook and that doesn't make me happy.'

'Happy?' Mary-Beth scoffed. 'This will solidify you as a household name plus make you a bunch of money. You telling me that's not important?' Her disbelief was absolute.

An unexpected lightness flooded through Lily's system. 'No, it's not. I never set out to be a celebrity chef. It was all Patrick's idea and I got caught up in his vision. All I've ever wanted is for people to enjoy my cooking.'

'Boy, you've changed your tune,' Mary-Beth exclaimed.

Lily understood her bitterness. Her assistant had hooked her star to Lily believing she would be pulled along in her wake.

'Of course I'll do what you ask, but I think you're stark, raving crazy. Tons of chefs would give their eye teeth for your good fortune.'

'I know, but it's not for me and I'm sorry if you feel I've let you down,' Lily apologised.

'You have,' Mary-Beth's reply was blunt and uncompromising. 'I'll get you the phone numbers as soon as possible. Bye.'

Lily set her phone down and had a brief flash of panic. She conjured up pictures of Kenan and her kitchen and smiled. She *would* make this work. She typed in a text message and hit the Send button. Lily needed an ally and hopefully she'd picked the right person.

CHAPTER 29

'Welcome aboard, mate.' Pete pumped Kenan's hand vigorously, a massive smile spreading over his genial face. 'This deserves a drink.' He strode across to the fridge and grabbed a couple of beers. 'Get that down you.'

Kenan popped open the bottle and took a long, deep swallow. 'Cheers.'

'Here's to a long partnership.' Pete raised his own bottle and nodded in his direction.

'Evelyn's good with this, I guess?' Kenan asked.

Pete wiped the froth off his mouth and grinned. 'Come on, mate, do you honestly think this would've gone past drunken speculation on my part without her approval? Get real.'

'What are you two reprobates up to now?' Evelyn stepped into the kitchen and changed her muddy boots for a pair of flat shoes. 'I can't trust you for a minute. It's ten o'clock in the morning. You should be working instead of drinking.'

Kenan lowered his glass to the table.

'I'm joking, you idiot,' she teased. 'I thought Lily revived your sense of humour.'

He struggled to drag up a smile but knew it was an abject failure.

'I assume you've signed on the dotted line and are now part of Burton's?' Evelyn asked.

'Yes, and I'm grateful for the—'

Evelyn shushed him. 'We're the grateful ones, Kenan. We need your expertise and we'd rather work with a friend.' She gave him a shrewd look. 'We've another idea too. If you don't like it we won't be offended, but you said you needed a place for you and Mandy to live and we might have a solution.'

'I haven't really thought it through yet.'

'Well, we have,' Evelyn stated bluntly. 'My mother's old cottage next door is vacant. One of the workers lived there for a while, but he's bought a place over in Gorran and I hate to see it gathering dust.'

'I don't need—'

'Charity?' she scoffed. 'Don't insult us, please. We've got an empty house to rent and you're looking for somewhere to live. It's a business prop-osition – plain and simple.'

Kenan bit his tongue and prepared to grovel, something he'd made a habit of recently. 'Sorry, both of you. I'm too prickly, I know.'

'If you like we can go over and take a look, if you're interested?' Evelyn asked, back to her usual easy warmth.

'That'd be good.' Kenan quickly finished off his beer.

'I'd better go and get today's orders out or our

new Financial Officer will have me on the carpet,' Pete joked.

'About time you did some work and . . . thanks.' Kenan's throat tightened and he couldn't say any more.

'No problem. See you later.' Pete grabbed Evelyn for a quick kiss, making her blush, and hurried off outside.

Kenan hated envying his friends, but their obvious, easy love sent a shaft of loneliness slicing through him. Lily had offered him all that on a plate and he'd turned her down, unable to see past the multitude of obstacles in the way.

'Penny for them.' Evelyn's quiet words startled him back to reality.

'They're not worth it, trust me.' He pulled himself together. 'Right, let's see this cottage.'

Evelyn scrutinised him with her bright blue eyes, then turned and led the way out of the farmhouse. 'Another plus, if you take it, is that one of us is usually around if you need an eye kept on Mandy. I'd enjoy spending time with her.'

Kenan caught the edge of wistfulness in her voice. After a few drinks one night Pete had confided how they couldn't have children and that it had almost broken their marriage apart. Everyone had their sorrows. Some hid it better than others is all.

'That'd be a great help,' he replied. 'It's easy now being there with Mum and Dad, but we need our own place.' He frowned and went silent.

'You aren't doing this alone, you know. Just

because you'll live under a different roof doesn't mean your family won't be there for you and we'll do anything we can to make it easier.' She cleared her throat. 'Single parenting is tough, but so are you.'

'Am I? I'm not so sure any more.' The words slipped out before he could stop them. He hadn't been tough the morning he had left Lily. Kenan had bawled his eyes out in the car like a baby.

'Is she coming back?'

Kenan didn't need to ask who they were discussing. 'She'll have to get her things from Betty's, but apart from that . . . no.'

'You want to talk about it?' Evelyn asked, then broke into a raspy laugh. 'Oh, I forgot, you're a man and men don't do such girly things. You're a dolt like Pete. Keep it all in and let it eat away at you.'

He could've told her about Pete's drunken revelations, but held his tongue. 'That's right, but you love us anyway.' Kenan tried to turn it into a joke but by the pity written all over her face, it was another miserable failure.

'Here's the key.' She stopped outside the first building they came to. 'Why don't you have a poke around by yourself and come back to tell me what you think afterwards? I need to check on lunch.'

'Thanks.' He let her go and stood outside the small, solid granite cottage for a moment and admired its traditional design and the fresh white paint gleaming in the sunlight. Turning the key in the lock, Kenan stepped inside and immediately something odd happened. He wasn't a fanciful man, far from it, and he'd never admit this to another soul, but the house welcomed him. The closest to peace he'd experienced in years settled around him.

He remembered Pete doing extensive renovations when Evelyn's mother came to live there, although she hadn't got to enjoy them for long. He'd knocked the two small downstairs rooms together into one comfortable living/dining area. The compact kitchen would work as long as they didn't do any cat swinging, and the new downstairs toilet tucked in under the stairs was a welcome bonus. Kenan's hand rested on the oak banister, smoothing the old wood, and then he slowly climbed the narrow stairs. He checked out the smaller bedroom first, deciding the blue paint could easily be changed to pink, Mandy's new favourite colour. Opening the larger room his gaze landed on the large brass-framed bed, covered with a softly worn quilt and stacked with pillows. It was a bed made for a loving couple and he swallowed hard.

Kenan retreated, slamming the door shut behind him and had a quick look in the neat, modern bathroom across the landing. He leaned against the door frame and closed his eyes for a few seconds. A worthwhile new job and a house to share with his daughter. Lucky, he was very lucky. He shook off the lingering sadness and headed back downstairs.

Before he could think too much, Kenan strode

briskly across the yard and into the farmhouse. 'It's perfect.' The words died in his throat and he barely managed to save himself from stumbling over the doormat.

'Look who's turned up. I swear the woman smells good food cooking a mile off,' Evelyn joked, as she pulled a steaming dish from the oven and set it on the counter.

'Hi, Kenan.'

Lily's soft, sultry voice wrapped around him and Kenan drank in the sight of her, totally poleaxed. There was no hiding behind *Luscious Lily* today. No glittery tight pink outfit melded her curves, instead a loose white shirt and pale blue drawstring trousers only hinted at what lay beneath. With no make-up and her hair drawn back into a loose ponytail, the natural beauty he'd always seen shone through.

'Kenan, go over to the shed and tell Pete to get a move on. If my lasagne gets cold and gluey I won't be a happy woman.' Evelyn pushed at his arm.

He turned to leave but as he reached the door he stupidly turned around.

Lily's sapphire eyes bored right through him, her lush mouth curved with amusement, and challenge written all across her gorgeous face.

He jerked his gaze away and ran from the house.

Lily sat down in the nearest chair. 'That didn't go as I expected.'

Evelyn grabbed a handful of cutlery from the drawer and started to lay the table. 'Did you really think he'd throw himself at your feet and declare undying love?'

Her candid words hit home.

'Just changing your appearance isn't going to do the trick. You need to pull in the big guns.'

'What do you mean?' Lily asked.

'Who means the absolute most to Kenan – apart from you?'

'Mandy, I guess, but I can hardly use a child.' Lily wanted Kenan, but not enough to take advantage of his daughter.

Evelyn piled the plates in front of her at the table, ready to dish up the lunch, and moved four glasses into place, going over to the sink and filling up a water jug. Finally she turned back around and fixed Lily with a pitying stare. 'Do you want him or not?'

'Of course I do. I wouldn't be here making a fool of myself otherwise,' Lily declared with vehemence. 'I've taken a risk no sane woman would – so I'd go with a yeah on that.'

'You might have to play dirty.' Evelyn gave her a thoughtful look. 'That's what I had to do with Pete.'

'I thought you were childhood sweethearts?'

Evelyn threw her a withering glance. 'He was mine, but it wasn't reciprocated. I was always good old Evelyn, his best friend and indistinguishable from his male friends. I could drink him under the table and plough a field in half the time. It wasn't a recipe for romance.'

Lily gawped, hardly able to believe what she was hearing.

'By the time Pete was eighteen he had put the moves on all my friends and come whining to me every time when none of them worked out.' Evelyn reached for the bread knife and sliced a freshly made baguette into neat slices, tossing them into a wicker basket. 'You know what his weakness was?' She didn't wait for an answer. 'His mother. In the nicest possible way Pete is, and always has been, a mother's boy.'

'What did you do?' Lily found her voice again.

'I made her my friend, baked her favourite coffee and walnut cake and we went shopping together. Every time Pete turned around I was at the house. She wasn't stupid and knew exactly what I was doing, but she approved and went along with my scheme.' Evelyn's smug smile amused Lily.

'I assume it worked.'

'Oh yes. When he needed a date for the Young Farmer's Christmas dance his mother suggested he take me. She steamrollered over his objections and he gave in to please her.' Evelyn's misty gaze hinted that she'd drifted back in time to be that young girl again.

'But how did you get him to see you differently?' That was the root of Lily's problem.

'A certain red silk dress, stilettos and killer perfume helped. Along with the slugs of whisky I kept adding to his beer when he wasn't looking. By the time I suggested going outside for some fresh air he didn't stand a chance. One devastating kiss up against the barn wall when I let him discover the fact I was wearing stockings and he was toast.' Evelyn's smile cracked wide open.

'But as *Luscious Lily* I have already tapped in to Kenan's baser instincts so I don't see that's going to work for me?'

'Flip it around, Lily. He needs to see you as a nurturing, gentle woman. I'm not saying get rid of the sex kitten – there's definitely a place for her, but everyone doesn't need to see her. Keep her for the two of you.'

Lily realised the plain spoken Englishwoman made complete sense. She wasn't *Luscious Lily* deep down, but she'd become her 24/7. 'I think Mandy likes me.'

'I'm certain she does,' Evelyn agreed. 'She chattered about you non-stop when I saw her last week. I'm not telling you to use her, but be her friend.' She grinned. 'Be that to Kenan, too. Nothing more and it'll drive him mad.'

Lily wasn't totally convinced but she'd run out of options and time was ticking away. 'All right, I'll give it a try. I've nothing to lose.' Tears pressed at her eyes.

'They're on their way. Buck up and put on a smile.' Evelyn straightened down her T-shirt and quickly ran a hand over her short, honey-brown hair.

Pete stomped in, pulled off his muddy boots and headed for the sink. Turning on the tap he began to methodically wash his hands, soaping them well and scrubbing his nails with a small brush.

'Where's Kenan?' Evelyn asked.

'Gone home. Said to give you his apologies, but he promised Mandy he'd be home for lunch.' Pete grabbed a towel and dried off his hands. 'Lasagne?' He sniffed appreciatively.

Despite everything Lily smiled, this was the simple joy of cooking, giving pleasure to other people.

'Yes, sit down, it's ready.' Evelyn slammed the dish onto a trivet and sat, raising her eyebrows at Lily.

Lily wasn't sorry Kenan had chickened out because she was feeling pretty chicken herself at the moment. Facing him again would hopefully be easier when she'd got her act together.

'I just need to make a quick phone call while you dish up, Evelyn. I'm starving and this smells delicious,' Lily said, flashing a brilliant smile and dipping back into her alter ego one last time.

CHAPTER 30

Kenan staggered against the gate under the force of Mandy's cannonball run straight at his legs.

'Daddy!' She flung her arms around his waist, jumping up and down on the tops of his feet. 'Guess what?'

He swung her up to him, smelling her special little girl scent and kicking himself yet again for missing so much of her life.

'Miss Lily's taking me to the beach tomorrow. We're going to swim and eat ice cream and—'

'I'm not sure that's a good idea.' Kenan eased back and frowned. A very Olivia-like coolness swept over Mandy's face and she wriggled out of his embrace, standing and glaring at him with her hands placed strategically on her hips.

'Why not? She's my friend. Granny said it'd be all right.'

He bit back a curse. He'd have to speak to his mother and, nicely, make it clear who was the parent. 'All right. You can go, but another time you have to ask me first. I'm responsible for you when you're not with Mummy.'

'Yes, Daddy.' Her instant agreement made him suspicious. Women did this to him all the time and then proceeded to go their own way.

'Let's go inside. I've got some exciting news, too.'

'Okay, I'll beat you. Granny Eileen's got chicken nuggets and salad ready for lunch.' Mandy took off racing up the path and Kenan followed, already grouchy about the thought of having to see Lily again tomorrow.

Around the kitchen table he munched away at the salad in front of him and mentally thanked Olivia. Kenan hadn't realised how much Mandy's loss had meant to his parents, as well as to himself, until now. Seeing them laughing and fussing over the little girl and the joy she got out of being with them was incredible. He laid down his knife and fork.

'I've something to tell you all.' A sly smile creased his mother's face and he guessed the unfortunate way her mind was going. *Sorry, Mum. No wedding bells.* 'You're looking at the new Financial Officer at Burton's. Pete and Evelyn offered me the job last week and I've decided to take it.' He smiled at Mandy. 'And guess what, poppet, you and Daddy are going to have a house of our own. It's a lovely cottage right next to Miss Evelyn and Mr Pete's farmhouse.'

She stopped with a chicken nugget halfway to her mouth and frowned at him. 'I don't want another new house. I like it here. I'm not going,'

Mandy declared and carried on eating as though that was decided.

Kenan caught his mother's eye. He needed her to help him convince Mandy this was a good thing even though he knew she'd miss having her granddaughter around as much.

'What a lucky girl you are,' Eileen proclaimed with a breezy smile. 'You'll have lots of room to play around the farm, and I bet your Daddy will paint your new bedroom whatever colour you like.'

'Yep, anything,' Kenan quickly agreed. 'I was thinking dark green. It's your favourite, isn't it?' he teased.

'You're silly.' She laughed and then gave him a shrewd look. 'Barbie pink, or I'm not coming.'

If only winning over grown-up women was as simple. Kenan held out his hand. 'Shake on it. We've got a deal.'

'It's not far, Mandy, and we'll still see you lots and lots,' Eileen reassured. 'We'll come to visit you and I'll keep your bedroom here exactly as it is so you can come and stay anytime.'

Kenan smiled at his mother, more grateful than he could say while wishing he didn't have an empty place deep inside of him.

'Mandy, when you're finished eating, would you like to walk into the village with me?' Eileen asked. 'If Daddy says it's all right we could go to the ice cream shop.' She glanced over at him, and Kenan nodded his approval. He could do with some quiet time to process the day.

Mandy shoved the last chicken nugget in her mouth, chewed quickly and swallowed. 'I'm done, Granny.'

In a whirlwind of activity they disappeared leaving Kenan alone with his father, who had been very quiet all the way through lunch.

'What's up, son?' his father asked. 'Are you regretting taking on the Burton's job?'

Kenan shook his head, but couldn't answer.

'The cottage?'

He gave in. 'No. They're both ideal.'

His father's fingers tapped idly on the kitchen table. 'So, you going to tell me or do I have to drag it out of you?'

'Take a wild guess. What's always the root of any man's problems?' Kenan didn't bother to hide his bitterness. 'Bloody women.'

'Taking a wild guess, I'd say you mean one in particular?'

'You're good. Ever thought of going in for mind-reading?' His sarcasm made his father laugh out loud. 'Thanks a bunch. I'm glad I opened up to you.'

'You didn't, boy, it's written all over your pitiful face. I hoped one day you'd find the one who'd do this to you. Olivia never did and, take my word for it, it's the only thing worth having. Family is everything. Without your mother I'd be a sorry creature.'

Kenan kept up his moody silence, but his father rattled on, telling him nothing he didn't already know. Blah. Blah. A great marriage. Best friends. Partners in life. He wasn't dumb. He got it, but it wasn't that simple.

'You think I don't understand, but it's not easy for anyone, son. Your mother gave me the run-around too, but she was worth it so I hung in there.'

He'd heard the story millions of times before, how she had been engaged to someone else and teased his father for ages before admitting she'd never intended to marry the other poor devil, but wanted him all along.

'It's more complicated with us,' Kenan insisted.

'If you want it enough all the obstacles fall away.'

'Yeah, right.' He slumped forward, cradling his head in his hands and wishing his father would just go away.

'All right, I'll give in and let you wallow in self-pity.' He pushed back the chair and stood up, resting a hand on Kenan's shoulder.

'Sorry, Dad.' He hadn't felt this much of a heel since . . . he dumped Lily. 'Mandy's got to be my priority. There'll be time for the rest later.'

'You know better than that. Is tomorrow a guarantee?' he persisted.

'No, but Mandy needs my full attention. I neglected her for far too long and I'm not letting her down again.' Kenan stubbornly clung on to the only constant in this whole mess.

His father held up his hands. 'Okay, son. I'll back off, for now.'

'Thanks.'

Over at the door, William hesitated. 'Don't wait too long, that's the last I'm saying.' He strode away before Kenan could think up a smart reply.

There wasn't one anyway.

Lily's heart raced as she sensed Kenan enter the room but she kept her attention fixed on Mandy. 'Sweetheart, go and get your swimming things and I'll check everything's okay with your Dad before we leave.'

'Two minutes. I'll only be two minutes,' Mandy declared and raced off.

Lily slowly stood up, smoothed down her cheery yellow sundress and slowly turned around.

The sight of Kenan with his hair still damp from a shower, smart as ever in dark dress trousers, a crisp white shirt, grey silk tie, and highly polished black shoes made every cell in her body curl up in protection against his simple, straightforward masculinity.

'This is kind of you,' Kenan stated with no hint of a smile.

'It'll be my pleasure. We'll have fun. I hope you don't mind.' *Tell me you do. Say you want to come with us.* Evelyn would smack her for being such a weak-willed ninny. *Friends. You're supposed to convince him you're a friend. Yeah right.*

'Not at all,' he replied, his face still hard and unrevealing. 'Where are you planning on going?'

'Back to Charlestown, on the bus.'

Kenan nodded. 'I'd like Mandy home no later than four. You have my mobile number?'

It's engraved in my brain. 'Yes.'

'Ring if you have any problems. Anything. Understand?' His eyes darkened to slate-grey.

'Of course.'

'I'll be at work, but I'll drop everything if you need help,' he insisted.

'Work?' *What was he talking about?*

Kenan's rigid features softened. 'I'm the new Financial Officer at Burton's starting today. Pete and Evelyn asked me to join them because they want to grow the business.' He hesitated briefly. 'Mandy and I will be moving into a cottage on the property soon.'

'That's wonderful.' Lily plastered on a bright smile while her heart cracked into tiny pieces. *Why hadn't Evelyn told her any of this?* 'Sounds like you've got it all figured out.' *With no room for me in the plan.* Fleeing on the first plane back to Nashville was a real tempting proposition right now.

Kenan shrugged and slid his glance over to the window. 'Not sure I'd go that far, but it's a start.'

'I'm ready.' Mandy raced back into the room, seizing Lily's hand and pulling hard. 'Come on or we'll miss the bus.'

Lily jerked back to reality and picked up her overstuffed pink bag from the table. 'Sure thing, kiddo. Let's go and have fun. Say goodbye to your daddy and wish him luck with his new job.' She caught Kenan looking at her and held his gaze for several long seconds. 'Don't worry, I'll take good care of her.'

'I know you will or you wouldn't be taking her,' he said, his voice dropping to a soft rumble.

If she didn't get out of here in the next few minutes all her sensible plans would fly out of the window and she'd throw herself at him and kiss him beyond crazy. She ached for the touch of his big, sure hands again all over her.

'Come on, Miss Lily.' Mandy tugged hard on her hand. 'Bye, Daddy, have fun.'

Lily tried not to brush against Kenan as they walked by him, but the scent of the simple, familiar pine soap he always used invaded her senses. *Damn him*.

Outside the front door Lily finally dared to breathe again. Evelyn hadn't warned her how hard this would be. Her new friend rose in her estimation because she'd kept it up for a solid year before Pete cracked. Lily would be carried off in a straightjacket if it took that long.

Kenan leaned against the kitchen cabinet and groaned under his breath. Why didn't she just leave? Go back to Nashville and be *Luscious Lily* again? The new, softer woman, the real Lily, was killing him. The other he could maybe dismiss as sex on legs and getting to him on a purely physical level, but now she was something else and he didn't have a clue how to cope.

'Coffee, sweetheart?' His mother's voice came out of the blue and Kenan straightened back up.

'No, thanks. I'll grab some up at the farm.' He'd concentrate on the task at hand and push Lily back in a locked box in his head.

Kenan grabbed his keys, phone and wallet from the counter, shoved them into his pockets and stalked out from the house.

Ten minutes later he slowed the car down, taking it easy up the gravel road into Burton's. He parked in the courtyard and jumped out, looking all around him. Kenan breathed in the soft air, laced with a mixture of earth and sun and for the first time appreciated his good fortune.

'Hey, mate, isn't this better than working up in the smog of London or being stuck in some damn desert?' Pete strode across the yard and slapped him on the shoulders. 'Boy, you're going to show us all up dressing like that.' He grinned, checking out Kenan. 'Don't feel you have to go with the business attire if you don't want to. We're farmers when all's said and done.'

'You might be, but I'm supposed to be the business end of things. I'll see how it goes. Easy enough to dress down if this puts people off,' Kenan explained.

Pete gave an easy shrug. 'Do what you like, pal.'

Kenan grinned. 'Don't worry, I've got rubber boots and rain gear in the car. You know I'm always prepared.'

'Except when it comes to women,' Pete retorted with a laugh.

'Yeah, well, we've all got our faults.' Kenan managed to laugh back. 'Come on, show me this office so I can get to work.'

'You want breakfast first?'

'Never eat the stuff by choice.' He needed to make it clear so he wouldn't have Evelyn trying to shove bacon and eggs down him every day. 'Does my new digs have a coffee machine?'

'No. I keep a kettle and a box of tea bags there, that's all. Evelyn will fix you a mug in the kitchen.'

'Okay, I'll run over there now and get one, then tomorrow I'll arrange something. If I don't get my caffeine fix first thing, plus regular infusions throughout the day you won't get any decent work out of me.' Kenan chuckled and started to relax. He hadn't looked forward to work in a long time and was ready for the challenge.

'I'll meet you in the trailer.' Pete gestured towards an oversized caravan parked near the distribution shed. 'That's one thing we need to discuss – a proper building.'

'We'll look at the balance sheets first,' Kenan said with a dry tone.

'Oh hell, I've stirred up a hornet's nest hiring you. Evelyn said you'd kick us into shape. The damn woman's always right.'

Most of them are. 'Thought you'd know that after God knows how many years of marriage.'

Pete smirked. 'Fifteen next month. Not bad going.'

'You're a lucky man.' Kenan fought to keep the

envy from his voice. 'I'll get that coffee before my brain cells shrivel up.'

Pete grabbed hold of his arm, not letting him move. 'I know I'm lucky but it takes hard work like everything else. Wouldn't have it any other way though.'

Kenan tried to avoid his friend's piercing stare but failed.

'It's worth it,' Pete declared.

'I'll take your word for it.' He wasn't in the mood for another lecture on his failings where women were concerned so walked away without another word.

CHAPTER 31

By two in the afternoon Lily had a new respect for parents. Who would have thought that taking care of one eight-year-old girl would be harder work than cooking a dinner service for two hundred people? She hadn't relaxed for a second, partly because if she considered the idea she saw Kenan's worried face. The responsibility really was life or death, unlike a fallen soufflé or a burnt chicken.

'I'm starving. Can we have some ice cream please?' Mandy asked, as they walked up the road from the beach.

Lily burst out laughing and ruffled the little girl's hair. 'You must have hollow legs.'

'Don't be silly. They're made of muscles and blood and bones and stuff.' Mandy launched into a far more detailed explanation than Lily needed, the result of a biology lesson she remembered from school.

'I only meant you haven't stopped eating all day.'

'I did when we went in swimming,' Mandy asserted with a smug expression on her face, so like her father's it made Lily choke.

'You win. Let's go to the toilet and wash our hands. We've got half an hour before the bus comes.' Lily prided herself on not saying restroom, she could get the hang of this strange lingo. *Stop it. You aren't going to be here long enough for it to matter.*

'I want a ninety-nine, please.'

Lily stared at the kid. What was she talking about now? 'Even you can't eat that many.'

Mandy threw her a scathing look. 'You are silly sometimes. I suppose you don't have them in America. It's an ice cream with a chocolate flake stuck in the top and it's yummy.'

'Ice cream and chocolate. Sounds good to me, kid. Sign me up. We'll get two of them.' She took a firm hold of Mandy's hand and they walked on. The sun warmed her back and Lily had a memory flash of Kenan hauling her in from the garden, angry and worried about her sunburn.

'Well, look who it isn't. My favourite girl. Lovely day isn't it?'

Lily yanked Mandy close, almost falling over her own feet as she ground to a halt. 'Patrick?' Handsome in crisply ironed khakis and an open-necked blue shirt, he stood smiling at her and totally at ease. 'What on earth are you doing here?'

He removed his sunglasses, immediately piercing her with his startling deep green eyes. 'I told you I wouldn't give up, so I can't believe you're *that* surprised. A little bird passed on some disturbing information to me and I decided another trip to Cornwall was on the cards.'

Something tugged at her hand and Lily suddenly remembered Mandy. 'What is it, sweetheart?'

'I need to pee, you promised me ice cream and if we miss the bus Daddy will be cross,' she said with a pout.

Patrick patted her head and Mandy wriggled away, snuggling closer to Lily and throwing him a typical Kenan glare.

'Why don't you see to this young lady, then we'll have ice cream together and I can give you a lift home?' he suggested.

Not in this lifetime. 'No, thank you. We've made our plans.'

Patrick grasped her arm and Lily bit back a yell. 'I think you'd better change them. We have things to discuss. Business.'

Lily put on a fake smile. 'Why don't you come to my bed and breakfast later? This isn't the time, Patrick.' He still held on, but added one of his charming smiles.

'All right, but you'd better be there. Seven o'clock. That should give you time to fulfil your other obligations.' He glanced dismissively at Mandy.

Lily nodded, hating him more than ever.

'Don't be late and make sure you're alone. No goon this time.' Patrick let go of her, slipped his sunglasses back on and sauntered away.

'Miss Lily. I really need the toilet.' Mandy hopped from one foot to the other. 'Is the nasty man gone?'

She came to her senses. 'Yes, he is, don't worry about him. Come on.'

They headed for the toilets and were soon done and washing their hands. Once Lily had Mandy busy eating ice cream she made a much needed move. 'Let's not say anything about meeting that man, okay? Daddy doesn't like him and we don't want to spoil his first day at work.'

'Okay. I don't like him either.' Mandy wrinkled up her nose. 'Do you?'

'No, I don't.'

They sat on the wall overlooking the harbour and licked their ice creams, but Lily's mind filled with dread about the evening to come.

'Managed not to turn into a boiled lobster this time I see,' Kenan teased, his only defence against Lily standing inches away from him, a vision in something soft, yellow and floaty.

'I'm not a complete moron.' Her cool tone told him she didn't appreciate his attempt at humour.

'Daddy, we had so much fun.' Mandy chattered away.

He swung her up into his arms. 'Good, that's what little girls are supposed to do.' He kissed her warm neck and she giggled, snuggling in closer.

'What about big girls?' Lily's soft drawl ran over him and Kenan blushed to the roots of his hair. 'It's all right, you don't need to answer.'

'I think someone needs a bath to get rid of all the salt water. Why don't you run out to the garden and ask your Granny if she'll help wash your hair?' Kenan suggested, sliding Mandy back down to standing.

'Okay, Daddy.' Mandy turned and threw herself at Lily. 'Are you going to ask Daddy about tomorrow?' she pleaded.

Lily fixed her attention back on him and he couldn't think clearly under the devastating power of her smile.

'Would it be okay if I took Mandy shopping in Truro tomorrow morning? She's grown out of a lot of her summer clothes and after our previous experience I'd say shopping makes you want to spit nails.'

Her laughing eyes drew him in and Kenan plastered his hands against his thighs to stop them from grabbing hold of her beautiful face and kissing her glossy, tempting mouth.

'I suppose it'd be all right,' he grudgingly agreed, wishing she'd just go away and leave them alone.

'Don't be too keen.'

'Sorry, I didn't mean to sound ungrateful.'

The scathing look she sent his way said Lily understood only too well what he'd meant.

'I'd better be going. I'll pick Mandy up at ten. If you don't mind I'll take her for lunch while we're out.'

'Sure, that'd be fine and thanks again for today.' Kenan struggled not to come across as a complete grouch.

'It was my pleasure. Bye.'

Kenan knew she meant every word, which only made him feel worse. 'Bye.'

He didn't walk her to the door but as soon as she left, he strolled over to the window and eased back the corner of the lace curtain. He drank in the sight of her walking down the path, her hips swaying under the gauzy cotton dress and tempting him beyond belief.

At the gate she turned and waved, catching him out, so Kenan gave in and waved back. One point to her.

'Your visitor's here,' Betty's disapproving voice floated upstairs.

Lily rested her shaking hands on the dressing table. She mustn't show any sign of weakness in front of Patrick.

'Coming,' she called back down and headed out of the bedroom before she lost her nerve.

'Good grief, Lily, what's with the hippy look?' Patrick stared up at her from where he stood in the hall. 'Couldn't you have changed? That might be suitable for wearing on the beach with a child, but *I'm* not taking you out looking like a gypsy.' Patrick's sneering gaze skimmed over the bright yellow dress she'd picked up at the Flea Market in Truro.

'For a start it's none of your business what I wear and secondly I don't intend going anywhere with you, so you won't have to be *ashamed* of me in public.' She headed down the stairs and reached the bottom step. She'd already decided to suggest they sit in the garden.

He grabbed her arm. 'Oh, yes, we are going out,' Patrick hissed under his breath. 'I'm not discussing business here with your nosey landlady around. Get your purse and we'll be off if you insist on staying in those drab clothes.'

Lily stood her ground. 'What if I say no?'

'I didn't ask,' he growled. 'We have a table booked at the Water's Edge. It'll give me a chance to check out one of the chefs you've got lined up and see if I approve.'

'I need to go back upstairs for my purse,' Lily said.

'Be quick and don't do anything stupid,' Patrick snarled.

She would have cracked a joke at his attempt to sound like a New York mob boss, but something about his cold demeanour made her hold her tongue.

Turning away from him she walked back up with a studied casualness she certainly didn't feel and headed back to her bedroom. Lily picked up the cheap straw bag she'd bought at the same time as the dress, dug around for her cellphone and sent a short text message. One of her mother's multitude of orders when she was a teenager had stuck with her. *Always let someone know where you're going.*

'Lily, now,' Patrick shouted up and she hurried to join him. It would be unwise to get him any more agitated if she wanted to end their business relationship for good with as little hassle as possible. 'My car's outside.'

'You're driving on these crazy roads? You're braver than I am.' Lily tried to keep it light, but he scowled right back at her.

'Necessity, Lily.'

She didn't ask any more and Patrick took hold of her arm and steered her towards the front door.

'Have a nice time, dears.' Betty breezed out from the kitchen, wiping her flour-covered hands on her apron.

'Thanks.' Lily flashed another fake smile, they were getting to be a specialty of hers. Patrick's hand pushed on her lower back and they walked out together into the evening.

CHAPTER 32

'Daddy, why aren't you and Miss Lily friends anymore?' Mandy interrupted the fifth reading of the new book she'd got in Charlestown.

If it hadn't been for the awkwardness of the question, Kenan wouldn't have been sorry – there was only so much a man could take of a dancing mouse. 'Is that what she said?' He carefully edged his way around the subject, not about to say any more than he had to.

'No, but my friend Tally was all funny with me when she wanted to be friends with Susan instead. She made up excuses not to play and wouldn't hold my hand when we went to lunch,' Mandy declared.

Nailed by his own daughter. How did children reduce everything to the simplest common denominator without even trying?

'Miss Lily's going back to America soon and Daddy's busy with his new job. It's hard to stay friends with someone who lives a long way away.' It was the best explanation he could drag up.

'But she likes Cornwall lots and lots. I bet she'd

stay here if you asked. I'd like that. I need her for girly things when I'm not with Mummy.'

A wry smile tugged at Kenan. If only it was that easy.

'I know she likes you, Daddy, and she doesn't like the nasty man, she told me so. He's got mean eyes.'

What was the kid talking about now? Kenan put the book down.

'Oops.' Mandy's face reddened. 'I'm not supposed to say anything. It's a secret.' Tears pooled in her large, sky-blue eyes. 'I promised.'

Kenan pulled her closer and stroked her hair. 'It's all right. I won't tell.' She must be talking about Patrick O'Brian. 'The nasty man is in America, sweetheart, and when she goes back Miss Lily doesn't have to be his friend if she doesn't want to.'

Mandy opened her mouth then slammed her lips shut again.

A chill ran through Kenan and he picked his next words with care. 'What made you ask about the nasty man, sweetheart?'

'I can't tell you,' she whined, giving him a mutinous stare.

'Can Daddy try to guess?' He didn't get a no so carried on. 'If you nod or shake your head that's different from telling me.' Encouraging his daughter to break a promise because of his own jealousy was unethical, but he justified it in his head by saying he was concerned about Lily. 'Did you see him today?'

Mandy nodded and a knot of anger formed in Kenan's stomach.

'Is Miss Lily meeting him?'

She nodded again, wriggling around and he knew she wanted to talk, but was torn. Kenan waited.

'He told her she had to and she wasn't happy, but she said yes,' Mandy blurted out, slapping a hand across her mouth.

'It's okay. This can be our secret. If we think our friends are unhappy it's our job to help them.'

She frowned, obviously not convinced.

'It's bedtime for little princesses. Lie down and I'll tuck you in.' Kenan laid the book on the table and pulled the covers up around Mandy. He found the worn pink rabbit she never slept without and tucked it in next to her. 'Right, your turn first tonight. Surprise me with one thing I don't know about you.' He loved this part of the day. By pure chance he'd suggested it the first night she arrived, lost and bewildered by her mother leaving and being left with a father she didn't know. Now it had become their ritual.

'Don't tell Mummy, but I broke her nasty blue vase. It was sort of an accident,' Mandy said with a naughty smile.

'Sort of?'

'Mm.' She nibbled at her lip, 'I was running in the house and I'm not supposed to do that. I bumped into the table and it fell over. So, Daddy, I knocked over the table really.'

'And the vase was on the table?' Kenan struggled not to laugh.

'Well, it was, but it was a co . . . co . . . you know when things happen and you can't help it.'

'A coincidence?'

She grinned, lighting up her whole face. 'That's right. Now it's your turn, Daddy.'

Kenan guessed he should tell her off, but would rather cut his heart out. 'Daddy doesn't tell very good jokes. I always forget the punch line – that's the funny bit of the joke.'

Mandy threw her arms around his neck. 'It's okay, Daddy. I love you anyway.'

Every night she brought him close to tears and he swore he'd never take this second chance for granted. He reluctantly gave her a last kiss and got up to leave. 'Good night, sleep tight, don't let the bed bugs bite.' He walked over to the doorway and made sure the soft night light glowed before he turned away to head downstairs.

'Hey, big brother, how's it going?' Jane popped out from her bedroom.

'Pretty good. You fancy a beer?' He didn't want to be alone and brood about Lily.

'You smooth talker. No wonder women fall over themselves around you,' Jane teased, poking his arm. 'All right, you've talked me into it. Let's sit out in the garden. Mum and Dad are watching TV.'

They headed downstairs and poked around in the kitchen, putting together a tray with drinks, cheese and crackers.

'You carry this and I'll go first and turn the lights on,' Jane instructed him and he followed orders.

The dusk settled around them and for a while they didn't talk, enjoying the mild summer air. Kenan stretched out his legs and took a deep swallow of beer. Getting drunk wasn't a bad idea tonight.

'Hey, I got a strange text from Lily just now.' Jane passed over her phone. 'Check that out.'

He scanned the message and cursed.

'Why would she tell *me* where she's going?' Jane smiled mischievously. 'Unless of course she expected me to pass it on to you and make you jealous.' She grinned. 'Succeeded, didn't she?'

'Not at all. She can go out with who she damn well likes. I've got no hold on her.' *Unfortunately.* 'If she's still interested in that brain-dead moron it's her concern, not mine.'

'Who do you think you're fooling?' Jane's raspy laughter made Kenan cringe. 'Not me, that's for sure. You're a dead man where Lily's concerned. Why you just don't admit it and marry the woman. I really don't—'

'That's right, you don't, and it's nothing to do with you. I have my reasons and I'm not discussing them with you or anyone else.' Kenan knocked back the rest of his drink and jumped up to standing, shoving the chair roughly out of the way. 'Will you keep an ear out for Mandy? I need to go out.'

'Sure thing. You'll never get a table you know,' she said casually.

'Don't need one. I don't plan on eating,' Kenan retorted.

'Are you going to thump him again? That worked real well last time from what I remember,' Jane prodded.

'Mind your own business.' He strode off across the patio and into the house, slamming the door behind him. Forcing himself to stop he went into planning mode. It never did to let emotions cloud a mission and that's what he was on tonight. Kenan checked his pockets for his car keys, wallet and phone. He hadn't ever got around to changing after work, so was dressed suitably. What he would say when he arrived was another story, but he'd plan it out on the way.

Very calmly he walked outside, got into his car and started up the engine. Kenan quietly put the car into gear, released the brake and eased away from the kerb.

Lily wanted him to step up so she might just get what she asked for.

'Miss Redman, what a pleasant surprise. I thought you'd returned to the United States.' Fiona Madden appeared from the dining room and Lily managed to dredge up a smile.

'Not yet.' Lily flinched as Patrick squeezed her arm. 'I'd like you to meet Patrick O'Brian. He's a producer on the Cooking Network and my manager.' She didn't think mentioning she'd fired him as her manager would be a wise move.

As he vigorously shook Fiona's hand, Lily sensed her immediate distaste.

'It's a pleasure to meet you, Miss Madden. May I call you Fiona?' He smoothly carried on, totally oblivious to her stony face. 'Fiona, I'm heavily involved with Lily's wonderful new show and it's sure going to be a pleasure working with you.'

'How can you possibly know that?' Fiona cut through his practised charm in one second. 'You don't know me from Adam.'

'I'm sure we'll remedy that very soon.'

Fiona pulled her hand away, wiping it on her apron. Lily suppressed a smile as the woman fixed Patrick with a remorseless glare. She was obviously unimpressed by his smooth patter. 'We'll see about that. I have work to do. Enjoy your meal.' She turned to Lily and a furrow of worry shaded her brow. 'Do let me know if there's anything I can do for you.'

A rush of heat warmed Lily's neck and face at the unexpected kindness. 'Thanks, I sure do appreciate it.'

Patrick subtly tugged on her hand and pulled her towards the dining room.

'Decent place. A bit sparse but suits the woman,' he said, as he checked out the room with a quick, decisive sweep. 'Good choice, Lily.'

She wasn't consoled by his softening stance because they had been here before. Patrick was waiting his moment.

Over their crab appetiser he started and never

let up all through the meal. It might as well have been sawdust for all Lily tasted. His recitation of everything he planned to do with the show and the role she'd play was relentless. With coffee in front of them she finally got the nerve to speak up.

'Patrick. The information you heard about me backing out of being the face of *Celebrity Chef Swap* was correct. I'm not happy with Mary-Beth for telling you, but it's done now. I'll still be involved in a consulting role, of course.'

'Oh, but I don't think so. I believe you've forgotten the small matter of a contract,' he smirked. 'I got this show put on the schedule for next year remember.'

'Check the small print, Patrick. There's a thirty-day out clause on both our sides. I'm invoking mine to part company, as far as you being my personal manager is concerned. You'll get the formal copy from my attorney by the end of the week.'

'Don't be ridiculous. What're you going to do with your time? Your "friend" Kenan is busy playing daddy now. He hasn't got time to romance you,' he said dismissively and Lily seethed.

'How the heck do you know what's going on with him?'

Patrick tapped the side of his nose. 'Information, Lily. It always pays to keep your finger on the pulse.'

'That's irrelevant anyway and nothing to do with my decision.'

He smirked. 'Come on. We both know you've got the hots for him. I'm sure you've got visions of being one happy family with you as the much-loved stepmother. Grow up, Lily.'

'I'm not changing my mind,' she said firmly. 'I've had enough of the whole celebrity chef thing. It was never what I really wanted. I let you talk me into a lot of things, Patrick.'

'Finish your coffee. We're going for a walk,' he snarled. 'Don't think you're going to get away with screwing me over. Others have tried and regretted it.'

Lily picked up the coffee pot and poured herself another cup, slowly adding cream and sugar. 'Go and suck eggs,' she murmured under her breath.

Something cold and hard pressed on her wrist and she glanced down. The breath left her body and Lily struggled against the wave of nausea sweeping through her. Patrick, still smiling and calm, rested a small, sharp knife against her skin.

'Unwise, Lily. I'm going to ask for the cheque. If your friendly chef comes out you'll make our excuses and say we're going for a walk on the beach. Do you understand me?'

His low, lethal tone scared her and she could only nod. Her usual smarts had deserted Lily big-time. Patrick had proved himself to be ruthless and uncaring, but he'd never shown any hint of violence before. Jane was her only hope, but it was so remote as to be almost impossible. The girl would read her text and laugh. She would think Lily sent it to tease Kenan.

Fifteen minutes later they had left Water's Edge and were back in Patrick's car.

'We're going to talk, Lily, and if we don't come to a satisfactory agreement, things will very likely take an unpleasant turn.'

Patrick's emotionless voice sent chills though her and Lily didn't answer, only slumped down in the seat and prayed. There was nothing else left to do.

CHAPTER 33

'Where is she?' Kenan seized Fiona Madden's arm as she wandered out through the restaurant.

'I'm glad to see you,' she said with a sharp nod.

'Why?'

'Join me in a drink and we'll talk,' Fiona ordered, and he reined in his anxiety enough to drag out a smile.

'It'd be a pleasure.'

'Will whisky suit you? A good single malt is my vice at the end of dinner service. Only one, of course,' she added primly.

Kenan nodded agreement and moved to join her at the bar, where the barman immediately slid two glasses in front of them.

'Cheers, Mr Rowse.'

He needed to be conciliatory. 'Call me Kenan, please.'

A slight smile tinged her severe features. 'I assume you're looking for Lily Redman?'

He nodded.

'May I ask why?'

Kenan hesitated, knowing his worries would

sound ridiculous. 'I understand Lily was coming here for dinner with a Mr Patrick O'Brian.' She didn't contradict him so he continued. 'I've reason to believe she may not be comfortable with having his . . . company.'

Fiona's eyes darkened and her fingers tapped on the marble counter.

'I wanted to check she was okay, that's all.'

She indicated to the barman to pour them another drink and he remembered her earlier statement. Something was very wrong. A woman like Fiona didn't break her own rules without good reason.

'Lily was on edge tonight, not her usual bubbly self,' Fiona explained. 'She introduced me to her companion, although I got the distinct impression she didn't want to. Mr O'Brian is a nasty piece of work. I saw through his fake Irish charm the minute he opened his mouth. I wouldn't trust the man an inch and as for working for him . . . Lily will find my contract torn into tiny pieces if he's involved with the show.'

Kenan leaned back in his chair and took in a deep breath, astounded by Fiona's calm, vitriolic summing up. 'I hit him the first time we met,' he admitted.

'I don't blame you in the least,' she stated bluntly. 'I had the urge to do the same, but it's not good for business.'

He burst out laughing at her unexpected dry humour. 'You're right there.'

'Much as I'm enjoying our conversation you didn't come here to chat with me.'

Kenan didn't bother denying the fact.

'They've left already, I'm afraid. They hurried through dinner and Mr O'Brian was impatient for the bill. Lily was . . . very pale when they went and I got the impression she would rather not go with him. I'm guessing he wasn't giving her any choice, but what could I do?'

Kenan's stomach knotted painfully. 'Nothing. I don't suppose you know where they went?'

She frowned. 'No, but let me get their waitress. She listens too much for her own good sometimes.' Fiona glanced over at the barman. 'Ask Suzy to come here right away.'

Kenan kept his amusement to himself as within seconds a young, dark-haired woman ran into the bar, stopping by them with a scared look on her face.

'Suzy, the couple who were at table ten, I don't suppose you heard them say where they were going next?'

The girl flushed and Kenan was pretty sure she expected to be chewed out by her boss.

'You're not in trouble.' Fiona gave a dry laugh. 'For once I want you to have been nosey.'

'I'm not certain, but I think the man mentioned the beach. The woman looked miserable. I thought it odd because he was cute and seemed to be doting on her,' she ran on, grinding to a halt when she realised she might have said too much.

Fiona dismissed her and turned back to Kenan. 'My best guess is Porthcurnow beach. It's at the far end of the village, and it's small and isolated.

Most people go to the south beach, but on summer evenings it's a non-stop party spot – not ideal for anything private.'

'It might not be my business, but I'm going anyway.' Kenan jumped up to standing.

'Good. Is there anything I can do to help?'

He raced through different scenarios in his head, determined to stay focused. 'Give me your phone number. If I don't ring in say . . . half an hour, I'd like you to ring the police.'

'Police? You don't think you might be over-reacting?' Fiona questioned.

'Hopefully I am, but that'll be long enough for me to find out.' She shrugged and took a business card from a holder on top of the bar, passing it over to him. Kenan stowed it safely in his pocket and got ready to leave. 'Thanks, Fiona. I really appreciate your help. You could've told me I was being stupid and jealous and sent me home.'

Her face creased into a wide smile. 'You might well be but I'm giving you the benefit of the doubt. Off with you, Mr Rowse.'

Kenan nodded and hurried out of the restaurant.

Back in the car he quickly texted Jane two words, *Plan B*. Starting up, he shoved the car into gear and peeled out of the car park, ignored any notion of a speed limit and raced through the street, heading out towards Porthcurnow.

As he turned onto the beach road he slowed down, not wanting to draw attention to himself until he was ready. The only other car in sight was a grey Volvo with a rental agency sticker parked by the steps down to the beach. Kenan put two and two together and only hoped his maths was on target tonight. He opened up the boot and swapped his dress shoes for an old pair of trainers and his white shirt for a less conspicuous dark T-shirt. Kenan turned his phone on vibrate.

Before making any rash moves he stood and did a visual sweep of the area. It was high tide so only a small portion of the beach was exposed. Large sand dunes on the right hand side led back up to the cliffs and there was another set of steps over by the closed up shop and deckchair stand. He checked his watch and glanced up at the sky and the sunset creeping in over the horizon. Not bad light for the element of surprise.

Kenan could just about make out two figures at the far end of the beach, close to the inky black water. Moving soundlessly down the stairs he pressed back against the cold, damp sea wall and began to inch his way along. Kenan was relieved he hadn't forgotten all the tricks. His army mates hadn't called him Stealth for nothing.

His heart raced but he took deliberate steady breaths to slow it down, adrenaline was a good thing in moderation but too much and you made mistakes. Reaching halfway along the wall he stopped to re-evaluate. Soon there would be the risk of them spotting him and Kenan needed to plan his reaction. There would be no use in pretending he'd come for a friendly chat.

Suddenly angry voices drifted through the still air and any doubts he'd had were eroded.

'This is your last chance, Lily. I made you what you are today and if you think I'm letting you run off to play Happy Families with your English thug, you're very wrong.'

Patrick's features had turned granite hard and Lily no longer recognised the man she'd once agreed to marry.

'I don't intend to be a bankrupt has-been in the industry.' He wound an arm around her waist and yanked her hard up against his chest, the tip of the knife glinting in his free hand.

'You've got other stars in your stable, Patrick. Why the obsession with me?' Lily asked, frightened and puzzled equally.

'You're on the brink of stardom and *Celebrity Chef Swap* will put you over the edge. Give you a couple of years and you'll put all the top chefs out to grass. You'll solve my money problems on your own, sweetheart.'

By the hysterical edge to his voice Lily realised that Patrick was beyond any logical thread of conversation. Strangely enough the knowledge freed her because it meant she didn't need to bother thinking up sensible arguments any longer. Surviving unhurt was her priority now.

'Do you really think so?' Even without wearing the right clothes she slipped her voice into sultry *Luscious Lily* and forced her body to soften against

Patrick. He responded by pressing into her, his arousal hard and insistent. Bile rose in her throat and for a second she didn't know if she could go through with this. *Save yourself, Lily. Do whatever it takes.* She heard Kenan's quiet instructions running through her head as clearly as if he was standing next to her.

'Oh, yeah, baby. You're something else.' He ground his hips and she forced herself to give a small moan. He grabbed her backside and squeezed. 'That woman was a slut, Lily. She tempted me beyond reason. You're the only one I've ever loved.'

'I know, honey. I never stopped loving you either. Now put the silly knife away and kiss me.'

He glanced down at his hand as if he'd forgotten the knife was there. 'You screwed me over big-time, Lily.' Patrick stared back at her with blank eyes. 'I think you need to be taught a lesson.' His ice-cold tones made Lily's stomach churn. 'I'm not a man to be messed with.'

You're not a real man at all, you moron.

Lily's head jerked back as he grabbed a handful of her hair. Patrick held the knife in front of her face and very slowly began to draw it down over her cheek just hard enough to break the skin. She steeled herself not to cry out as a trickle of warm blood ran down the side of her neck.

'Next time it'll be your throat if you don't do what I say.' Patrick dragged her deeper out into the freezing water and pushed her to her knees, still keeping the knife at her throat. 'I want a promise, Lily. You'll reinstate me as your manager and there'll be no more of this nonsense.' Suddenly he pushed her head down into the cold water and Lily flailed her hands around, desperately trying to grab hold of his legs. He jerked her back up to bang painfully against his body and Lily sucked in deep breaths while she struggled to wipe the stinging salt water from her eyes.

'Enjoy that, did you?' Patrick's manic laughter rang in her ears.

'Let go of her.'

At the sound of Kenan's deep, steady voice from behind Lily almost cried out but she forced herself to slump, hoping to buy them precious extra seconds by not fighting back.

'Might have guessed you'd turn up on your white horse,' Patrick jeered. 'Guess who's on top this time?' He pulled harder on Lily's hair as he turned around, dragging her with him.

'That would be you,' Kenan replied calmly. 'For now.'

'Very good, but I do believe the little lady needs to be sure of it too.' Patrick viciously shoved her back down and Lily quickly grabbed a deep breath before her face hit the water, her chest swelling and tightening with the effort. She fought against panicking and after seemingly endless seconds Patrick hauled her up again and Lily sucked more air into her painful lungs, preparing for him to do it again. Kenan wouldn't let her die, not this way.

'Next time she stays down,' Patrick's voice held

a note of hysteria. 'I've nothing to lose now, so what the hell.'

Through stinging eyes Lily made out the shape of Kenan's blurred face and bit back tears. Her vision cleared enough to meet his smouldering gaze.

'I love you, Lily. I'm going to love you for the rest of our lives.'

She'd known it before tonight but hearing his declaration of love, so sure and steady, sent a surge of confidence through her. Lily felt the words he didn't need to say. *Be still. I've got you. I'll always have your back.*

'The police are on their way. If you let Lily go now you'll have time to get away.' Kenan edged closer until she spotted the dark material of his trousers almost within reach. 'If you don't make a run for it right now you're smart enough to know I'll take you down. You going to give me the knife?'

'You must think I'm bloody stupid,' Patrick sneered. 'Like I'm goin' to fall for that. If I'm goin' down I'll take her with me.'

Kenan shrugged. 'Up to you.' He glanced at his watch. 'I'd say you've got five minutes at the most. They should be coming over that way.' He pointed behind him and Lily sensed Patrick's gaze switch direction.

At that second a large wave hit them and Patrick stumbled, letting out a rough curse.

'You're welcome to the bitch,' Patrick yelled and gave her a hard shove.

Water rushed around Lily's head and she

struggled to stand back up but then Kenan's strong hands hauled her to him.

'Are you okay?'

She nodded, her eyes burning.

'Patrick's getting away. I've got to chase after him, Lily, for your sake.'

'But, the police are coming. Let them.' She clung onto him.

'He's running towards the dunes and I can't see anyone over there.' Kenan's warm, sure fingers stroked down her face. 'Jane's right here. She'll take care of you, okay?'

'Go on, big brother, we'll be fine.' Hearing Jane's reassuring voice made Lily's eyes fill with tears. Jane wrapped a thick woollen blanket around her and the uncontrollable shivers running through her body started to ease. 'The ambulance is here, they can check you over,' Jane said.

Lily tried to thank her but her mind swirled in a maddening fog and everything went black.

CHAPTER 34

Kenan's breath exploded from his chest as he took off running across the sand, never taking his eyes off of Patrick. Hell. This time last year he could run miles without breaking a sweat but he'd let himself get out of shape.

He firmly pushed away the horrifying picture that he knew would join the cast of his nightmares – of Lily's terror-stricken face as Patrick threatened to kill her. If he let anger take over he would screw up and that wasn't happening again. Kenan grasped a tuft of grass and pulled himself up to the top of the first dune.

In front of him Patrick stumbled on the rough ground and the mistake gave Kenan the chance he needed. He threw himself forward and made a grab for Patrick's ankle. He wrapped his hand around and held on as his adversary kicked and bucked. Kenan reared up and threw his whole weight on top of Patrick, grabbed a handful of his hair and jerked up on his head then slammed it repeatedly to the ground. 'That's for Lily, you bastard.'

A strong pair of arms yanked him back up to standing.

'If you kill him they'll lock you up.' Kenan stared into Mike Braithwaite's stony features. 'Jane wouldn't like that.' Mike let go of Kenan and moved to straddle Patrick, pressing a firm hold on the other man's shoulders. 'The police are here, they'll deal with the jerk.'

'Move away, sir, we've got him now.' A uniformed policeman appeared and several more policemen and a couple of paramedics swarmed around Patrick. Mike moved away as Patrick was turned back over.

'Take him out of my sight,' Kenan spat out the words. 'I'm going to check on the woman he nearly killed.'

'Good idea, sir. Leave him to us.'

Kenan picked up the touch of sympathy in the young policeman's voice and managed to throw out a word of thanks.

'It's Miss Fiona Madden at the Water's Edge you need to thank, sir. My boss tried to tell her we couldn't come out on a hunch and she—'

'Ripped him to shreds?' Kenan suggested, with a smile.

'You could say that, sir. We've had dealings with her before and – don't repeat this – but I wouldn't have been stupid enough to cross her myself.'

'Nor would I. Don't worry, I'll thank her.'

'I'll leave that to you, sir.' The policeman laughed. 'Cheers, mate.'

Kenan watched them carry a handcuffed Patrick away on a stretcher and a sudden rush of fatigue swept over him.

'We'll need a statement, sir, from you and the lady, but it'll be time enough in the morning,' another policeman chimed in.

'Thanks again.'

'Jane took care of Lily, she's doing okay,' Mike assured him. 'Come on, let's head back over and sort out these women of ours.'

Kenan bit his tongue. This wasn't the right moment to interrogate the other man about his intentions regarding Jane. 'Cheers.'

As they headed back Kenan scanned the beach but didn't see any sign of Lily.

'Hey, big brother, we're up here,' Jane called out from up on the road.

Kenan took off running and landed at his sister's feet. 'Where's Lily?' he gasped, dropping his head and clutching hold of his knees.

'Sitting in my car. She let the medics check her out but then she refused to leave until you got back. I told her she was stupid and would catch her death of cold but . . .'

Kenan brushed past and marched over to Jane's Volkswagen, flinging open the passenger door.

'Oh, thank goodness. I was so afraid for you,' Lily exclaimed, a brilliant smile lighting up her pale, drawn face. She threw her arms around his neck and he wrapped himself around her. Having her in his arms had never felt so wonderful.

'You were afraid for me? Oh, Lily. I could've taken Patrick down, but I had to try talking first. He'd cut you already and he was desperate. When

I pulled you up . . . I thought . . .' He choked on the awful words and tears pressed against his eyes.

She nuzzled into him, resting her head on his chest.

'Don't you ever do that to me again,' he ordered and Kenan tipped her chin back up to meet his gaze. 'If I haven't made it clear enough, I love you. I don't know how we're going to sort things out and in the morning I'll probably—'

Lily seized him in a fierce, hard kiss before pulling away slightly. 'Shut up, Kenan. Don't spoil it, okay. You've been my hero tonight. If I were you I'd revel in that and make the most of my gratitude.' Her sapphire-blue eyes shone. 'I'd prefer not to have been half-dead to get you to admit you love me, but I get the fact you're not the most verbal man. I love you too, you overgrown boy. It's not rocket science to work this out. Now kiss me again before I change my mind.'

'Yes, ma'am.' Kenan happily obeyed.

'For goodness sake, this woman just nearly drowned, stop pawing her,' Jane teased. 'She needs a hot bath and a good night's sleep.'

'Right.' Kenan reached in and scooped Lily up into his arms out of the car. 'She's coming with me.'

Lily gave him a mock-glare. 'Do I get any say in this?'

'No. My mother will take good care of you.'

'So would Betty,' she protested half-heartedly.

'Yeah, but I want you with me.' Kenan corrected

himself. 'I *need* you with me. Are you going to argue again?'

'I guess not.' Lily laughed over his shoulder at Jane. 'Sorry, but I'm giving in to the caveman tonight.'

Kenan didn't mind the touch of sarcasm because it showed his Lily was doing all right. 'I'd better throw you over my shoulder and haul you back to my lair,' he joked, and then turned to Jane. 'I don't know where Mike turned up from, but your suitor stopped me going too far back there. Maybe as thanks I'll give him permission to ask you out on a date.'

'Well, aren't you the generous one considering I'm twenty-one and my own woman. I'll let you know how it goes.'

'No details, please,' Kenan pleaded with a grin, and looked down at Lily. 'Right, woman, let's get you home and dry.'

There would be time enough to sort out everything else in the cold light of day.

CHAPTER 35

'Miss Lily, can we come in?'

Lily struggled to sit up in the bed. For a few seconds she couldn't work out where she was or why her face hurt. She rubbed her fingers over the plaster on her cheek and it all slammed back.

'Miss Lily, you have to be awake by now, it's nine o'clock,' Mandy's shrill voice yelled from outside the bedroom.

'Come in.' She flopped back on the pillows as the door was flung open, crashing back against the wall. Mandy flew into the room and hurled herself at Lily.

'Careful. What did Daddy say?' Kenan's handsome figure filled the doorway, concern written all over his face.

Mandy clambered onto the bed and threw her arms around Lily. 'Not to jump on Miss Lily because she might be hurting and tired.'

'So, what are you doing right now?' Kenan asked dryly.

'Hugging her to make her feel better,' she insisted.

'It's working perfectly. I'm cured.' Lily laughed and hugged Mandy back.

'See, I told you,' she gloated.

'You'll see Miss Lily again when you get back tonight. Off you go now and let her rest,' Kenan said in a firm, do-not-argue-with-me tone.

'What're you doing today?' Lily asked, not wanting the little girl to feel unwanted.

Mandy beamed. 'My new friend, Kayla, is nine today. She's asked me and four other girls to go out for the day. We're driving all the way to Plymouth to the Aquarium. There are sharks and all sorts of big fish. It's going to be masses of fun and we're going to have pizza and ice cream.'

'You're all set for an awesome day. I want to hear all about it when you get back.' Lily glanced around the strange room to see where her things had ended up. 'Give me my purse, sweetheart.'

'Where is it?' Mandy frowned.

'Over there.' Lily pointed to her straw bag on the floor.

'That's a handbag, silly. A purse is where you keep your money.'

Lily grinned. 'You got me there, kid. I'll have to learn the lingo better.'

'I'll teach you,' Mandy said earnestly, scrambling off the bed and rifling through the straw bag. 'Here you go.' She passed over Lily's glitter encrusted pink wallet.

Lily opened it and pulled out some money. 'There you go.'

'You don't have to do that, she's already wheedled money out of me and her grandparents,'
Kenan intervened.

Lily shook her head sadly. 'He doesn't get it,
honey. A day out with the girls is bound to involve
shopping and a lady should always be prepared.
Enjoy it and don't take any notice of your spoilsport
father.'

Kenan's dark eyes immediately lightened and the
frown lines left his face.

'I give up. You're ganging up on me again. Mandy,
say thank you and go and get ready. Kayla's parents
will be here in a minute,' he said with a grin.

Lily laughed as Mandy treated her to another
massive hug. 'You have lots of fun, sweetheart, and
don't let the sharks get you.' She snapped her jaw
and mock-chewed on Mandy's arm, making her
dissolve into fits of giggles.

'Right, let's leave Miss Lily in peace.' Kenan came
across and swooped Mandy up into his arms.
'Mum's bringing you up some breakfast and then
she and Dad are off out for the day. They're going
to visit my aunt in Newquay. I've been in touch
with the police and told them we'll be in after lunch.'

Kenan reached the door and fixed his steely gaze
on her. 'I'll be back when everything's quiet.'

Lily gave him a smile and laid contentedly back
on the pillows.

Kenan waved his parents off and headed back into
the house. He crept back upstairs and quietly

opened Lily's door in case she'd gone back to sleep.

'Is the coast clear?' she gazed at him longingly, and Kenan swallowed hard.

'Yep.'

'You gonna stand there all day?' Lily beckoned him over.

'I guess we need to talk, uh, first.' He didn't have much hope she'd say no. Lily was a woman to face things head on. Normally they had that in common but when it came to relationship talk he'd rather face a Taliban fire-fight unarmed.

Lily patted the bed next to her. 'I'd prefer some delicious life-affirming lovemaking first, if that's all right with you, of course? Then I'll do the talking and you can do the listening.'

Kenan cleared his throat. 'It might help if you took off my mother's nightdress.'

A throaty laugh broke out of Lily and he couldn't stop himself from joining in.

'Not very romantic, I guess?' she replied and instantly tossed back the sheet, raised her arms and peeled off the offending garment to toss it on the floor. 'Is that better?'

He couldn't stop staring, and didn't know how to force out an answer that didn't make him sound a complete prat.

'I'm taking that as a yes.' Lily preened. 'Break the ice. Kiss me.'

Kenan somehow got his feet to work and walked the needed couple of steps across the carpet. He perched on the edge of the bed and reached one hand up to touch her face, resting his fingers for a moment on the small plaster covering the cut on her cheek. Leaning in he brushed his lips against hers and sunk into the wonderful soft lure of Lily's mouth. Her soft moan undid him and he deepened the kiss, losing himself in her as he always did when they touched.

Minutes later they came up for breath and he tried unsuccessfully to wipe the satisfied smile from his face.

'Join me,' she pleaded, and he was helpless. If the woman wanted love he'd give it to her.

Lily couldn't take her eyes from Kenan as he quickly stripped off his clothes and sat on the edge of the bed – the shallow side of her confirming he really was yummy eye candy.

'Are you sure you're not too sore? I couldn't bear to hurt you,' he murmured, picking up her hand and stroking her fingers. Even that light touch on her skin sent shivers rippling through her and Lily decided she'd waited long enough.

'Lay down.' She pointed to the empty space next to her on the bed. 'You want proof I'm fine?' Kenan opened his mouth to answer but she reached up and kissed him, stopping whatever he was going to say. 'Do what you're told,' she said with a teasing laugh.

'Yes, ma'am.' Kenan grinned and shifted himself over, lying back on the pillow and giving her a decided smirk.

Lily moved to kneel over him and the breath caught in her throat as he gazed up at her, his dark eyes burning.

'I'm yours.' The rough words dragged from him and she swallowed hard.

Very slowly and deliberately she made them one and as Kenan reached up and cupped her face with large sure hands, Lily trembled. He moved deep inside her and she gasped, making him suddenly hold still.

'For heaven's sake, don't stop. It just felt so good,' she reassured him.

'Thank goodness.' Kenan's relief at not having to be noble made her smile.

Soon everything else disappeared as a wave of pleasure engulfed them both. Lily cried out Kenan's name and leaned down to seize him in a deep, needy kiss. Collapsing onto his chest she gave herself up to the joy of being wrapped around with love.

Lily itched to bake something, anything, to take her mind off 'The Talk'. Purposely not channelling *Luscious Lily* when they finally got up out of bed, she'd chosen to go with no make-up and redone her hair in a simple braid. Thankfully Jane had retrieved some clean clothes for her from Betty's earlier so she'd put on a simple white cotton camisole, dark jeans and flip-flops.

'Hey, gorgeous.' Kenan strolled in, rubbing his freshly shaved jaw and she smelled his familiar pine soap from the shower she'd left him to have in peace, while she put some coffee on to brew.

She backed into the counter and held up her hands in warning. 'Don't touch me, please.'

'Why? Drive you crazy, do I? Good to know,' he teased, folding his arms and giving in to a deep warm chuckle.

'You've known it forever,' Lily muttered. 'Now behave yourself and sit down. Once I've got our coffee we'll have a civilised conversation.'

He studied her hard for a moment, nodded and pulled out a kitchen chair to sit down, stretching out his long legs and clasping his hands behind his head.

Lily poured their two cups, forcing her hand to be steady. 'There you go.' She pushed his across the table and picked up her own for something to hold onto. 'Aren't you going to say anything?' she badgered him.

'When we were in bed you told me I had to listen while you talked, and only then would I be allowed to speak.'

His calm, steady voice made her want to scream. 'Fine.' Lily sucked in a deep breath and forced her brain to remember the first thing she wanted to get out of the way and decided to go for it. 'Before we start I take it you don't believe the nonsense about rehab and my mother?'

'I never did,' he mumbled.

She wagged her finger. 'You wondered, admit it.'

'Well, maybe for a minute, I'm sorry I—'

Lily planted a kiss on his open mouth and didn't let up until he'd stopped trying to talk back. 'Enough.' She let go and sat back in the chair. 'For now all I'm asking you to do is listen. I love you. I didn't want to but I can't help it. I do, more than anything and I know you love me.'

He sipped his coffee and nodded but didn't say a word.

'That makes everything else straightforward. As far as I can see the main reason you're reluctant to commit to me is because of Mandy. For some reason you have this warped idea being a good father means giving up your own chance of a personal life. That's a load of baloney. I love Mandy too, and don't think I'm bragging when I say she's pretty fond of me as well. Am I making sense?' she probed, desperate for some feedback.

Kenan sighed. 'Lily, make up your mind. Either you want me to talk or you don't. Let me know where I stand. I'm trying to do the right thing here.' His quiet, logical words shouldn't have annoyed her, but they did.

'You are such a man,' her frustration bubbled over.

'Um, yes. I believe that's why you love me, but do correct me if I'm wrong.'

She counted to ten under her breath to calm herself down. 'Right. I'll carry on.'

Kenan nodded, the tease of a smile shading his unrevealing eyes.

'The other thing you keep harping on about is simple geography. You'd think no one else from different countries ever fell in love and made it work. I know Olivia won't let you take Mandy abroad to live, and I'm good with that. I'm a cook, Kenan, not a NASA rocket scientist. I can cook anywhere. I'd already decided not to star in the new show myself – not because of you – but because of me. I'm tired of the whole *Luscious Lily* act. I want to be me again.'

Lily fought back tears. 'I rarely get to cook these day and I spend half the time on publicity ventures.' She sucked in a deep, calming breath before continuing. 'Even if you don't want to marry me, and I don't have a clue why you wouldn't, I'm still laying my alter-ego to rest.' Lily clasped her hands together and stared at him trying to work out what Kenan's stoic expression meant. 'Well?'

'Are you finished?' he asked quietly.

'Yes,' Lily yelled.

'I agree.' Kenan nodded.

'To what?'

'Marry you,' he replied very slowly and carefully, as if he was explaining something complicated to Mandy.

'That's it?' Lily screamed. 'You agree? You've nothing more to say?'

Kenan seized hold of her hands and the intensity of his dark eyes focusing on her sent a rush of blood to Lily's face. 'I'm not a man for fancy words. If you want those you'd better retract your offer. Otherwise I'm agreeing with you. I'd already thought it through and decided I was a moron. So, are we good?'

Lily sat back a little and laughed loudly. 'Did we just decide to get married?'

'Yeah, I'd say so.'

'But I didn't get any protestation of undying love, any proposal on a bent knee, or a flashy diamond,' Lily sort-of protested.

'Didn't Patrick do all that?' he probed.

'Well, yeah, he did.'

'And he proved to be an unfaithful jerk. So do you think all that nonsense proves anything?' Kenan asked, resting his warm hand against her cheek.

She shook her head, leaning into his comforting strength.

'If it helps, sweetheart, I love you so much it drives me insane. If it'll make you happier I'll get down on one knee to tell you exactly the same, but I don't buy jewellery unsupervised. Trust me when I say you wouldn't want whatever I chose. I'll go with you and buy whatever your heart desires and promise not to rush you.' Kenan grinned. 'By the way, it's the only time you'll get such a generous offer. Other shopping trips, if they include me, will have set time limits.'

'Deal,' Lily agreed. This had to be the most unorthodox proposal going.

'I've just got one request,' Kenan said seriously, and her heart wobbled.

'What's that?'

'Well, it's like this,' he said with a frown. 'I've got a bit of a thing for *Luscious Lily*. In fact, you could say I fell for her before I fell for you.' A mischievous smile crept across his face. 'I've no problem with you getting rid of her as far as your career's concerned, but I wondered if she might still appear occasionally – let's say in the bedroom or um . . . other fun places – to keep me happy?'

Hell, she loved this man. What could a woman say to such a request apart from the obvious? 'I promise you shall have your fantasy woman at regular intervals. After all, it'd be a shame to waste all those outfits, wouldn't it?'

Kenan swooped in, dropping light kisses all over her face until she burst into uncontrollable giggles. 'You're my fantasy, you, Lily Redman. In fact you're much better than any fantasy because I could never have dreamed up anything half as wonderful.'

'How can you say you're not a romantic? That's the loveliest thing anyone's ever said to me,' Lily declared. 'I ought to have recorded it on my phone because you'll probably never say anything that amazing for the rest of our lives.'

'I'll agree with you again – it's very doubtful,' Kenan stated with a resigned air. 'I suppose you want the whole big wedding thing?'

He might be describing an act of torture and for a minute she considered teasing him for a bit longer, but they'd messed around enough.

Lily shook her head. 'I'd prefer something casual and fun. There's only one non-negotiable.'

'What's that?' She caught the looming dread in his voice.

'Mandy. She'll never forgive us if we don't let her be a bridesmaid. She needs a princess dress, flowers, the whole nine yards.'

Kenan beamed, it was the only word to describe his face-splitting smile. 'No problem. I'll buy every piece of tawdry jewellery she wants without complaint . . . as long as you take her shopping for it all.'

'I think we've about wrapped up the pesky details.' Lily threw her arms around his neck, gazing up into his handsome face. 'I suggest we go back upstairs and seal our engagement.'

'I'd love to, sweetheart, but—'

'But what?' she said crossly.

'We've got to go to the police station. I'm sorry.'

He sounded awful and Lily was instantly swamped with guilt. 'No, I'm the one who's sorry. I've spoiled—'

'Don't you dare apologise. It is what it is and not anybody's fault. We'll deal with this together and move on.' Kenan reached out and pulled off the ribbon holding her braid in place. 'I like it loose and seeing as you've just talked me into marrying you, I get this small reward.' He trailed his fingers through the heavy mass, separating the strands and fanning them out around her shoulders. 'Why don't you do what you do best and find something for our lunch, and then we'll get this over with?'

'What're you going to do while I'm slaving away?'

Kenan's wolfish grin made her blush all over. 'Watch. You're incredibly sexy when you're cooking.'

'Only when I'm cooking? I must be slipping,' Lily teased and flounced over to the fridge, making sure to give an extra shake of her hips as she bent over.

'Witch,' Kenan hissed.

She glanced over her shoulder and stuck her tongue out at him in fun. He was as happy to delay the next task as she was.

CHAPTER 36

'Are you ready?' Kenan took hold of Lily's trembling hand.

'Yeah. Let's get this over with.' She pulled back her shoulders and allowed him to lead the way into the police station.

An hour later he couldn't help but think this wasn't how an engagement should be celebrated – in separate rooms being questioned by the police. Kenan read through the statement the detective thrust under his nose and signed his name at the bottom.

'You can wait for Miss Redman in the lobby.'

'Thanks.' Kenan left and made his way back out to the entrance and sat down.

'Okay, I'm done. Let's get out of here.'

Lily appeared in front of him, smiling and relaxed, but over her shoulder Kenan caught the detective glowering at them.

'Is everything all right?' He aimed his question at them both, and the man spoke up before Lily could open her mouth.

'Against our advice, Miss Redman refuses to press charges.' He snapped out the words, obviously displeased. 'We could force the issue but my governor decided not to. Mr O'Brian will be placed on a plane back to the United States and strongly discouraged from returning any time soon.'

Kenan caught Lily's pleading glance. 'If that's her decision I completely support her.'

'Your choice, sir.' The words *henpecked* and *wimp* hung between them, but Kenan didn't need validation from any policeman regarding his masculinity.

'Thanks again for your help last night,' Kenan said, and shook hands with the detective. 'Come on, Lily, let's go.' She didn't protest and they walked back outside together.

'Are you mad at me?' she asked, her voice small and uncertain.

Kenan swung her into his arms. 'No, sweetheart, I'm not. It's your choice to make and I respect that. I might have chosen differently but that's not the point. You're an independent woman and you'll always be that way – married or not – and it's one of the reasons I love you.'

Lily burrowed into his chest and broke into loud, gut-wrenching sobs. Kenan helplessly patted her back. 'Shush. It's all right. Let's go home.'

She gazed up at him, her eyes shimmering with tears and love. 'That sounds wonderful. I've got to plan out a special meal to fix for us tonight.' She frowned, nibbling at her lip.

'Oh, Lily, I do love you. I can't think of any other woman after the twenty-four hours you've had fretting about what to cook.' Kenan swept them both along the pavement towards his car. 'Mum and Dad will be home soon, and so will Mandy. No privacy I'm afraid,' he said ruefully.

'No problem. I can't wait to hear Mandy scream when we tell her our news. She'll have her brides-maid's dress planned by bedtime.' A satisfied smile crept across her face. 'I'm going to surprise you with supper tonight. Your only task is to go home and invite your parents, Mandy, Jane, and Mike if he's still around, to come to Betty's house at six this evening. We'll announce our engagement then.'

'Anything else, boss?' he joked.

'Stay out of the way. I don't need you distracting me.'

Kenan shrugged. 'Okay. I'll obey orders although I'd rather be with you.'

'Me too, but I know my limits and this will take all my concentration,' she insisted.

'What on earth are you up to now?'

She grinned and wagged a finger in his face. 'That's for me to know and you to find out. Now drive us back to St Dinas and drop me down by the shops.'

Kenan bent to the steamroller force of the woman he loved and did what he was told.

Lily took another nervous peek in the oven.

'Go on, take them out, they should be ready and you want them to cool down some before we eat,'

Betty declared as the doorbell rang. 'I'll shoo everyone out into the garden. You finish off here and come join us when you're ready.' She bustled away laughing as she went.

Lily mentally crossed her fingers and got everything organised then checked her hair in the small mirror by the kitchen door. *Right Kenan Rowse. You may not be that interested in food, but I think I've found the way to your heart.*

She stepped out on to the patio and Kenan instantly jumped up and pulled her into his arms.

'Here's the lady of the hour,' he declared with a big grin. 'I hope the food will wait until we've shared our news?'

Lily nodded. 'Won't hurt at all.' Everyone stared at them and a flush of heat crept up her neck. 'Go ahead,' she urged him.

Kenan cleared his throat and clutched her hand tightly. 'I'm not one for fancy words so I'll spit it out. Lily's agreed to marry me and we're . . .' Mandy leapt up from her grandmother's lap and threw herself at him, wrapping her arms around his waist.

'Yes, yes, I knew she loved us. This is the best news ever.' She giggled and beamed up at Lily.

'I certainly do, sweetheart.' Lily struggled to choke back tears. 'We need you to do something very special for us.' She caught Kenan's eye and he nodded. 'You see the problem is we need a bridesmaid and—'

Mandy let go of Kenan and bounced up and down. 'Me, me, me.'

'It'll mean wearing a pretty dress and you'll need fancy shoes and flowers in your hair,' Kenan said in a serious voice, trying to sound worried, but the little girl only laughed.

'Oh, Daddy, you're being silly again. I know all that and I'll be the best bridesmaid ever,' she declared.

Lily smirked at Kenan. 'She's right, you know. I think we'd better say yes before she changes her mind.'

'Goodie, goodie, goodie.' Mandy jumped back on her grandmother's lap.

'Now we've got that out of the way, let's eat. I've made a recipe tonight for the first time so I want honest opinions,' Lily stated, staring around at them all.

'You'll get that all right, luv,' Mike declared, his muscular arm draped around Jane's slender shoulders.

'I'm sure I will, but don't be too rude. I'm a newly engaged woman and have to be indulged.'

Mike snorted and shook his head in mock-sadness.

'Come on, I'm starving.' Kenan took hold of her hand and they headed for the door.

Mandy ran on ahead and reached the kitchen first. 'Pasties!' she squealed, looking at the plates set out all ready for them.

Lily glanced at Kenan and his loving smile lit up her heart.

'How did you know?' he rasped.

'Know what?'

'The one food I can't resist.' He sniffed the air appreciatively.

'You're a Cornishman, and Betty informed me there's not one living who can say no to a decent pasty,' Lily declared hopefully. 'Evelyn gave me a crash course on pastry making and Betty supervised the rest, so you can thank them as well if they're good or blame them if they're bad.'

By now everyone had found somewhere to sit and Betty rushed around pouring cups of tea for the grown-ups and getting a glass of orange squash for Mandy. Kenan pulled out the nearest spare chair and sat down, picked up the warm pasty in his hands and flashed a quick grin at Lily.

'Here goes.'

She held her breath as he took a large bite, chewed and swallowed.

'Brilliant. Bloody brilliant. My God, get a license so I can marry you right now.' He wiped his mouth, put down the pasty and reached around to yank her down onto his lap. Ignoring the cheers and whistles from everyone he kissed her unmercifully.

'Leave the woman alone for a minute. These are damn good, Lily. We'll turn you into a proper English cook yet,' Mike jested.

Jane leaned over to poke him in the ribs and he chuckled, giving her an indulgent smile.

Kenan tipped Lily off his lap and gave her backside a quick smack. 'Eat yours and see what you think. I'm sure you'll need to analyse it and make notes afterwards,' he teased.

She flounced to the other end of the table to grab the only empty seat. Kenan was spot on as usual because he'd guessed exactly what she intended to do. How cool was it to be understood so well? Lily ignored her knife and fork and picked up her pasty and took a bite. Maybe a touch more seasoning next time, and the onion could be cut a little less fine and . . .

'You've done a proper job. Nobody would know they weren't made by a Cornishwoman,' Betty declared.

Lily wanted to hug her. 'Thanks,' she whispered, not trusting herself to say anything more.

Suddenly Kenan's father stood up. 'Congratulations, you pair. This is the best news I've had in years. I think it's time we took this little lady home,' he patted Mandy's head, 'and we'll put her to bed.'

Lily was relieved when Kenan didn't protest, but then glanced around at all the mess. 'I need to clear up.'

'Get on with you and go somewhere on your own while you've got willing babysitters. There's only a few plates and cups,' Betty insisted.

'We'll help,' Jane declared, giving Mike's hand a tug.

'How would you like to come and see my new cottage?' Kenan asked with a mischievous gleam in his eye.

She just about managed a respectable nod in reply.

'Clear off, mate,' Mike asserted. 'We're good here.'

'Thanks.' Lily grinned and seized hold of Kenan. 'Let's go before they change their minds.'

CHAPTER 37

If Kenan thought Lily was obsessed with food before they started wedding planning he'd been very wrong. He'd always understood brides fretted and fussed about finding the perfect wedding dress, but apparently that was a minor detail compared to what food to serve at the reception.

Several of Lily's chef friends were coming to the wedding and she informed him this meant the food would be picked apart and then reported on to the ones who couldn't be there. Once, when she was nearly tearing her beautiful hair out, he'd stupidly suggested they have a pasty supper. The scathing look he received would have stripped rust from corroded metal in a matter of seconds.

'Are you ready?' Lily breezed into his mother's kitchen with a determined glint in her eye. 'Scrub your hands and let's get busy.'

Kenan didn't bother to say he'd already washed them and walked over to the sink. This wasn't how he'd expected to spend his last few hours as a single man, but strangely enough she'd worked on him over the last couple of months and today he was ready to prove himself.

'I'll start on the buns. You're in charge of the butterflies.' She stated bluntly.

'Do I get a kiss first?'

'Ask again when you've piped two hundred chocolate butterflies,' Lily declared and flounced over to the oven.

They worked almost in silence for the next two hours, only asking for each other's opinion when necessary but otherwise just getting on with it. Once, when he was stirring the chocolate to make sure it was lump-free and slipping in the thermometer to check he had the temperature right, Kenan caught Lily watching him. The joy lighting up her face made all his efforts worthwhile. They'd practised this so many times since Lily decided she didn't want a traditional wedding cake that Kenan was totally sick of eating raspberry, dark chocolate butterfly buns.

He ignored her and poured chocolate into the piping bag he had ready. Concentrating hard he made the first one, holding his breath because it usually went wrong but not today. With a satisfied sigh he carried on, finally piping the last butterfly exactly on schedule.

'Pleased with yourself, aren't you?' Lily teased. 'I suppose for an amateur you haven't done a bad job.'

'Very generous of you to say so,' Kenan replied, bending low in a sweeping bow.

She beckoned him closer and he didn't need asking twice. Lily reached up and popped a quick kiss on his mouth but it wasn't enough and he seized hold of her for a proper, satisfying, long one.

'That's much better,' he declared with a grin.

'Playtime over. We've got an hour to put these together and get the kitchen clean. You can't be here when my mother arrives to get changed or she'll be convinced you've jinxed our marriage. This has to be our secret.'

'Mike has everything else under control?' he asked and she nodded.

'Yep. It's goin' to be amazing. People will be talking about the food for years,' Lily announced.

No. They'll be talking about how beautiful you looked. Kenan kept the traitorous thought to himself. His heart did a flip at the idea of standing at the altar waiting for Lily in four short hours. He'd never understand what he'd done to deserve her loving him, but would spend the rest of his life proving she'd made the right choice.

'Back to work,' she ordered, and Kenan happily did what he was told.

The pale autumn sun warmed Lily's back as she waited outside the church. She crept forward and took a peek in through the open door at the waiting guests. Olivia and Henry Cunningham sat together in the second row. Lily could have done without Kenan's glamorous ex turning up, but it made Mandy happy, and that was all that mattered.

She stepped back and smoothed down the front of her knee-length white silk dress. Lily had chosen the Marilyn Monroe style with its halter neck and full skirt because the soft folds would unfurl around her when she danced with Kenan later.

'Do you wish you'd chosen a more traditional dress?' her mother asked anxiously.

Her decision to go for short and flirty caused a few tense mother/daughter discussions. She'd shattered Tricia Redman's long held dream of Lily floating down the aisle in a white tulle ball gown with a tiara and cathedral length veil, preceded by at least six bridesmaids.

Lily laughed. 'No, Mom. I love my dress. Mandy's doing enough princess for us both, aren't you, honey?' She turned and smiled at the little girl who was fighting a losing battle to stand still behind them. Apparently at English weddings the bride entered first and Lily wasn't about to buck the system.

Mandy spun around, showing off her bright pink and silver dress, silver shoes and the pink glittery flowers in her hair. The first time Lily spotted her own dress she'd known it was the one, not even trying on any others, but Mandy was her mother's daughter when it came to clothes and they'd spent weeks putting together the perfect outfit. Mandy had insisted that she find something to match the famous princess necklace they bought in Charlestown, and how could she and Kenan argue with that?

The vicar swept out of the church, smiling broadly and Lily straightened up. 'Are we ready, ladies?'

Lily nodded, somehow oddly calm. She knew the reason she didn't have the usual wedding nerves was because she had absolutely no doubts.

'As soon as the music starts you come on in. I'll meet you at the altar.' He left them and a couple of minutes later the organ struck up the first chords of Handel's *Water Music* – Kenan's choice.

'Ready, Mom?' Lily took hold of her mother's shaking hands. 'You don't have to worry. Look at him. They don't come any better.' She pointed at Kenan, waiting with his back to her, ramrod straight in the new dark grey suit they'd chosen together.

'He's a good man,' her mother agreed. 'You're a lucky girl.'

'I know,' Lily said fervently. 'Don't worry, I know. Let's go and do this.' They linked arms and stepped down the two granite steps into the church and onto the dark blue carpet.

The small crowd all turned to look at them, but Lily focused solely on Kenan. Once she reached his side he faced her, his dark eyes overflowing with love and passion. She stifled a giggle as her gaze locked in on the bright pink silk tie he'd insisted on buying. Kenan's gaze travelled down over her and a smouldering smile crept across his face. He'd spotted her hot pink stilettos, adorned with their combined initials in sparkling diamonds.

Every man deserved a fantasy on his wedding day, and she was determined to always be his.

His strong, warm hand wrapped around hers and they faced the vicar together.

'Dearly beloved, we are gathered . . .'

For Lily's sake Kenan tried to pay attention to the food, but really he couldn't take his eyes off his new wife. Laughing, joking, hugging and kissing their guests, Lily floated around the room, dragging him in her wake.

Kenan had dutifully eaten one of everything on the magnificent buffet and attempted to remember enough so he could hold an intelligent conversation when she questioned him later. And she would. It didn't matter if it was their wedding, Lily would make notes afterwards on what worked and what didn't. He'd be expected to give an opinion and would do his best because making her happy was what he intended to do for the rest of his life.

'Time for our dance,' Lily declared. 'Now you'll see why I chose this dress. It'll look so pretty when you do the swooping thing we practised.'

He just smiled. As far as he was concerned the dress looked pretty because she was wearing it, end of story. Not only had he been subjected to months of backwards and forward on today's menu but she'd also dragged him to dancing lessons after he shuffled her around at a party one night. She'd declared him to have at least three left feet, and possibly four. Tonight she'd selected a jazzy swing dance for their debut as Mr and Mrs Rowse and he was petrified he'd let her down. Possibly literally to the floor if he dropped her at a crucial moment.

Lily reached up to slide her fingers around his neck, and whispered in his ear. 'Any man who can create two hundred amazing chocolate butterflies for his wedding cakes will not be defeated by a simple dance.' She kissed him right on the mouth and let him taste her all the way to his toes before letting go. 'Trust me.'

Kenan eased back and held out his hand to her. 'Come on, Mrs Rowse. Time to show them what we're made of.'

'If you insist, Mr Rowse.' Lily laughed, giving her hips a quick, tempting shimmy.

'Oh, I do.'

'You said that once already today,' she teased.

'And I'll keep on saying it to keep my *Luscious Lily* happy,' Kenan declared, and nodded over at the DJ. With a triumphant laugh he swung her up into his arms and headed for the dance floor as the first notes of music started.

EPILOGUE

'**H**urry up, Kenan, it's starting,' Lily yelled up the stairs to him and raced back into the living room. She flung herself on the sofa and turned on the TV. Mandy put the bowl of popcorn they'd fixed on the coffee table, grabbing a handful and cramming it into her mouth. She snuggled in next to Lily and grinned.

The theme music started as he came into the room, cradling baby Daniel in one arm, and a beer bottle in the other hand. 'Who's on tonight again?' He sat down by her and stretched out his legs to one side.

'Mike Braithwaite and Jonathan Cabot, my preppy Bostonian. Mike will have the women swooning and set the ratings on fire. Fiona and Martin Farrell did great, but this should send them through the roof.'

Kenan's hand covered hers and Lily turned to face him, meeting his steel-grey eyes straight on.

'Any regrets?'

He didn't have to spell it out. In only the first couple of programmes *Celebrity Chef Swap* had become *the* show to watch. Marianna Firenze, the host, was flying high and that would have been Lily's job.

'None. I'm thrilled it's a success, and I've enjoyed my consultant role, but this is celebrity enough for me.' She gestured to him and the children. 'An amazing husband, the best daughter ever,' she ruffled Mandy's hair, 'and our sweet honeymoon baby. What more could any woman want?'

'Uh, maybe the award-winning restaurant she's started at Burton's, plus the thriving organic food shop. And how about the charity for schooling Afghan girls she helped so-called amazing husband to organise?'

'Yeah, I guess I could've mentioned those too.' Lily chuckled and popped a quick kiss on his forehead.

Kenan leaned closer and whispered in her ear. 'It's okay, I'll refresh your memory tonight.'

'Is that a promise, Mr Rowse?'

'It certainly is, Mrs Rowse.' His heavy gaze dragged over her and Lily shivered in anticipation. 'I think it's time *Luscious Lily* came out to play again,' he murmured low enough so Mandy couldn't hear.

Lily leaned in closer. 'She has a set of pink diamante lingerie a certain man hasn't seen yet.'

Kenan groaned. 'You're an evil woman.'

'What a thing to say to me.' She reached out to Daniel. 'Give me that poor child and drink your beer. Let's see how your future brother-in-law does.'

'Do you know something I don't?' Kenan's brow furrowed.

'No, but trust me it won't be long. Jane told me she's only waiting until she gets her master's degree next summer.'

'How does she know Mike is ready to commit?' he asked.

Lily chuckled. 'Because he's as besotted as you were and look where you ended up.'

Kenan dropped a kiss on her forehead. 'Exactly where I want to be.'